The Story of Waitst

Kate Douglas Smith Wiggin

Alpha Editions

This edition published in 2024

ISBN : 9789362994196

Design and Setting By
Alpha Editions
www.alphaedis.com
Email - info@alphaedis.com

As per information held with us this book is in Public Domain.
This book is a reproduction of an important historical work. Alpha Editions uses the best technology to reproduce historical work in the same manner it was first published to preserve its original nature. Any marks or number seen are left intentionally to preserve its true form.

Contents

SPRING I. SACO WATER .... - 1 -

II. THE SISTERS .... - 4 -

III. DEACON BAXTER'S WIVES .... - 9 -

IV. SOMETHING OF A HERO .... - 13 -

V. PATIENCE AND IMPATIENCE .... - 20 -

VI. A KISS .... - 27 -

VII. "WHAT DREAMS MAY COME" .... - 33 -

SUMMER VIII. THE JOINER'S SHOP .... - 37 -

IX. CEPHAS SPEAKS .... - 41 -

X. ON TORY HILL .... - 45 -

XI. A JUNE SUNDAY .... - 52 -

XII. THE GREEN-EYED MONSTER .... - 58 -

XIII. HAYING-TIME .... - 63 -

XIV. UNCLE BART DISCOURSES .... - 67 -

XV. IVORY'S MOTHER .... - 71 -

XVI. LOCKED OUT .... - 77 -

AUTUMN XVII. A BRACE OF LOVERS .... - 84 -

XVIII. A STATE O' MAINE PROPHET .... - 91 -

XIX. AT THE BRICK STORE .... - 97 -

XX. THE ROD THAT BLOSSOMED .... - 104 -

XXI. LOIS BURIES HER DEAD .... - 111 -

XXII. HARVEST-TIME .... - 114 -

XXIII. AUNT ABBY'S WINDOW .... - 118 -

XXIV. PHOEBE TRIUMPHS .... - 122 -

XXV. LOVE'S YOUNG DREAMS .... - 125 -

WINTER XXVI. A WEDDING-RING .... - 132 -

XXVII. THE CONFESSIONAL .... - 136 -

XXVIII. PATTY IS SHOWN THE DOOR .... - 141 -

XXIX. WAITSTILL SPEAKS HER MIND .... - 146 -

XXX. A CLASH OF WILLS .... - 150 -

XXXI. SENTRY DUTY .... - 154 -

XXXII. THE HOUSE OF AARON .... - 159 -

XXXIII. AARON'S ROD .... - 165 -

XXXIV. THE DEACON'S WATERLOO .... - 172 -

XXXV. TWO HEAVENS .... - 179 -

SPRING
I. SACO WATER

FAR, far up, in the bosom of New Hampshire's granite hills, the Saco has its birth. As the mountain rill gathers strength it takes

"Through Bartlett's vales its tuneful way,

Or hides in Conway's fragrant brakes,

Retreating from the glare of day."

Now it leaves the mountains and flows through "green Fryeburg's woods and farms." In the course of its frequent turns and twists and bends, it meets with many another stream, and sends it, fuller and stronger, along its rejoicing way. When it has journeyed more than a hundred miles and is nearing the ocean, it greets the Great Ossipee River and accepts its crystal tribute. Then, in its turn, the Little Ossipee joins forces, and the river, now a splendid stream, flows onward to Bonny Eagle, to Moderation and to Salmon Falls, where it dashes over the dam like a young Niagara and hurtles, in a foamy torrent, through the ragged defile cut between lofty banks of solid rock.

Widening out placidly for a moment's rest in the sunny reaches near Pleasant Point, it gathers itself for a new plunge at Union Falls, after which it speedily merges itself in the bay and is fresh water no more.

At one of the falls on the Saco, the two little hamlets of Edgewood and Riverboro nestle together at the bridge and make one village. The stream is a wonder of beauty just here; a mirror of placid loveliness above the dam, a tawny, roaring wonder at the fall, and a mad, white-flecked torrent as it dashes on its way to the ocean.

The river has seen strange sights in its time, though the history of these two tiny villages is quite unknown to the great world outside. They have been born, waxed strong, and fallen almost to decay while Saco Water has tumbled over the rocks and spent itself in its impetuous journey to the sea.

It remembers the yellow-moccasined Sokokis as they issued from the Indian Cellar and carried their birchen canoes along the wooded shore. It was in those years that the silver-skinned salmon leaped in its crystal depths; the otter and the beaver crept with sleek wet skins upon its shore; and the brown deer came down to quench his thirst at its brink while at twilight the stealthy forms of bear and panther and wolf were mirrored in its glassy surface.

Time sped; men chained the river's turbulent forces and ordered it to grind at the mill. Then houses and barns appeared along its banks, bridges were built, orchards planted, forests changed into farms, white-painted meetinghouses gleamed through the trees and distant bells rang from their steeples on quiet Sunday mornings.

All at once myriads of great hewn logs vexed its downward course, slender logs linked together in long rafts, and huge logs drifting down singly or in pairs. Men appeared, running hither and thither like ants, and going through mysterious operations the reason for which the river could never guess: but the mill-wheels turned, the great saws buzzed, the smoke from tavern chimneys rose in the air, and the rattle and clatter of stage-coaches resounded along the road.

Now children paddled with bare feet in the river's sandy coves and shallows, and lovers sat on its alder-shaded banks and exchanged their vows just where the shuffling bear was wont to come down and drink.

The Saco could remember the "cold year," when there was a black frost every month of the twelve, and though almost all the corn along its shores shrivelled on the stalk, there were two farms where the vapor from the river saved the crops, and all the seed for the next season came from the favored spot, to be known as "Egypt" from that day henceforward.

Strange, complex things now began to happen, and the river played its own part in some of these, for there were disastrous freshets, the sudden breaking-up of great jams of logs, and the drowning of men who were engulfed in the dark whirlpool below the rapids.

Caravans, with menageries of wild beasts, crossed the bridge now every year. An infuriated elephant lifted the side of the old Edgewood Tavern barn, and the wild laughter of the roistering rum-drinkers who were tantalizing the animals floated down to the river's edge. The roar of a lion, tearing and chewing the arm of one of the bystanders, and the cheers of the throng when a plucky captain of the local militia thrust a stake down the beast's throat,—these sounds displaced the former war-whoop of the Indians and the ring of the axe in the virgin forests along the shores.

There were days, and moonlight nights, too, when strange sights and sounds of quite another nature could have been noted by the river as it flowed under the bridge that united the two little villages.

Issuing from the door of the Riverboro Town House, and winding down the hill, through the long row of teams and carriages that lined the roadside, came a procession of singing men and singing women. Convinced of sin, but entranced with promised pardon; spiritually intoxicated by the glowing eloquence of the latter-day prophet they were worshipping, the band of "Cochranites" marched down the dusty road and across the bridge, dancing, swaying, waving handkerchiefs, and shouting hosannas.

God watched, and listened, knowing that there would be other prophets, true and false, in the days to come, and other processions following them; and the river watched and listened too, as it hurried on towards the sea with its story of the present that was sometime to be the history of the past.

When Jacob Cochrane was leading his overwrought, ecstatic band across the river, Waitstill Baxter, then a child, was watching the strange, noisy company from the window of a little brick dwelling on the top of the Town-House Hill.

Her stepmother stood beside her with a young baby in her arms, but when she saw what held the gaze of the child she drew her away, saying: "We mustn't look, Waitstill; your father don't like it!"

"Who was the big man at the head, mother?"

"His name is Jacob Cochrane, but you mustn't think or talk about him; he is very wicked."

"He doesn't look any wickeder than the others," said the child. "Who was the man that fell down in the road, mother, and the woman that knelt and prayed over him? Why did he fall, and why did she pray, mother?"

"That was Master Aaron Boynton, the schoolmaster, and his wife. He only made believe to fall down, as the Cochranites do; the way they carry on is a disgrace to the village, and that's the reason your father won't let us look at them."

"I played with a nice boy over to Boynton's," mused the child.

"That was Ivory, their only child. He is a good little fellow, but his mother and father will spoil him with their crazy ways."

"I hope nothing will happen to him, for I love him," said the child gravely. "He showed me a humming-bird's nest, the first ever I saw, and the littlest!"

"Don't talk about loving him," chided the woman. "If your father should hear you, he'd send you to bed without your porridge."

"Father couldn't hear me, for I never speak when he's at home," said grave little Waitstill. "And I'm used to going to bed without my porridge."

II. THE SISTERS

THE river was still running under the bridge, but the current of time had swept Jacob Cochrane out of sight, though not out of mind, for he had left here and there a disciple to preach his strange and uncertain doctrine. Waitstill, the child who never spoke in her father's presence, was a young woman now, the mistress of the house; the stepmother was dead, and the baby a girl of seventeen.

The brick cottage on the hilltop had grown only a little shabbier. Deacon Foxwell Baxter still slammed its door behind him every morning at seven o'clock and, without any such cheerful conventions as good-byes to his girls, walked down to the bridge to open his store.

The day, properly speaking, had opened when Waitstill and Patience had left their beds at dawn, built the fire, fed the hens and turkeys, and prepared the breakfast, while the Deacon was graining the horse and milking the cows. Such minor "chores" as carrying water from the well, splitting kindling, chopping pine, or bringing wood into the kitchen, were left to Waitstill, who had a strong back, or, if she had not, had never been unwise enough to mention the fact in her father's presence. The almanac day, however, which opened with sunrise, had nothing to do with the real human day, which always began when Mr. Baxter slammed the door behind him, and reached its high noon of delight when he disappeared from view.

"He's opening the store shutters!" chanted Patience from the heights of a kitchen chair by the window. "Now he's taken his cane and beaten off the Boynton puppy that was sitting on the steps as usual,—I don't mean Ivory's dog" (here the girl gave a quick glance at her sister), "but Rodman's little yellow cur. Rodman must have come down to the bridge on some errand for Ivory. Isn't it odd, when that dog has all the other store steps to sit upon, he should choose father's, when every bone in his body must tell him how father hates him and the whole Boynton family."

"Father has no real cause that I ever heard of; but some dogs never know when they've had enough beating, nor some people either." said Waitstill, speaking from the pantry.

"Don't be gloomy when it's my birthday, Sis!—Now he's opened the door and kicked the cat! All is ready for business at the Baxter store."

"I wish you weren't quite so free with your tongue, Patty."

"Somebody must talk," retorted the girl, jumping down from the chair and shaking back her mop of red-gold curls. "I'll put this hateful, childish, round comb in and out just once more, then it will disappear forever. This very after-noon up goes my hair!"

"You know it will be of no use unless you braid it very plainly and neatly. Father will take notice and make you smooth it down."

"Father hasn't looked me square in the face for years; besides, my hair won't braid, and nothing can make it quite plain and neat, thank goodness! Let us be thankful for small mercies, as Jed Morrill said when the lightning struck his mother-in-law and skipped his wife."

"Patty, I will not permit you to repeat those tavern stories; they are not seemly on the lips of a girl!" And Waitstill came out of the pantry with a shadow of disapproval in her eyes and in her voice.

Patty flung her arms round her sister tempestuously, and pulled out the waves of her hair so that it softened her face.—"I'll be good," she said, "and oh, Waity! let's invent some sort of cheap happiness for to-day! I shall never be seventeen again and we have so many troubles! Let's put one of the cows in the horse's stall and see what will happen! Or let's spread up our beds with the head at the foot and put the chest of drawers on the other side of the room, or let's make candy! Do you think father would miss the molasses if we only use a cupful? Couldn't we strain the milk, but leave the churning and the dishes for an hour or two, just once? If you say 'yes' I can think of something wonderful to do!"

"What is it?" asked Waitstill, relenting at the sight of the girl's eager, roguish face.

"PIERCE MY EARS!" cried Patty. "Say you will!"

"Oh! Patty, Patty, I am afraid you are given over to vanity! I daren't let you wear eardrops without father's permission."

"Why not? Lots of church members wear them, so it can't be a mortal sin. Father is against all adornments, but that's because he doesn't want to buy them. You've always said I should have your mother's coral pendants when I was old enough. Here I am, seventeen today, and Dr. Perry says I am already a well-favored young woman. I can pull my hair over my ears for a few days and when the holes are all made and healed, even father cannot make me fill them up again. Besides, I'll never wear the earrings at home!"

"Oh! my dear, my dear!" sighed Waitstill, with a half-sob in her voice. "If only I was wise enough to know how we could keep from these little deceits, yet have any liberty or comfort in life!"

"We can't! The Lord couldn't expect us to bear all that we bear," exclaimed Patty, "without our trying once in a while to have a good time in our own way. We never do a thing that we are ashamed of, or that other girls don't do every day in the week; only our pleasures always have to be taken behind father's back. It's only me that's ever wrong, anyway, for you are always an angel. It's a burning shame and you only twenty-one yourself. I'll pierce your ears if you say so, and let you wear your own coral drops!"

"No, Patty; I've outgrown those longings years ago. When your mother died and left father and you and the house to me, my girlhood died, too, though I was only thirteen."

"It was only your inside girlhood that died," insisted Patty stoutly, "The outside is as fresh as the paint on Uncle Barty's new ell. You've got the loveliest eyes and hair in Riverboro, and you know it; besides, Ivory Boynton would tell you so if you didn't. Come and bore my ears, there's a darling!"

"Ivory Boynton never speaks a word of my looks, nor a word that father and all the world mightn't hear." And Waitstill flushed.

"Then it's because he's shy and silent and has so many troubles of his own that he doesn't dare say anything. When my hair is once up and the coral pendants are swinging in my ears, I shall expect to hear something about MY looks, I can tell you. Waity, after all, though we never have what we want to eat, and never a decent dress to our backs, nor a young man to cross the threshold, I wouldn't change places with Ivory Boynton, would you?" Here Patty swept the hearth vigorously with a turkey wing and added a few corncobs to the fire.

Waitstill paused a moment in her task of bread-kneading. "Well," she answered critically, "at least we know where our father is."

"We do, indeed! We also know that he is thoroughly alive!"

"And though people do talk about him, they can't say the things they say of Master Aaron Boynton. I don't believe father would ever run away and desert us."

"I fear not," said Patty. "I wish the angels would put the idea into his head, though, of course, it wouldn't be the angels; they'd be above it. It would have to be the 'Old Driver,' as Jed Morrill calls the Evil One; but whoever did it, the result would be the same: we should be deserted, and live happily ever after. Oh! to be deserted, and left with you alone on this hilltop, what joy it would be!"

Waitstill frowned, but did not interfere further with Patty's intemperate speech. She knew that she was simply serving as an escape-valve, and that after the steam was "let off" she would be more rational.

"Of course, we are motherless," continued Patty wistfully, "but poor Ivory is worse than motherless."

"No, not worse, Patty," said Waitstill, taking the bread-board and moving towards the closet. "Ivory loves his mother and she loves him, with all the mind she has left! She has the best blood of New England flowing in her veins, and I suppose it was a great come down for her to marry Aaron Boynton, clever and gifted though he was. Now Ivory has to protect her, poor, daft, innocent creature, and hide her away from the gossip of the village. He is surely the best of sons, Ivory Boynton!"

"She is a terrible care for him, and like to spoil his life," said Patty.

"There are cares that swell the heart and make it bigger and warmer, Patty, just as there are cares that shrivel it and leave it tired and cold. Love lightens Ivory's afflictions but that is something you and I have to do without, so it seems."

"I suppose little Rodman is some comfort to the Boyntons, even if he is only ten." Patty suggested.

"No doubt. He's a good little fellow, and though it's rather hard for Ivory to be burdened for these last five years with the support of a child who's no nearer kin than a cousin, still he's of use, minding Mrs. Boynton and the house when Ivory's away. The school-teacher says he is wonderful at his books and likely to be a great credit to the Boyntons some day or other."

"You've forgot to name our one great blessing, Waity, and I believe, anyway, you're talking to keep my mind off the earrings!"

"You mean we've each other? No, Patty, I never forget that, day or night. 'Tis that makes me willing to bear any burden father chooses to put upon us.—Now the bread is set, but I don't believe I have the courage to put a needle into your tender flesh, Patty; I really don't."

"Nonsense! I've got the waxed silk all ready and chosen the right-sized needle and I'll promise not to jump or screech more than I can help. We'll make a tiny lead-pencil dot right in the middle of the lobe, then you place the needle on it, shut your eyes, and JAB HARD! I expect to faint, but when I 'come to,' we can decide which of us will pull the needle through to the other side. Probably it will be you, I'm such a coward. If it hurts dreadfully, I'll have only one pierced to-day and take the other to-morrow; and if it hurts very dreadfully, perhaps I'll go through life with one ear-ring. Aunt Abby Cole will say it's just odd enough to suit me!"

"You'll never go through life with one tongue at the rate you use it now," chided Waitstill, "for it will never last you. Come, we'll take the work-basket and go out in the barn where no one will see or hear us."

"Goody, goody! Come along!" and Patty clapped her hands in triumph. "Have you got the pencil and the needle and the waxed silk? Then bring the camphor bottle to revive me, and the coral pendants, too, just to give me courage. Hurry up! It's ten o'clock. I was born at sun-rise, so I'm 'going on' eighteen and can't waste any time!"

III. DEACON BAXTER'S WIVES

FOXWELL BAXTER was ordinarily called "Old Foxy" by the boys of the district, and also, it is to be feared, by the men gathered for evening conference at the various taverns, or at one of the rival village stores.

He had a small farm of fifteen or twenty acres, with a pasture, a wood lot, and a hay-field, but the principal source of his income came from trading. His sign bore the usual legend: "WEST INDIA GOODS AND GROCERIES," and probably the most profitable articles in his stock were rum, molasses, sugar, and tobacco; but there were chests of rice, tea, coffee, and spices, barrels of pork in brine, as well as piles of cotton and woolen cloth on the shelves above the counters. His shop window, seldom dusted or set in order, held a few clay pipes, some glass jars of peppermint or sassafras lozenges, black licorice, stick-candy, and sugar gooseberries. These dainties were seldom renewed, for it was only a very bold child, or one with an ungovernable appetite for sweets, who would have spent his penny at Foxy Baxter's store.

He was thought a sharp and shrewd trader, but his honesty was never questioned; indeed, the only trait in his character that ever came up for general discussion was his extraordinary, unbelievable, colossal meanness. This so eclipsed every other passion in the man, and loomed so bulkily and insistently in the foreground, that had he cherished a second vice no one would have observed it, and if he really did possess a casual virtue, it could scarcely have reared its head in such ugly company.

It might be said, to defend the fair name of the Church, that Mr. Baxter's deaconhood did not include very active service in the courts of the Lord. He had "experienced religion" at fifteen and made profession of his faith, but all well-brought-up boys and girls did the same in those days; their parents saw to that! If change of conviction or backsliding occurred later on, that was not their business! At the ripe age of twenty-five he was selected to fill a vacancy and became a deacon, thinking it might be good for trade, as it was, for some years. He was very active at the time of the "Cochrane craze," since any defence of the creed that included lively detective work and incessant spying on his neighbors was particularly in his line; but for many years now, though he had been regular in attendance at church, he had never officiated at communion, and his diaconal services had gradually lapsed into the passing of the contribution-box, a task of which he never wearied; it was such a keen pleasure to make other people yield their pennies for a good cause, without adding any of his own!

Deacon Baxter had now been a widower for some years and the community had almost relinquished the idea of his seeking a fourth wife. This was a matter of some regret, for there was a general feeling that it would be a good thing for the Baxter girls to have some one to help with the housework and act as a buffer between them and their grim and irascible parent. As for the women of the village, they were mortified that the Deacon had been able to secure three wives, and refused to believe that the universe held anywhere a creature benighted enough to become his fourth.

The first, be it said, was a mere ignorant girl, and he a beardless youth of twenty, who may not have shown his true qualities so early in life. She bore him two sons, and it was a matter of comment at the time that she called them, respectively, Job and Moses, hoping that the endurance and meekness connected with these names might somehow help them in their future relations with their father. Pneumonia, coupled with profound discouragement, carried her off in a few years to make room for the second wife, Waitstill's mother, who was of different fibre and greatly his superior. She was a fine, handsome girl, the orphan daughter of up-country gentle-folks, who had died when she was eighteen, leaving her alone in the world and penniless.

Baxter, after a few days' acquaintance, drove into the dooryard of the house where she was a visitor and, showing her his two curly-headed boys, suddenly asked her to come and be their stepmother. She assented, partly because she had nothing else to do with her existence, so far as she could see, and also because she fell in love with the children at first sight and forgot, as girls will, that it was their father whom she was marrying.

She was as plucky and clever and spirited as she was handsome, and she made a brave fight of it with Foxy; long enough to bring a daughter into the world, to name her Waitstill, and start her a little way on her life journey,— then she, too, gave up the struggle and died. Typhoid fever it was, combined with complete loss of illusions, and a kind of despairing rage at having made so complete a failure of her existence.

The next year, Mr. Baxter, being unusually busy, offered a man a good young heifer if he would jog about the country a little and pick him up a housekeeper; a likely woman who would, if she proved energetic, economical, and amiable, be eventually raised to the proud position of his wife. If she was young, healthy, smart, tidy, capable, and a good manager, able to milk the cows, harness the horse, and make good butter, he would give a dollar and a half a week. The woman was found, and, incredible as it may seem, she said "yes" when the Deacon (whose ardor was kindled at having paid three months' wages) proposed a speedy marriage. The two boys by this time had reached the age of discretion, and one of them evinced the fact by promptly running away to parts unknown, never to be heard from afterwards; while the other, a reckless and unhappy lad, was drowned while running on the logs in the river. Old Foxy showed little outward sign of his loss, though he had brought the boys into the world solely with the view of having one of them work on the farm and the other in the store.

His third wife, the one originally secured for a housekeeper, bore him a girl, very much to his disgust, a girl named Patience, and great was Waitstill's delight at this addition to the dull household. The mother was a timid, colorless, docile creature, but Patience nevertheless was a sparkling, bright-eyed baby, who speedily became the very centre of the universe to the older child. So the months and years wore on, drearily enough, until, when Patience was nine, the third Mrs. Baxter succumbed after the manner of her predecessors, and slipped away from a life that had grown intolerable. The trouble was diagnosed as "liver complaint," but scarcity of proper food, no new frocks or kind words, hard work, and continual bullying may possibly have been contributory causes. Dr. Perry thought so, for he had witnessed three most contented deaths in the Baxter house. The ladies were all members of the church and had presumably made their peace with God, but the good doctor fancied that their pleasure in joining the angels was mild compared with their relief at parting with the Deacon.

"I know I hadn't ought to put the care on you, Waitstill, and you only thirteen," poor Mrs. Baxter sighed, as the young girl was watching with her one night when the end seemed drawing near. "I've made out to live till now when Patience is old enough to dress herself and help round, but I'm all beat out and can't try any more."

"Do you mean I'm to take your place, be a mother to Patience, and keep house, and everything?" asked Waitstill quaveringly.

"I don't see but you'll have to, unless your father marries again. He'll never hire help, you know that!"

"I won't have another mother in this house," flashed the girl. "There's been three here and that's enough! If he brings anybody home, I'll take Patience and run away, as Job did; or if he leaves me alone, I'll wash and iron and scrub and cook till Patience grows up, and then we'll go off together and hide somewhere. I'm fourteen; oh, mother, how soon could I be married and take Patience to live with me? Do you think anybody will ever want me?"

"Don't marry for a home, Waitstill! Your own mother did that, and so did I, and we were both punished for it! You've been a great help and I've had a sight of comfort out of the baby, but I wouldn't go through it again, not even for her! You're real smart and capable for your age and you've done your full share of the work every day, even when you were at school. You can get along all right."

"I don't know how I'm going to do everything alone," said the girl, forcing back her tears. "You've always made the brown bread, and mine will never suit father. I suppose I can wash, but don't know how to iron starched clothes, nor make pickles, and oh! I can never kill a rooster, mother, it's no use to ask me to! I'm not big enough to be the head of the family."

Mrs. Baxter turned her pale, tired face away from Waitstill's appealing eyes.

"I know," she said faintly. "I hate to leave you to bear the brunt alone, but I must!... Take good care of Patience and don't let her get into trouble.... You won't, will you?"

"I'll be careful," promised Waitstill, sobbing quietly; "I'll do my best."

"You've got more courage than ever I had; don't you s'pose you can stiffen up and defend yourself a little mite?... Your father'd ought to be opposed, for his own good... but I've never seen anybody that dared do it." Then, after a pause, she said with a flash of spirit,—"Anyhow, Waitstill, he's your father after all. He's no blood relation of mine, and I can't stand him another day; that's the reason I'm willing to die."

IV. SOMETHING OF A HERO

IVORY BOYNTON lifted the bars that divided his land from the highroad and walked slowly toward the house. It was April, but there were still patches of snow here and there, fast melting under a drizzling rain. It was a gray world, a bleak, black-and-brown world, above and below. The sky was leaden; the road and the footpath were deep in a muddy ooze flecked with white. The tree-trunks, black, with bare branches, were lined against the gray sky; nevertheless, spring had been on the way for a week, and a few sunny days would bring the yearly miracle for which all hearts were longing.

Ivory was season-wise and his quick eye had caught many a sign as he walked through the woods from his schoolhouse. A new and different color haunted the tree-tops, and one had only to look closely at the elm buds to see that they were beginning to swell. Some fat robins had been sunning about in the school-yard at noon, and sparrows had been chirping and twittering on the fence-rails. Yes, the winter was over, and Ivory was glad, for it had meant no coasting and skating and sleighing for him, but long walks in deep snow or slush; long evenings, good for study, but short days, and greater loneliness for his mother. He could see her now as he neared the house, standing in the open doorway, her hand shading her eyes, watching, always watching, for some one who never came.

"Spring is on the way, mother, but it isn't here yet, so don't stand there in the rain," he called. "Look at the nosegay I gathered for you as I came through the woods. Here are pussy willows and red maple blossoms and Mayflowers, would you believe it?"

Lois Boynton took the handful of budding things and sniffed their fragrance.

"You're late to-night, Ivory," she said. "Rod wanted his supper early so that he could go off to singing-school, but I kept something warm for you, and I'll make you a fresh cup of tea."

Ivory went into the little shed room off the kitchen, changed his muddy boots for slippers, and made himself generally tidy; then he came back to the living-room bringing a pine knot which he flung on the fire, waking it to a brilliant flame.

"We can be as lavish as we like with the stumps now, mother, for spring is coming," he said, as he sat down to his meal.

"I've been looking out more than usual this afternoon," she replied. "There's hardly any snow left, and though the walking is so bad I've been rather expecting your father before night. You remember he said, when he went away in January, that he should be back before the Mayflowers bloomed?"

It did not do any good to say: "Yes, mother, but the Mayflowers have bloomed ten times since father went away." He had tried that, gently and persistently when first her mind began to be confused from long grief and hurt love, stricken pride and sick suspense.

Instead of that, Ivory turned the subject cheerily, saying, "Well, we're sure of a good season, I think. There's been a grand snow-fall, and that, they say, is the poor man's manure. Rod and I will put in more corn and potatoes this year. I shan't have to work single-handed very long, for he is growing to be quite a farmer."

"Your father was very fond of green corn, but he never cared for potatoes," Mrs. Boynton said, vaguely, taking up her knitting. "I always had great pride in my cooking, but I could never get your father to relish my potatoes."

"Well, his son does, anyway," Ivory replied, helping himself plentifully from a dish that held one of his mother's best concoctions, potatoes minced fine and put together into the spider with thin bits of pork and all browned together.

"I saw the Baxter girls to-day, mother," he continued, not because he hoped she would give any heed to what he said, but from the sheer longing for companionship. "The Deacon drove off with Lawyer Wilson, who wanted him to give testimony in some case or other down in Milltown. The minute Patty saw him going up Saco Hill, she harnessed the old starved Baxter mare and the girls started over to the Lower Corner to see some friends. It seems it's Patty's birthday and they were celebrating. I met them just as they were coming back and helped them lift the rickety wagon out of the mud; they were stuck in it up to the hubs of the wheels. I advised them to walk up the Town-House Hill if they ever expected to get the horse home."

"Town-House Hill!" said Ivory's mother, dropping her knitting. "That was where we had such wonderful meetings! Truly the Lord was present in our midst, and oh, Ivory! the visions we saw in that place when Jacob Cochrane first unfolded his gospel to us. Was ever such a man!"

"Probably not, mother," remarked Ivory dryly.

"You were speaking of the Baxters. I remember their home, and the little girl who used to stand in the gateway and watch when we came out of meeting. There was a baby, too; isn't there a Baxter baby, Ivory?"

"She didn't stay a baby; she is seventeen years old to-day, mother."

"You surprise me, but children do grow very fast. She had a strange name, but I cannot recall it."

"Her name is Patience, but nobody but her father calls her anything but Patty, which suits her much better."

"No, the name wasn't Patience, not the one I mean."

"The older sister is Waitstill, perhaps you mean her?"—and Ivory sat down by the fire with his book and his pipe.

"Waitstill! Waitstill! that is it! Such a beautiful name!"

"She's a beautiful girl."

"Waitstill! 'They also serve who only stand and wait.' 'Wait, I say, on the Lord and He will give thee the desires of thy heart.'—Those were wonderful days, when we were caught up out of the body and mingled freely in the spirit world." Mrs. Boynton was now fully started on the topic that absorbed her mind and Ivory could do nothing but let her tell the story that she had told him a hundred times.

"I remember when first we heard Jacob Cochrane speak." (This was her usual way of beginning.) "Your father was a preacher, as you know, Ivory, but you will never know what a wonderful preacher he was. My grandfather, being a fine gentleman, and a governor, would not give his consent to my marriage, but I never regretted it, never! Your father saw Elder Cochrane at a revival meeting of the Free Will Baptists in Scarboro', and was much impressed with him. A few days later we went to the funeral of a child in the same neighborhood. No one who was there could ever forget it. The minister had made his long prayer when a man suddenly entered the room, came towards the coffin, and placed his hand on the child's forehead. The room, in an instant, was as still as the death that had called us together. The stranger was tall and of commanding presence; his eyes pierced our very hearts, and his marvellous voice penetrated to depths in our souls that had never been reached before."

"Was he a better speaker than my father?" asked Ivory, who dreaded his mother's hours of complete silence even more than her periods of reminiscence.

"He spoke as if the Lord of Hosts had given him inspiration; as if the angels were pouring words into his mouth just for him to utter," replied Mrs. Boynton. "Your father was spell-bound, and I only less so. When he ceased speaking, the child's mother crossed the room, and swaying to and fro, fell at his feet, sobbing and wailing and imploring God to forgive her sins. They carried her upstairs, and when we looked about after the confusion and excitement the stranger had vanished. But we found him again! As Elder Cochrane said: 'The prophet of the Lord can never be hid; no darkness is thick enough to cover him!' There was a six weeks' revival meeting in North Saco where three hundred souls were converted, and your father and I were among them. We had fancied ourselves true believers for years, but Jacob Cochrane unstopped our ears so that we could hear the truths revealed to him by the Almighty!—It was all so simple and easy at the beginning, but it grew hard and grievous afterward; hard to keep the path, I mean. I never quite knew whether God was angry with me for backsliding at the end, but I could not always accept the revelations that Elder Cochrane and your father had!"

Lois Boynton's hands were now quietly folded over the knitting that lay forgotten in her lap, but her low, thrilling voice had a note in it that did not belong wholly to earth.

There was a long silence; one of many long silences at the Boynton fireside, broken only by the ticking of the clock, the purring of the cat, and the clicking of Mrs. Boynton's needles, as, her paroxysm of reminiscence over, she knitted ceaselessly, with her eyes on the window or the door.

"It's about time for Rod to be coming back, isn't it?" asked Ivory.

"He ought to be here soon, but perhaps he is gone for good; it may be that he thinks he has made us a long enough visit. I don't know whether your father will like the boy when he comes home. He never did fancy company in the house."

Ivory looked up in astonishment from his Greek grammar. This was an entirely new turn of his mother's mind. Often when she was more than usually confused he would try to clear the cobwebs from her brain by gently questioning her until she brought herself back to a clearer understanding of her own thought. Thus far her vagaries had never made her unjust to any human creature; she was uniformly sweet and gentle in speech and demeanor.

"Why do you talk of Rod's visiting us when he is one of the family?" Ivory asked quietly.

"Is he one of the family? I didn't know it," replied his mother absently.

"Look at me, mother, straight in the eye; that's right: now listen, dear, to what I say."

Mrs. Boynton's hair that had been in her youth like an aureole of corn-silk was now a strange yellow-white, and her blue eyes looked out from her pale face with a helpless appeal.

"You and I were living alone here after father went away," Ivory began. "I was a little boy, you know. You and father had saved something, there was the farm, you worked like a slave, I helped, and we lived, somehow, do you remember?"

"I do, indeed! It was cold and the neighbors were cruel. Jacob Cochrane had gone away and his disciples were not always true to him. When the magnetism of his presence was withdrawn, they could not follow all his revelations, and they forgot how he had awakened their spiritual life at the first of his preaching. Your father was always a stanch believer, but when he started on his mission and went to Parsonsfield to help Elder Cochrane in his meetings, the neighbors began to criticize him. They doubted him. You were too young to realize it, but I did, and it almost broke my heart."

"I was nearly twelve years old; do you think I escaped all the gossip, mother?"

"You never spoke of it to me, Ivory."

"No, there is much that I never spoke of to you, mother, but sometime when you grow stronger and your memory is better we will talk together.— Do you remember the winter, long after father went away, that Parson Lane sent me to Fairfield Academy to get enough Greek and Latin to make me a schoolmaster?"

"Yes," she answered uncertainly.

"Don't you remember I got a free ride down-river one Friday and came home for Sunday, just to surprise you? And when I got here I found you ill in bed, with Mrs. Mason and Dr. Perry taking care of you. You could not speak, you were so ill, but they told me you had been up in New Hampshire to see your sister, that she had died, and that you had brought back her boy, who was only four years old. That was Rod. I took him into bed with me that night, poor, homesick little fellow, and, as you know, mother, he's never left us since."

"I didn't remember I had a sister. Is she dead, Ivory?" asked Mrs. Boynton vaguely.

"If she were not dead, do you suppose you would have kept Rodman with us when we hadn't bread enough for our own two mouths, mother?" questioned Ivory patiently.

"No, of course not. I can't think how I can be so forgetful. It's worse sometimes than others. It's worse to-day because I knew the Mayflowers were blooming and that reminded me it was time for your father to come home; you must forgive me, dear, and will you excuse me if I sit in the kitchen awhile? The window by the side door looks out towards the road, and if I put a candle on the sill it shines quite a distance. The lane is such a long one, and your father was always a sad stumbler in the dark! I shouldn't like him to think I wasn't looking for him when he's been gone since January."

Ivory's pipe went out, and his book slipped from his knee unnoticed.

His mother was more confused than usual, but she always was when spring came to remind her of her husband's promise. Somehow, well used as he was to her mental wanderings, they made him uneasy to-night. His father had left home on a fancied mission, a duty he believed to be a revelation given by God through Jacob Cochrane. The farm did not miss him much at first, Ivory reflected bitterly, for since his fanatical espousal of Cochranism his father's interest in such mundane matters as household expenses had diminished month by month until they had no meaning for him at all. Letters to wife and boy had come at first, but after six months—during which he had written from many places, continually deferring the date of his return-they had ceased altogether. The rest was silence. Rumors of his presence here or there came from time to time, but though Parson Lane and Dr. Perry did their best, none of them were ever substantiated.

Where had those years of wandering been passed, and had they all been given even to an imaginary and fantastic service of God? Was his father dead? If he were alive, what could keep him from writing? Nothing but a very strong reason, or a very wrong one, so his son thought, at times.

Since Ivory had grown to man's estate, he understood that in the later days of Cochrane's preaching, his "visions," "inspirations," and "revelations" concerning the marriage bond were a trifle startling from the old-fashioned, orthodox point of view. His most advanced disciples were to hold themselves in readiness to renounce their former vows and seek "spiritual consorts," sometimes according to his advice, sometimes as their inclinations prompted.

Had Aaron Boynton forsaken, willingly, the wife of his youth, the mother of his boy? If so, he must have realized to what straits he was subjecting them. Ivory had not forgotten those first few years of grinding poverty, anxiety, and suspense. His mother's mind had stood the strain bravely, but it gave way at last; not, however, until that fatal winter journey to New Hampshire, when cold, exposure, and fatigue did their worst for her weak body. Religious enthusiast, exalted and impressionable, a natural mystic, she had probably always been, far more so in temperament, indeed, than her husband; but although she left home on that journey a frail and heartsick woman, she returned a different creature altogether, blurred and confused in mind, with clouded memory and irrational fancies.

She must have given up hope, just then, Ivory thought, and her love was so deep that when it was uprooted the soil came with it. Now hope had returned because the cruel memory had faded altogether. She sat by the kitchen window in gentle expectation, watching, always watching.

And this is the way many of Ivory Boynton's evenings were spent, while the heart of him, the five-and-twenty-year-old heart of him, was longing to feel the beat of another heart, a girl's heart only a mile or more away. The ice in Saco Water had broken up and the white blocks sailed majestically down towards the sea; sap was mounting and the elm trees were budding; the trailing arbutus was blossoming in the woods; the robins had come;- everything was announcing the spring, yet Ivory saw no changing seasons in his future; nothing but winter, eternal winter there!

V. PATIENCE AND IMPATIENCE

PATTY had been searching for eggs in the barn chamber, and coming down the ladder from the haymow spied her father washing the wagon by the well-side near the shed door. Cephas Cole kept store for him at meal hours and whenever trade was unusually brisk, and the Baxter yard was so happily situated that Old Foxy could watch both house and store.

There never was a good time to ask Deacon Baxter a favor, therefore this moment would serve as well as any other, so, approaching him near enough to be heard through the rubbing and splashing, but no nearer than was necessary Patty said:—

"Father, can I go up to Ellen Wilson's this afternoon and stay to tea? I won't start till I've done a good day's work and I'll come home early."

"What do you want to go gallivantin' to the neighbors for? I never saw anything like the girls nowadays; highty-tighty, flauntin', traipsin', triflin' trollops, ev'ry one of 'em, that's what they are, and Ellen Wilson's one of the triflin'est. You're old enough now to stay to home where you belong and make an effort to earn your board and clothes, which you can't, even if you try."

Spunk, real, Simon-pure spunk, started somewhere in Patty and coursed through her blood like wine.

"If a girl's old enough to stay at home and work, I should think she was old enough to go out and play once in a while." Patty was still too timid to make this remark more than a courteous suggestion, so far as its tone was concerned.

"Don't answer me back; you're full of new tricks, and you've got to stop 'em, right where you are, or there'll be trouble. You were whistlin' just now up in the barn chamber; that's one of the things I won't have round my premises,—a whistlin' girl."

"'T was a Sabbath-School hymn that I was whistling!" This with a creditable imitation of defiance.

"That don't make it any better. Sing your hymns if you must make a noise while you're workin'."

"It's the same mouth that makes the whistle and sings the song, so I don't see why one's any wickeder than the other."

"You don't have to see," replied the Deacon grimly; "all you have to do is to mind when you're spoken to. Now run 'long 'bout your work."

"Can't I go up to Ellen's, then?"

"What's goin' on up there?"

"Just a frolic. There's always a good time at Ellen's, and I would so like the sight of a big, rich house now and then!"

"'Just a frolic.' Land o' Goshen, hear the girl! 'Sight of a big, rich house,' indeed!—Will there be any boys at the party?"

"I s'pose so, or 't wouldn't be a frolic," said Patty with awful daring; "but there won't be many; only a few of Mark's friends."

"Well, there ain't going to be no more argyfyin'!"

"Well, there ain't goin' to be no more argyfyin'! I won't have any girl o' mine frolickin' with boys, so that's the end of it. You're kind o' crazy lately, riggin' yourself out with a ribbon here and a flower there, and pullin' your hair down over your ears. Why do you want to cover your ears up? What are they for?"

"To hear you with, father," Patty replied, with honey-sweet voice and eyes that blazed.

"Well, I hope they'll never hear anything worse," replied her father, flinging a bucket of water over the last of the wagon wheels.

"THEY COULDN'T!" These words were never spoken aloud, but oh! how Patty longed to shout them with a clarion voice as she walked away in perfect silence, her majestic gait showing, she hoped, how she resented the outcome of the interview.

"I've stood up to father!" she exclaimed triumphantly as she entered the kitchen and set down her yellow bowl of eggs on the table. "I stood up to him, and answered him back three times!"

Waitstill was busy with her Saturday morning cooking, but she turned in alarm.

"Patty, what have you said and done? Tell me quickly!"

"I 'argyfied,' but it didn't do any good; he won't let me go to Ellen's party."

Waitstill wiped her floury hands and put them on her sister's shoulders.

"Hear what I say, Patty: you must not argue with father, whatever he says. We don't love him and so there isn't the right respect in our hearts, but at least there can be respect in our manners."

"I don't believe I can go on for years, holding in, Waitstill!" Patty whimpered.

"Yes, you can. I have!"

"You're different, Waitstill."

"I wasn't so different at sixteen, but that's five years ago, and I've got control of my tongue and my temper since then. Sometime, perhaps, when I have a grievance too great to be rightly borne, sometime when you are away from here in a home of your own, I shall speak out to father; just empty my heart of all the disappointment and bitterness and rebellion. Somebody ought to tell him the truth, and perhaps it will be me!"

"I wish it could be me," exclaimed Patty vindictively, and with an equal disregard of grammar.

"You would speak in temper, I'm afraid, Patty, and that would spoil all. I'm sorry you can't go up to Ellen's," she sighed, turning back to her work; "you don't have pleasure enough for one of your age; still, don't fret; something may happen to change things, and anyhow the weather is growing warmer, and you and I have so many more outings in summer-time. Smooth down your hair, child; there are straws in it, and it's all rough with the wind. I don't like flying hair about a kitchen."

"I wish my hair was flying somewhere a thousand miles from here; or at least I should wish it if it did not mean leaving you; for oh. I'm so miserable and disappointed and unhappy!"

Waitstill bent over the girl as she flung herself down beside the table and smoothed her shoulder gently.

"There, there, dear; it isn't like my gay little sister to cry. What is the matter with you to-day, Patty?"

"I suppose it's the spring," she said, wiping her eyes with her apron and smiling through her tears. "Perhaps I need a dose of sulphur and molasses."

"Don't you feel well as common?"

"Well? I feel too well! I feel as if I was a young colt shut up in an attic. I want to kick up my heels, batter the door down, and get out into the pasture. It's no use talking, Waity;—I can't go on living without a bit of pleasure and I can't go on being patient even for your sake. If it weren't for you, I'd run away as Job did; and I never believed Moses slipped on the logs; I'm sure he threw himself into the river, and so should I if I had the courage!"

"Stop, Patty, stop, dear! You shall have your bit of pasture, at least. I'll do some of your indoor tasks for you, and you shall put on your sunbonnet and go out and dig the dandelion greens for dinner. Take the broken knife and a milkpan and don't bring in so much earth with them as you did last time. Dry your eyes and look at the green things growing. Remember how young you are and how many years are ahead of you! Go along, dear!"

Waitstill went about her work with rather a heavy heart. Was life going to be more rather than less difficult, now that Patty was growing up? Would she he able to do her duty both by father and sister and keep peace in the household, as she had vowed, in her secret heart, always to do? She paused every now and then to look out of the window and wave an encouraging hand to Patty. The girl's bonnet was off, and her uncovered head blazed like red gold in the sunlight. The short young grass was dotted with dandelion blooms, some of them already grown to huge disks of yellow, and Patty moved hither and thither, selecting the younger weeds, deftly putting the broken knife under their roots and popping them into the tin pan. Presently, for Deacon Baxter had finished the wagon and gone down the hill to relieve Cephas Cole at the counter, Patty's shrill young whistle floated into the kitchen, but with a mischievous glance at the open window she broke off suddenly and began to sing the words of the hymn with rather more emphasis and gusto than strict piety warranted.

"There'll be SOMEthing in heav-en for chil-dren to do,

None are idle in that bless-ed land:

There'll be WORK for the heart. There'll be WORK for the mind,

And emPLOYment for EACH little hand.

  "There'll be SOME-thing to do,

   There'll be SOME-thing to do,

There'll be SOME-thing for CHIL-dren to do!

On that bright blessed shore where there's joy evermore,

There'll be SOME-thing for CHIL-DREN to do."

Patty's young existence being full to the brim of labor, this view of heaven never in the least appealed to her and she rendered the hymn with little sympathy. The main part of the verse was strongly accented by jabs at the unoffending dandelion roots, but when the chorus came she brought out the emphatic syllables by a beat of the broken knife on the milkpan.

This rendition of a Sabbath-School classic did not meet Waitstill's ideas of perfect propriety, but she smiled and let it pass, planning some sort of recreation for a stolen half-hour of the afternoon. It would have to be a walk through the pasture into the woods to see what had grown since they went there a fortnight ago. Patty loved people better than Nature, but failing the one she could put up with the other, for she had a sense of beauty and a pagan love of color. There would be pale-hued innocence and blue and white violets in the moist places, thought Waitstill, and they would have them in a china cup on the supper-table. No, that would never do, for last time father had knocked them over when he was reaching for the bread, and in a silent protest against such foolishness got up from the table and emptied theirs into the kitchen sink.

"There's a place for everything," he said when he came back, "and the place for flowers is outdoors."

Then in the pine woods there would be, she was sure, Star of Bethlehem, Solomon's Seal, the white spray of groundnuts and bunchberries. Perhaps they could make a bouquet and Patty would take it across the fields to Mrs. Boynton's door. She need not go in, and thus they would not be disobeying their father's command not to visit that "crazy Boynton woman."

Here Patty came in with a pan full of greens and the sisters sat down in the sunny window to get them ready for the pot.

"I'm calmer," the little rebel allowed. "That's generally the way it turns out with me. I get into a rage, but I can generally sing it off!"

"You certainly must have got rid of a good deal of temper this morning, by the way your voice sounded."

"Nobody can hear us in this out-of-the-way place. It's easy enough to see that the women weren't asked to say anything when the men settled where the houses should be built! The men weren't content to stick them on the top of a high hill, or half a mile from the stores, but put them back to the main road, taking due care to cut the sink-window where their wives couldn't see anything even when they were washing dishes."

"I don't know that I ever thought about it in that way"; and Waitstill looked out of the window in a brown study while her hands worked with the dandelion greens. "I've noticed it, but I never supposed the men did it intentionally."

"No, you wouldn't," said Patty with the pessimism of a woman of ninety, as she stole an admiring glance at her sister. Patty's own face, irregular, piquant, tantalizing, had its peculiar charm, and her brilliant skin and hair so dazzled the masculine beholder that he took note of no small defects; but Waitstill was beautiful; beautiful even in her working dress of purple calico. Her single braid of hair, the Foxwell hair, that in her was bronze and in Patty pale auburn, was wound once around her fine head and made to stand a little as it went across the front. It was a simple, easy, unconscious fashion of her own, quite different from anything done by other women in her time and place, and it just suited her dignity and serenity. It looked like a coronet, but it was the way she carried her head that gave you the fancy, there was such spirit and pride in the poise of it on the long graceful neck. Her eyes were as clear as mountain pools shaded by rushes, and the strength of the face was softened by the sweetness of the mouth.

Patty never let the conversation die out for many seconds at a time and now she began again. "My sudden rages don't match my name very well, but, of course, mother didn't know how I was going to turn out when she called me Patience, for I was nothing but a squirming little bald, red baby; but my name really is too ridiculous when you think about it."

Waitstill laughed as she said: "It didn't take you long to change it! Perhaps Patience was a hard word for a baby to say, but the moment you could talk you said, 'Patty wants this' and 'Patty wants that.'"

"Did Patty ever get it? She never has since, that's certain! And look at your name: it's 'Waitstill,' yet you never stop a moment. When you're not in the shed or barn, or chicken-house, or kitchen or attic, or garden-patch, you are working in the Sunday School or the choir."

It seemed as if Waitstill did not intend to answer this arraignment of her activities. She rose and crossed the room to put the pan of greens in the sink, preparing to wash them.

Taking the long-handled dipper from the nail, she paused a moment before plunging it into the water pail; paused, and leaning her elbow on a corner of the shelf over the sink, looked steadfastly out into the orchard.

Patty watched her curiously and was just going to offer a penny for her thoughts when Waitstill suddenly broke the brief silence by saying: "Yes, I am always busy; it's better so, but all the same, Patty, I'm waiting,—inside! I don't know for what, but I always feel that I am waiting!"

VI. A KISS

"SHALL we have our walk in the woods on the Edgewood side of the river, just for a change, Patty?" suggested her sister. "The water is so high this year that the river will be splendid. We can gather our flowers in the hill pasture and then you'll be quite near Mrs. Boynton's and can carry the nosegay there while I come home ahead of you and get supper. I'll take to-day's eggs to father's store on the way and ask him if he minds our having a little walk. I've an errand at Aunt Abby's that would take me down to the bridge anyway."

"Very well," said Patty, somewhat apathetically. "I always like a walk with you, but I don't care what becomes of me this afternoon if I can't go to Ellen's party."

The excursion took place according to Waitstill's plan, and at four o'clock she sped back to her night work and preparations for supper, leaving Patty with a great bunch of early wildflowers for Ivory's mother. Patty had left them at the Boyntons' door with Rodman, who was picking up chips and volunteered to take the nosegay into the house at once.

"Won't you step inside?" the boy asked shyly, wishing to be polite, but conscious that visitors, from the village very seldom crossed the threshold.

"I'd like to, but I can't this afternoon, thank you. I must run all the way down the hill now, or I shan't be in time to supper."

"Do you eat meals together over to your house?" asked the boy.

"We're all three at the table if that means together."

"We never are. Ivory goes off early and takes lunch in a pail. So do I when I go to school. Aunt Boynton never sits down to eat; she just stands at the window and takes a bite of something now 'and then. You haven't got any mother, have you?"

"No, Rodman."

"Neither have I, nor any father, nor any relations but Aunt Boynton and Ivory. Ivory is very good to me, and when he's at home I'm never lonesome."

"I wish you could come over and eat with sister and me," said Patty gently. "Perhaps sometime, when my father is away buying goods and we are left alone, you could join us in the woods, and we would have a picnic? We would bring enough for you; all sorts of good things; hard-boiled eggs, doughnuts, apple-turnovers, and bread spread with jelly."

"I'd like it fine!" exclaimed Rodman, his big dark eyes sparkling with anticipation. "I don't have many boys to play with, and I never went to a picnic Aunt Boynton watches for uncle 'most all the time; she doesn't know he has been away for years and years. When she doesn't watch, she prays. Sometimes she wants me to pray with her, but praying don't come easy to me."

"Neither does it to me," said Patty.

"I'm good at marbles and checkers and back-gammon and jack-straws, though."

"So am I," said Patty, laughing, "so we should be good friends. I'll try to get a chance to see you soon again, but perhaps I can't; I'm a good deal tied at home."

"Your father doesn't like you to go anywheres, I guess," interposed Rodman. "I've heard Ivory tell Aunt Boynton things, but I wouldn't repeat them. Ivory's trained me years and years not to tell anything, so I don't."

"That's a good boy!" approved Patty. Then as she regarded him more closely, she continued, "I'm sorry you're lonesome, Rodman, I'd like to see you look brighter."

"You think I've been crying," the boy said shrewdly. "So I have, but not because I've been punished. The reason my eyes are so swollen up is because I killed our old toad by mistake this morning. I was trying to see if I could swing the scythe so's to help Ivory in haying-time. I've only 'raked after' and I want to begin on mowing soon's I can. Then somehow or other the old toad came out from under the steps; I didn't see him, and the scythe hit him square. I cried for an hour, that's what I did, and I don't care who knows it except I wouldn't like the boys at school to hector me. I've buried the toad out behind the barn, and I hope Ivory'll let me keep the news from Aunt Boynton. She cries enough now without my telling her there's been a death in the family. She set great store by the old toad, and so did all of us."

"It's too bad; I'm sorry, but after all you couldn't help it."

"No, but we should always look round every-wheres when we're cutting; that's what Ivory says. He says folks shouldn't use edged tools till they're old enough not to fool with 'em."

And Rodman looked so wise and old-fashioned for his years that Patty did not know whether to kiss him or cry over him, as she said: "Ivory's always right, and now good-bye; I must go this very minute. Don't forget the picnic."

"I won't!" cried the boy, gazing after her, wholly entranced with her bright beauty and her kindness. "Say, I'll bring something, too,—white-oak acorns, if you like 'em; I've got a big bagful up attic!"

Patty sped down the long lane, crept under the bars, and flew like a lapwing over the high-road.

"If father was only like any one else, things might be so different!" she sighed, her thoughts running along with her feet. "Nobody to make a home for that poor lonesome little boy and that poor lonesome big Ivory.... I am sure that he is in love with Waitstill. He doesn't know it; she doesn't know it; nobody does but me, but I'm clever at guessing. I was the only one that surmised Jed Morrill was going to marry again.... I should almost like Ivory for myself, he is so tall and handsome, but of course he can never marry anybody; he is too poor and has his mother to look after. I wouldn't want to take him from Waity, though, and then perhaps I couldn't get him, anyway.... If I couldn't, he'd be the only one! I've never tried yet, but I feel in my bones, somehow, that I could have any boy in Edgewood or Riverboro, by just crooking my forefinger and beckoning to him.. .. I wish—I wish—they were different! They don't make me want to beckon to them! My forefinger just stays straight and doesn't feel like crooking!... There's Cephas Cole, but he's as stupid as an owl. I don't want a husband that keeps his mouth wide open whenever I'm talking, no matter whether it's sense or nonsense. There's Phil Perry, but he likes Ellen, and besides he's too serious for me; and there's Mark Wilson; he's the best dressed, and the only one that's been to college. He looks at me all the time in meeting, and asked me if I wouldn't take a walk some Sunday afternoon. I know he planned Ellen's party hoping I'd be there!—Goodness gracious, I do believe that is his horse coming behind me! There's no other in the village that goes at such a gait!"

It was, indeed, Mark Wilson, who always drove, according to Aunt Abby Cole, "as if he was goin' for a doctor." He caught up with Patty almost in the twinkling of an eye, but she was ready for him. She had taken off her sunbonnet just to twirl it by the string, she was so warm with walking, and in a jiffy she had lifted the clustering curls from her ears, tucked them back with a single expert movement, and disclosed two coral pendants just the color of her ear-tips and her glowing cheeks.

"Hello, Patty!" the young man called, in brusque country fashion, as he reined up beside her. "What are you doing over here? Why aren't you on your way to the party? I've been over to Limington and am breaking my neck to get home in time myself."

"I am not going; there are no parties for me!" said Patty plaintively. "Not going! Oh! I say, what's the matter? It won't be a bit of fun without you! Ellen and I made it up expressly for you, thinking your father couldn't object to a candy-pull!"

"I can't help it; I did the best I could. Wait-still always asks father for me, but I wouldn't take any chances to-day, and I spoke to him myself; indeed I almost coaxed him!"

"He's a regular old skinflint!" cried Mark, getting out of the wagon and walking beside her.

"You mustn't call him names," Patty interposed with some dignity. "I call him a good many myself, but I'm his daughter."

"You don't look it," said Mark admiringly. "Come and have a little ride, Won't you?"

"Oh, I couldn't possibly, thank you. Some one would be sure to see us, and father's so strict."

"There isn't a building for half a mile! Just jump in and have a spin till we come to the first house; then I'll let you out and you can walk the rest of the way home. Come, do, and make up to me a little for my disappointment. I'll skip the candy-pull if you say the word."

It was an incredibly brief drive, at Mark's rate of speed; and as exciting and blissful as it was brief and dangerous, Patty thought. Did she imagine it, or did Mark help her into the wagon differently from—old Dr. Perry, for instance?

The fresh breeze lifted the gold thread of her curls and gave her cheeks a brighter color, while her breath came fast through her parted lips and her eyes sparkled at the unexpected, unaccustomed pleasure. She felt so grown up, so conscious of a new power as she sat enthroned on the little wagon seat (Mark Wilson always liked his buggies "courtin' size" so the neighbors said), that she was almost courageous enough to agree to make a royal progress through the village; almost, but not quite.

"Come on, let's shake the old tabbies up and start 'em talking, shall we?" Mark suggested. "I'll give you the reins and let Nero have a flick of the whip."

"No, I'd rather not drive," she said. "I'd be afraid of this horse, and, anyway, I must get out this very minute; yes, I really must. If you hold Nero I can just slip down between the wheels; you needn't help me."

Mark alighted notwithstanding her objections, saying gallantly, "I don't miss this pleasure, not by a jugful! Come along! Jump!"

Patty stretched out her hands to be helped, but Mark forestalled her by putting his arms around her and lifting her down. A second of time only was involved, but in that second he held; her close and kissed her warm cheek, her cheek that had never felt the touch of any lips but those of Waitstill. She pulled her sunbonnet over her flaming face, while Mark, with a gay smile of farewell, sprang into the wagon and gave his horse a free rein.

Patty never looked up from the road, but walked faster and faster, her heart beating at breakneck speed. It was a changed world that spun past her; fright, triumph, shame, delight, a gratified vanity swam over her in turn.

A few minutes later she heard once more the rumble of wheels on the road. It was Cephas Cole driving towards her over the brow of Saco Hill. "He'll have seen Mark," she thought, "but he can't know I've talked and driven with him. Ugh! how stupid and common he looks!" "I heard your father blowin' the supper-horn jest as I come over the bridge," remarked Cephas, drawing up in the road. "He stood in the door-yard blowin' like Bedlam. I guess you 're late to supper."

"I'll be home in a few minutes," said Patty, "I got delayed and am a little behindhand."

"I'll turn right round if you'll git in and lemme take you back-along a piece; it'll save you a good five minutes," begged Cephas, abjectly.

"All right; much obliged; but it's against the rules and you must drop me at the foot of our hill and let me walk up."

"Certain; I know the Deacon 'n' I ain't huntin' for trouble any more'n you be; though I 'd take it quick enough if you jest give me leave! I ain't no coward an' I could tackle the Deacon to-morrow if so be I had anything to ask him."

This seemed to Patty a line of conversation distinctly to be discouraged under all the circumstances, and she tried to keep Cephas on the subject of his daily tasks and his mother's rheumatism until she could escape from his over-appreciative society.

"How do you like my last job?" he inquired as they passed his father's house. "Some think I've got the ell a little mite too yaller. Folks that ain't never handled a brush allers think they can mix paint better 'n them that knows their trade."

"If your object was to have everybody see the ell a mile away, you've succeeded," said Patty cruelly. She never flung the poor boy a civil word for fear of getting something warmer than civility in return.

"It'll tone down," Cephas responded, rather crestfallen. "I wanted a good bright lastin' shade. 'T won't look so yaller when father lets me paint the house to match, but that won't be till next year. He makes fun of the yaller color same as you; says a home's something you want to forget when you're away from it. Mother says the two rooms of the ell are big enough for somebody to set up housekeepin' in. What do you think?"

"I never think," returned Patty with a tantalizing laugh. "Good-night, Cephas; thank you for giving me a lift!"

VII. "WHAT DREAMS MAY COME"

SUPPER was over and the work done at last; the dishes washed, the beans put in soak, the hens shut up for the night, the milk strained and carried down cellar. Patty went up to her little room with the one window and the slanting walls and Waitstill followed and said good-night. Her father put out the lights, locked the doors, and came up the creaking stairs. There was never any talk between the sisters before going to bed, save on nights when their father was late at the store, usually on Saturdays only, for the good talkers of the village, as well as the gossips and loafers, preferred any other place to swap stories than the bleak atmosphere provided by old Foxy at his place of business.

Patty could think in the dark; her healthy young body lying not uncomfortably on the bed of corn husks, and the patchwork comforter drawn up under her chin. She could think, but for the first time she could not tell her thoughts to Waitstill. She had a secret; a dazzling secret, just like Ellen Wilson and some of the other girls who were several years older. Her afternoon's experience loomed as large in her innocent mind as if it had been an elopement.

"I hope I'm not engaged to be married to him, EVEN IF HE DID—" The sentence was too tremendous to be finished, even in thought. "I don't think I can be; men must surely say something, and not take it for granted you are in love with them and want to marry them. It is what they say when they ask that I should like much better than being married, when I'm only just past seventeen. I wish Mark was a little different; I don't like his careless ways! He admires me, I can tell one; that by the way he looks, but he admires himself just as much, and expects me to do the same; still, I suppose none of them are perfect, and girls have to forgive lots of little things when they are engaged. Mother must have forgiven a good many things when she took father. Anyway, Mark is going away for a month on business, so I shan't have to make up my mind just yet!" Here sleep descended upon the slightly puzzled, but on the whole delightfully complacent, little creature, bringing her most alluring and untrustworthy dreams.

The dear innocent had, indeed, no need of haste! Young Mr. Marquis de Lafayette Wilson, Mark for short, was not in the least a gay deceiver or ruthless breaker of hearts, and, so far as known, no scalps of village beauties were hung to his belt. He was a likable, light-weight young chap, as indolent and pleasure-loving as the strict customs of the community would permit; and a kiss, in his mind, most certainly never would lead to the altar, else he had already been many times a bridegroom. Miss Patience Baxter's maiden meditations and uncertainties and perplexities, therefore, were decidedly premature. She was a natural-born, unconsciously artistic, highly expert, and finished coquette. She was all this at seventeen, and Mark at twenty-four was by no means a match for her in this field of effort, yet!—but sometimes, in getting her victim into the net, the coquette loses her balance and falls in herself. There wasn't a bit of harm in Marquis de Lafayette, but he was extremely agile in keeping out of nets!

Waitstill was restless, too, that night, although she could not have told the reason. She opened her window at the back of the house and leaned out. The evening was mild with a soft wind blowing. She could hear the full brook dashing through the edge of the wood-lot, and even the "ker-chug" of an occasional bull-frog. There were great misty stars in the sky, but no moon.

There was no light in Aunt Abby Cole's kitchen, but a faint glimmer shone through the windows of Uncle Bart's joiner's shop, showing that the old man was either having an hour of peaceful contemplation with no companion but his pipe, or that there might be a little group of privileged visitors, headed by Jed Morrill, busily discussing the affairs of the nation.

Waitstill felt troubled and anxious to-night; bruised by the little daily torments that lessened her courage but never wholly destroyed it. Any one who believed implicitly in heredity might have been puzzled, perhaps, to account for her. He might fantastically picture her as making herself out of her ancestors, using a free hand, picking and choosing what she liked best, with due care for the effect of combinations; selecting here and there and modifying, if advisable, a trait of Grandpa or Grandma Foxwell, of Great-Uncle or Great-Aunt Baxter; borrowing qualities lavishly from her own gently born and gently bred mother, and carefully avoiding her respected father's Stock, except, perhaps, to take a dash of his pluck and an ounce of his persistence. Jed Morrill remarked of Deacon Baxter once: "When Old Foxy wants anything he'll wait till hell freezes over afore he'll give up." Waitstill had her father's firm chin, but there the likeness ended. The proud curve of her nostrils, the clear well-opened eye with its deep fringe of lashes, the earnest mouth, all these came from the mother who was little more than a dim memory.

Waitstill disdained any vague, dreary, colorless theory of life and its meaning. She had joined the church at fifteen, more or less because other girls did and the parson had persuaded her; but out of her hard life she had somehow framed a courageous philosophy that kept her erect and uncrushed, no matter how great her difficulties. She had no idea of bringing a poor, weak, draggled soul to her Maker at the last day, saying "Here is all I have managed to save out of what you gave me!" That would be something, she allowed, immeasurably something; but pitiful compared with what she might do if she could keep a brave, vigorous spirit and march to the last tribunal strengthened by battles, struggles, defeats, victories; by the defense of weaker human creatures, above all, warmed and vitalized by the pouring out and gathering in of love.

Patty slept sweetly on the other side of the partition, the contemplation of her twopenny triumphs bringing a smile to her childish lips: but even so a good heart was there (still perhaps in the process of making), a quick wit, ready sympathy, natural charm; plenty, indeed, for the stronger sister to cherish, protect, and hold precious, as she did, with all her mind and soul.

There had always been a passionate loyalty in Waitstill's affection, wherever it had been bestowed. Uncle Bart delighted in telling an instance of it that occurred when she was a child of five. Maine had just separated amicably from her mother, Massachusetts, and become an independent state. It was in the middle of March, but there was no snow on the ground and the village boys had built a bonfire on a plot of land near Uncle Bart's joiner's shop. There was a large gathering in celebration of the historic event and Waitstill crept down the hill with her homemade rag doll in her arms. She stood on the outskirts of the crowd, a silent, absorbed little figure clad in a shabby woollen coat, with a blue knit hood framing her rosy face. Deborah, her beloved, her only doll, was tightly clasped in her arms, for Debby, like her parent, had few pleasures and must not be denied so great a one as this. Suddenly, one of the thoughtless young scamps in the group, wishing to create a new sensation and add to the general excitement, caught the doll from the child's arms, and running forward with a loud war-whoop, flung it into the flames. Waitstill did not lose an instant. She gave a scream Of anguish, and without giving any warning of her intentions, probably without realizing them herself, she dashed through the little crowd into the bonfire and snatched her cherished offspring from the burning pile. The whole thing was over in the twinkling of an eye, for Uncle Bart was as quick as the child and dragged her out of the imminent danger with no worse harm done than a good scorching.

He led the little creature up the hill to explain matters and protect her from a scolding. She still held the doll against her heaving breast, saying, between her sobs: "I couldn't let my Debby burn up! I couldn't, Uncle Bart; she's got nobody but me! Is my dress scorched so much I can't wear it? You'll tell father how it was, Uncle Bart, won't you?"

Debby bore the marks of her adventure longer than her owner, for she had been longer in the fire, but, stained and defaced as she was, she was never replaced, and remained the only doll of Waitstill's childhood. At this very moment she lay softly and safely in a bureau drawer ready to be lifted out, sometime, Waitstill fancied, and shown tenderly to Patty's children. Of her own possible children she never thought. There was but one man in the world who could ever be the father of them and she was separated from him by every obstacle that could divide two human beings.

SUMMER
VIII. THE JOINER'S SHOP

VILLAGE "Aunts" and "Uncles" were elected to that relationship by the common consent of the community; their fitness being established by great age, by decided individuality or eccentricity of character, by uncommon lovableness, or by the possession of an abundant wit and humor. There was no formality about the thing; certain women were always called "Aunt Sukie," or "Aunt Hitty," or what not, while certain men were distinguished as "Uncle Rish," or "Uncle Pel," without previous arrangement, or the consent of the high contracting parties.

Such a couple were Cephas Cole's father and mother, Aunt Abby and Uncle Bart. Bartholomew Cole's trade was that of a joiner; as for Aunt Abby's, it can only be said that she made all trades her own by sovereign right of investigation, and what she did not know about her neighbor's occupations was unlikely to be discovered on this side of Jordan. One of the villagers declared that Aunt Abby and her neighbor, Mrs. Abel Day, had argued for an hour before they could make a bargain about the method of disseminating a certain important piece of news, theirs by exclusive right of discovery and prior possession. Mrs. Day offered to give Mrs. Cole the privilege of Saco Hill and Aunt Betty-Jack's, she herself to take Guide-Board and Town-House Hills. Aunt Abby quickly proved the injustice of this decision, saying that there were twice as many families living in Mrs. Day's chosen territory as there were in that allotted to her, so the river road to Milliken's Mills was grudgingly awarded to Aunt Abby by way of compromise, and the ladies started on what was a tour of mercy in those days, the furnishing of a subject of discussion for long, quiet evenings.

Uncle Bart's joiner's shop was at the foot of Guide-Board Hill on the Riverboro side of the bridge, and it was the pleasantest spot in the whole village. The shop itself had a cheery look, with its weather-stained shingles, its small square windows, and its hospitable door, half as big as the front side of the building. The step was an old millstone too worn for active service, and the piles of chips and shavings on each side of it had been there for so many years that sweet-williams, clove pinks, and purple phlox were growing in among them in the most irresponsible fashion; while a morning-glory vine had crept up and curled around a long-handled rake that had been standing against the front of the house since early spring. There was an air of cosy and amiable disorder about the place that would have invited friendly confabulation even had not Uncle Bart's white head, honest, ruddy face, and smiling welcome coaxed you in before you were aware. A fine Nodhead apple tree shaded the side windows, and underneath it reposed all summer a bright blue sleigh, for Uncle Bart always described himself as being "plagued for shed room" and kept things as he liked at the shop, having a "p'ison neat" wife who did exactly the opposite at his house.

The seat of the sleigh was all white now with scattered fruit blossoms, and one of Waitstill's earliest remembrances was of going downhill with Patty toddling at her side; of Uncle Bart's lifting them into the sleigh and permitting them to sit there and eat the ripe red apples that had fallen from the tree. Uncle Bart's son, Cephas (Patty's secret adorer), was a painter by trade, and kept his pots and cans and brushes in a little outhouse at the back, while Uncle Bart himself stood every day behind his long joiner's bench almost knee-deep in shavings. How the children loved to play with the white, satiny rings, making them into necklaces, hanging them to their ears and weaving them into wreaths.

Wonderful houses could always be built in the corner of the shop, out of the little odds and ends and "nubbins" of white pine, and Uncle Bart was ever ready to cut or saw a special piece needed for some great purpose.

The sound of the plane was sweet music in the old joiner's ears. "I don't hardly know how I'd a made out if I'd had to work in a mill," he said confidentially to Cephas. "The noise of a saw goin' all day, coupled with your mother's tongue mornin's an' evenin's, would 'a' been too much for my weak head. I'm a quiet man, Cephas, a man that needs a peaceful shop where he can get away from the comforts of home now and then, without shirkin' his duty nor causin' gossip. If you should ever marry, Cephas,— which don't look to me likely without you pick out a dif'rent girl,—I'd advise you not to keep your stock o' paints in the barn or the shed, for it's altogether too handy to the house and the women-folks. Take my advice and have a place to yourself, even if it's a small one. A shop or a barn has saved many a man's life and reason Cephas, for it's ag'in' a woman's nature to have you underfoot in the house without hectorin' you. Choose a girl same's you would a horse that you want to hitch up into a span; 't ain't every two that'll stan' together without kickin'. When you get the right girl, keep out of her way consid'able an' there'll be less wear an' tear."

It was June and the countryside was so beautiful it seemed as if no one could be unhappy, however great the cause. That was what Waitstill Baxter thought as she sat down on the millstone step for a word with the old joiner, her best and most understanding friend in all the village.

"I've come to do my mending here with you," she said brightly, as she took out her well-filled basket and threaded her needle. "Isn't it a wonderful morning? Nobody could look the world in the face and do a wrong thing on such a day, could they, Uncle Bart?"

The meadows were a waving mass of golden buttercups; the shallow water at the river's edge just below the shop was blue with spikes of arrow-weed; a bunch of fragrant water-lilies, gathered from the mill-pond's upper levels, lay beside Waitstill's mending-basket, and every foot of roadside and field within sight was swaying with long-stemmed white and gold daisies. The June grass, the friendly, humble, companionable grass, that no one ever praises as they do the flowers, was a rich emerald green, a velvet carpet fit for the feet of the angels themselves. And the elms and maples! Was there ever such a year for richness of foliage? And the sky, was it ever so blue or so clear, so far away, or so completely like heaven, as you looked at its reflection in the glassy surface of the river?

"Yes, it's a pretty good day," allowed Uncle Bart judicially as he took a squint at his T-square. "I don' know's I should want to start out an' try to beat it! The Lord can make a good many kinds o' weather in the course of a year, but when He puts his mind on to it, an' kind o' gives Himself a free hand, He can turn out a June morning that must make the Devil sick to his stomach with envy! All the same, Waity, my cow ain't behavin' herself any better'n usual. She's been rampagin' since sun-up. I've seen mother chasin' her out o' Mis' Day's garden-patch twice a'ready!—It seems real good an' homey to see you settin' there sewin' while I'm workin' at the bench. Cephas is down to the store, so I s'pose your father's off somewheres?"

Perhaps the June grass was a little greener, the buttercups yellower, the foliage more lacey, the sky bluer, because Deacon Baxter had taken his luncheon in a pail under the wagon seat, and departed on an unwilling journey to Moderation, his object being to press the collection of some accounts too long overdue. There was something tragic in the fact, Waitstill thought, that whenever her father left the village for a whole day, life at once grew brighter, easier, more hopeful. One could breathe freely, speak one's heart out, believe in the future, when father was away.

The girls had harbored many delightful plans at early breakfast. As it was Saturday, Patty could catch little Rod Boynton, if he came to the bridge on errands as usual; and if Ivory could spare him for an hour at noon they would take their luncheon and eat it together on the river-bank as Patty had promised him. At the last moment, however, Deacon Baxter had turned around in the wagon and said: "Patience, you go down to the store and have a regular house-cleanin' in the stock-room. Git Cephas to lift what you can't lift yourself, move everything in the place, sweep and dust it, scrub the floor, wash the winder, and make room for the new stuff that they'll bring up from Mill-town 'bout noon. If you have any time left over, put new papers on the shelves out front, and clean up and fix the show winder. Don't stand round gabbin' with Cephas, and see't he don't waste time that's paid for by me. Tell him he might clean up the terbaccer stains round the stove, black it, and cover it up for the summer if he ain't too busy servin' cust'mers."

"The whole day spoiled!" wailed Patty, flinging herself down in the kitchen rocker. "Father's powers of invention beat anything I ever saw! That stockroom could have been cleaned any time this month and it's too heavy work for me anyway; it spoils my hands, grubbing around those nasty, sticky, splintery boxes and barrels. Instead of being out of doors, I've got to be shut up in that smelly, rummy, tobacco-y, salt-fishy, pepperminty place with Cephas Cole! He won't have a pleasant morning, I can tell you! I shall snap his head off every time he speaks to me."

"So I would!" Waitstill answered composedly. "Everything is so clearly his fault that I certainly would work off my temper on Cephas! Still, I can think of a way to make matters come out right. I've got a great basket of mending that must be done, and you remember there's a choir rehearsal for the new anthem this afternoon, but anyway I can help a little on the cleaning. Then you can make Rodman do a few of the odd jobs, it will be a novelty to him; and Cephas will work his fingers to the bone for you, as you well know, if you treat him like a human being."

"All right!" cried Patty joyously, her mood changing in an instant. "There's Rod coming over the bridge now! Toss me my gingham apron and the scrubbing-brush, and the pail, and the tin of soft soap, and the cleaning cloths; let's see, the broom's down there, so I've got everything. If I wave a towel from the store, pack up luncheon for three. You come down and bring your mending; then, when you see how I'm getting on, we can consult. I'm going to take the ten cents I've saved and spend it in raisins. I can get a good many if Cephas gives me wholesale price, with family discount subtracted from that. Cephas would treat me to candy in a minute, but if I let him we'd have to ask him to the picnic! Good-bye!" And the volatile creature darted down the hill singing, "There'll be something in heaven for children to do," at the top of her healthy young lungs.

IX. CEPHAS SPEAKS

THE waving signal, a little later on, showed that Rodman could go to the picnic, the fact being that he was having a holiday from eleven o'clock until two, and Ivory was going to drive to the bridge at noon, anyway, so his permission could then be asked.

Patty's mind might have been thought entirely on her ugly task as she swept and dusted and scrubbed that morning, but the reverse was true. Mark Wilson had gone away without saying good-bye to her. This was not surprising, perhaps, as she was about as much sequestered in her hilltop prison as a Turkish beauty in a harem; neither was it astonishing that Mark did not write to her. He never had written to her, and as her father always brought home the very infrequent letters that came to the family, Mark knew that any sentimental correspondence would be fraught with danger. No, everything was probably just as it should be, and yet,—well, Patty had expected during the last three weeks that something would happen to break up the monotony of her former existence. She hardly knew what it would be, but the kiss dropped so lightly on her cheek by Mark Wilson still burned in remembrance, and made her sure that it would have a sequel, or an explanation.

Mark's sister Ellen and Phil Perry were in the midst of some form of lover's quarrel, and during its progress Phil was paying considerable attention to Patty at Sabbath School and prayer-meeting, occasions, it must be confessed, only provocative of very indirect and long-distance advances. Cephas Cole, to the amazement of every one but his (constitutionally) exasperated mother, was "toning down" the ell of the family mansion, mitigating the lively yellow, and putting another fresh coat of paint on it, for no conceivable reason save that of pleasing the eye of a certain capricious, ungrateful young hussy, who would probably say, when her verdict was asked, that she didn't see any particular difference in it, one way or another.

Trade was not especially brisk at the Deacon's emporium this sunny June Saturday morning. Cephas may have possibly lost a customer or two by leaving the store vacant while he toiled and sweated for Miss Patience Baxter in the stockroom at the back, overhanging the river, but no man alive could see his employer's lovely daughter tugging at a keg of shingle nails without trying to save her from a broken back, although Cephas could have watched his mother move the house and barn without feeling the slightest anxiety in her behalf. If he could ever get the "heft" of the "doggoned" cleaning out of the way so that Patty's mind could be free to entertain his proposition; could ever secure one precious moment of silence when she was not slatting and banging, pushing and pulling things about, her head and ears out of sight under a shelf, and an irritating air of absorption about her whole demeanor; if that moment of silence could ever, under Providence, be simultaneous with the absence of customers in the front shop, Cephas intended to offer himself to Patience Baxter that very morning.

Once, during a temporary lull in the rear, he started to meet his fate when Rodman Boynton followed him into the back room, and the boy was at once set to work by Patty, who was the most consummate slave-driver in the State of Maine. After half an hour there was another Heavensent chance, when Rodman went up to Uncle Bart's shop with a message for Waitstill, but, just then, in came Bill Morrill, a boy of twelve, with a request for a gallon of molasses; and would Cephas lend him a stone jug over Sunday, for his mother had hers soakin' out in soap-suds 'cause 't wa'n't smellin' jest right. Bill's message given, he hurried up the road on another errand, promising to call for the molasses later.

Cephas put the gallon measure under the spigot of the molasses hogshead and turned on the tap. The task was going to be a long one and he grew impatient, for the stream was only a slender trickle, scarcely more than the slow dripping of drops, so the molasses must be very never low, and with his mind full of weightier affairs he must make a note to tell the Deacon to broach a new hogshead. Cephas feared that he could never make out a full gallon, in which case Mrs. Morrill would be vexed, for she kept mill boarders and baked quantities of brown bread and gingerbread and molasses cookies for over Sunday. He did wish trade would languish altogether on this particular morning. The minutes dragged by and again there was perfect quiet in the stock-room. As the door opened, Cephas, taking his last chance, went forward to meet Patty, who was turning down the skirt of her dress, taking the cloth off her head, smoothing her hair, and tying on a clean white ruffed apron, in which she looked as pretty as a pink.

"Patty!" stammered Cephas, seizing his golden opportunity, "Patty, keep your mind on me for a minute. I've put a new coat o' paint on the ell just to please you; won't you get married and settle down with me? I love you so I can't eat nor drink nor 'tend store nor nothin'!"

"Oh, I—I—couldn't, Cephas, thank you; I just couldn't,—don't ask me," cried Patty, as nervous as Cephas himself now that her first offer had really come; "I'm only seventeen and I don't feel like settling down, Cephas, and father wouldn't think of letting me get married."

"Don't play tricks on me, Patty, and keep shovin' me off so, an' givin' wrong reasons," pleaded Cephas. "What's the trouble with me? I know mother's temper's onsartain, but we never need go into the main house daytimes and father'd allers stand up ag'in' her if she didn't treat you right. I've got a good trade and father has a hundred dollars o' my savin's that I can draw out to-morrer if you'll have me."

"I can't, Cephas; don't move; stay where you are; no, don't come any nearer; I'm not fond of you that way, and, besides,—and, besides—"

Her blush and her evident embarrassment gave Cephas a new fear.

"You ain't promised a'ready, be you?" he asked anxiously; "when there ain't a feller anywheres around that's ever stepped foot over your father's doorsill but jest me?"

"I haven't promised anything or anybody,"

Patty answered sedately, gaining her self-control by degrees, "but I won't deny that I'm considering; that's true!"

"Considerin' who?" asked Cephas, turning pale.

"Oh,—SEVERAL, if you must know the truth"; and Patty's tone was cruel in its jauntiness.

"SEVERAL!" The word did not sound like ordinary work-a-day Riverboro English in Cephas's ears. He knew that "several" meant more than one, but he was too stunned to define the term properly in its present strange connection.

"Whoever 't is wouldn't do any better by you'n I would. I'd take a lickin' for you any day," Cephas exclaimed abjectly, after a long pause.

"That wouldn't make any difference, Cephas," said Patty firmly, moving towards the front door as if to end the interview. "If I don't love you UNlicked, I couldn't love you any better licked, now, could I?—Goodness gracious, what am I stepping in? Cephas, quick! Something has been running all over the floor. My feet are sticking to it."

"Good Gosh! It's Mis' Morrill's molasses!" cried Cephas, brought to his senses suddenly.

It was too true! Whatever had been the small obstruction in the tap, it had disappeared. The gallon measure had been filled to the brim ten minutes before, and ever since, the treacly liquid had been overflowing the top and spreading in a brown flood, unnoticed, over the floor. Patty's feet were glued to it, her buff calico skirts lifted high to escape harm.

"I can't move," she cried. "Oh! You stupid, stupid Cephas, how could you leave the molasses spigot turned on? See what you've done! You've wasted quarts and quarts! What will father say, and how will you ever clean up such a mess? You never can get the floor to look so that he won't notice it, and he is sure to miss the molasses. You've ruined my shoes, and I simply can't bear the sight of you!"

At this Cephas all but blubbered in the agony of his soul. It was bad enough to be told by Patty that she was "considering several," but his first romance had ended in such complete disaster that he saw in a vision his life blasted; changed in one brief moment from that of a prosperous young painter to that of a blighted and despised bungler, whose week's wages were likely to be expended in molasses to make good the Deacon's loss.

"Find those cleaning-cloths I left in the back room," ordered Patty with a flashing eye. "Get some blocks, or bits of board, or stones, for me to walk on, so that I can get out of your nasty mess. Fill Bill Morrill's jug, quick, and set it out on the steps for him to pick up. I don't know what you'd do without me to plan for you! Lock the front door and hang father's sign that he's gone to dinner on the doorknob. Scoop up all the molasses you can with one of those new trowels on the counter. Scoop, and scrape, and scoop, and scrape; then put a cloth on your oldest broom, pour lots of water on, pail after pail, and swab! When you've swabbed till it won't do any more good, then scrub! After that, I shouldn't wonder if you had to fan the floor with a newspaper or it'll never get dry before father comes home. I'll sit on the flour barrel a little while and advise, but I can't stay long because I'm going to a picnic. Hurry up and don't look as if you were going to die any minute! It's no use crying over spilt molasses. You don't suppose I'm going to tell any tales after you've made me an offer of marriage, do you? I'm not so mean as all that, though I may have my faults."

It was nearly two o'clock before the card announcing Deacon Baxter's absence at dinner was removed from the front doorknob, and when the store was finally reopened for business it was a most dejected clerk who dealt out groceries to the public. The worst feature of the affair was that every one in the two villages suddenly and contemporaneously wanted molasses, so that Cephas spent the afternoon reviewing his misery by continually turning the tap and drawing off the fatal liquid. Then, too, every inquisitive boy in the neighborhood came to the back of the store to view the operation, exclaiming: "What makes the floor so wet? Hain't been spillin' molasses, have yer? Bet yer have! Good joke on Old Foxy!"

X. ON TORY HILL

It had been a heavenly picnic the little trio all agreed as to that; and when Ivory saw the Baxter girls coming up the shady path that led along the river from the Indian Cellar to the bridge, it was a merry group and a transfigured Rodman that caught his eye. The boy, trailing on behind with the baskets and laden with tin dippers and wildflowers, seemed another creature from the big-eyed, quiet little lad he saw every day. He had chattered like a magpie, eaten like a bear, is torn his jacket getting wild columbines for Patty, been nicely darned by Waitstill, and was in a state of hilarity that rendered him quite unrecognizable.

"We've had a lovely picnic!" called Patty; "I wish you had been with us!"

"You didn't ask me!" smiled Ivory, picking up Waitstill's mending-basket from the nook in the trees where she had hidden it for safe-keeping.

"We've played games, Ivory," cried the boy. "Patty made them up herself. First we had the 'Landing of the Pilgrims,' and Waitstill made believe be the figurehead of the Mayflower. She stood on a great boulder and sang:—

> 'The breaking waves dashed high
>
> On a stern and rock-bound coast'—

and, oh! she was splendid! Then Patty was Pocahontas and I was Cap'n John Smith, and look, we are all dressed up for the Indian wedding!"

Waitstill had on a crown of white birch bark and her braid of hair, twined with running ever-green, fell to her waist. Patty was wreathed with columbines and decked with some turkey feathers that she had put in her basket as too pretty to throw away. Waitstill looked rather conscious in her unusual finery, but Patty sported it with the reckless ease and innocent vanity that characterized her.

"I shall have to run into father's store to put myself tidy," Waitstill said, "so good-bye, Rodman, we'll have another picnic some day. Patty, you must do the chores this afternoon, you know, so that I can go to choir rehearsal."

Rodman and Patty started up the hill gayly with their burdens, and Ivory walked by Waitstill's side as she pulled off her birch-bark crown and twisted her braid around her head with a heightened color at being watched.

"I'll say good-bye now, Ivory, but I'll see you at the meeting-house," she said, as she neared the store. "I'll go in here and brush the pine needles off, wash my hands, and rest a little before rehearsal. That's a puzzling anthem we have for to-morrow."

"I have my horse here; let me drive you up to the church."

"I can't, Ivory, thank you. Father's orders are against my driving out with any one, you know."

"Very well, the road is free, at any rate. I'll hitch my horse down here in the woods somewhere and when you start to walk I shall follow and catch up with you. There's luckily only one way to reach the church from here, and your father can't blame us if we both take it!"

And so it fell out that Ivory and Waitstill walked together in the cool of the afternoon to the meeting-house on Tory Hill. Waitstill kept the beaten path on one side and Ivory that on the other, so that the width of the country road, deep in dust, was between them, yet their nearness seemed so tangible a thing that each could feel the heart beating in the other's side. Their talk was only that of tried friends, a talk interrupted by long beautiful silences; silences that come only to a man and woman whose understanding of each other is beyond question and answer. Not a sound broke the stillness, yet the very air, it seemed to them, was shedding meanings: the flowers were exhaling a love secret with their fragrances, the birds were singing it boldly from the tree-tops, yet no word passed the man's lips or the girl's. Patty would have hung out all sorts of signals and lures to draw the truth from Ivory and break through the walls of his self-control, but Waitstill, never; and Ivory Boynton was made of stuff so strong that he would not speak a syllable of love to a woman unless he could say all. He was only five-and-twenty, but he had been reared in a rigorous school, and had learned in its poverty, loneliness, and anxiety lessons of self-denial and self-control that bore daily fruit now. He knew that Deacon Baxter would never allow any engagement to exist between Waitstill and himself; he also knew that Waitstill would never defy and disobey her father if it meant leaving her younger sister to fight alone a dreary battle for which she was not fitted. If there was little hope on her side there seemed even less on his. His mother's mental illness made her peculiarly dependent upon him, and at the same time held him in such strict bondage that it was almost impossible for him to get on in the world or even to give her the comforts she needed. In villages like Riverboro in those early days there was no putting away, even of men or women so demented as to be something of a menace to the peace of the household; but Lois Boynton was so gentle, so fragile, so exquisite a spirit, that she seemed in her sad aloofness simply a thing to be sheltered and shielded somehow in her difficult life journey. Ivory often thought how sorely she needed a daughter in her affliction. If the baby sister had only lived, the home might have been different; but alas! there was only a son,—a son who tried to be tender and sympathetic, but after all was nothing but a big, clumsy, uncomprehending man-creature, who ought to be felling trees, ploughing, sowing, reaping, or at least studying law, making his own fortune and that of some future wife. Old Mrs. Mason, a garrulous, good-hearted grandame, was their only near neighbor, and her visits always left his mother worse rather than better. How such a girl as Waitstill would pour comfort and beauty and joy into a lonely house like his, if only he were weak enough to call upon her strength and put it to so cruel a test. God help him, he would never do that, especially as he could not earn enough to keep a larger family, bound down as he was by inexorable responsibilities. Waitstill, thus far in life, had suffered many sorrows and enjoyed few pleasures; marriage ought to bring her freedom and plenty, not carking care and poverty. He stole long looks at the girl across the separating space that was so helpless to separate,—feeding his starved heart upon her womanly graces. Her quick, springing step was in harmony with the fire and courage of her mien. There was a line or two in her face,—small wonder; but an "unconquerable soul" shone in her eyes; shone, too, in no uncertain way, but brightly and steadily, expressing an unshaken joy in living. Valiant, splendid, indomitable Waitstill! He could never tell her, alas! but how he gloried in her!

It is needless to say that no woman could be the possessor of such a love as Ivory Boynton's and not know of its existence. Waitstill never heard a breath of it from Ivory's lips; even his eyes were under control and confessed nothing; nor did his hand ever clasp hers, to show by a tell-tale touch the truth he dared not utter; nevertheless she felt that she was beloved. She hid the knowledge deep in her heart and covered it softly from every eye but her own; taking it out in the safe darkness sometimes to wonder over and adore in secret. Did her love for Ivory rest partly on a sense of vocation?—a profound, inarticulate divining of his vast need of her? He was so strong, yet so weak because of the yoke he bore, so bitterly alone in his desperate struggle with life, that her heart melted like wax whenever she thought of him. When she contemplated the hidden mutiny in her own heart, she was awestruck sometimes at the almost divine patience of Ivory's conduct as a son.

"How is your mother this summer, Ivory?" she asked as they sat down on the meeting-house steps waiting for Jed Morrill to open the door. "There is little change in her from year to year, Waitstill.—By the way, why don't we get out of this afternoon sun and sit in the old graveyard under the trees? We are early and the choir won't get here for half an hour.—Dr. Perry says that he does not understand mother's case in the least, and that no one but some great Boston physician could give a proper opinion on it; of course, that is impossible at present."

They sat down on the grass underneath one of the elms and Waitstill took off her hat and leaned back against the tree-trunk.

"Tell me more," she said; "it is so long since we talked together quietly and we have never really spoken of your mother."

"Of course," Ivory continued, "the people of the village all think and speak of mother's illness as religious insanity, but to me it seems nothing of the sort. I was only a child when father first fell ill with Jacob Cochrane, but I was twelve when father went away from home on his 'mission,' and if there was any one suffering from delusions in our family it was he, not mother. She had altogether given up going to the Cochrane meetings, and I well remember the scene when my father told her of the revelation he had received about going through the state and into New Hampshire in order to convert others and extend the movement. She had no sympathy with his self-imposed mission, you may be sure, though now she goes back in her memory to the earlier days of her married life, when she tried hard, poor soul, to tread the same path that father was treading, so as to be by his side at every turn of the road.

"I am sure" (here Ivory's tone was somewhat dry and satirical) "that father's road had many turns, Waitstill! He was a schoolmaster in Saco, you know, when I was born but he soon turned from teaching to preaching, and here my mother followed with entire sympathy, for she was intensely, devoutly religious. I said there was little change in her, but there is one new symptom. She has ceased to refer to her conversion to Cochranism as a blessed experience. Her memory of those first days seems to have faded, As to her sister's death and all the circumstances of her bringing Rodman home, her mind is a blank. Her expectation of father's return, on the other hand, is much more intense than ever."

"She must have loved your father dearly, Ivory, and to lose him in this terrible way is much worse than death. Uncle Bart says he had a great gift of language!"

"Yes, and it was that, in my mind, that led him astray. I fear that the Spirit of God was never so strong in father as the desire to influence people by his oratory. That was what drew him to preaching in the first place, and when he found in Jacob Cochrane a man who could move an audience to frenzy, lift them out of the body, and do with their spirits as he willed, he acknowledged him as master. Whether his gospel was a pure and undefiled religion I doubt, but he certainly was a master of mesmeric control. My mother was beguiled, entranced, even bewitched at first, I doubt not, for she translated all that Cochrane said into her own speech, and regarded him as the prophet of a new era. But Cochrane's last 'revelations' differed from the first, and were of the earth, earthy. My mother's pure soul must have revolted, but she was not strong enough to drag father from his allegiance. Mother was of better family than father, but they were both well educated and had the best schooling to be had in their day. So far as I can judge, mother always had more 'balance' than father, and much better judgment,—yet look at her now!"

"Then you think it was your father's disappearance that really caused her mind to waver?" asked Waitstill.

"I do, indeed. I don't know what happened between them in the way of religious differences, nor how much unhappiness these may have caused. I remember she had an illness when we first came here to live and I was a little chap of three or four, but that was caused by the loss of a child, a girl, who lived only a few weeks. She recovered perfectly, and her head was as clear as mine for a year or two after father went away. As his letters grew less frequent, as news of him gradually ceased to come, she became more and more silent, and retired more completely into herself. She never went anywhere, nor entertained visitors, because she did not wish to hear the gossip and speculation that were going on in the village. Some of it was very hard for a wife to bear, and she resented it indignantly; yet never received a word from father with which to refute it. At this time, as nearly as I can judge, she was a recluse, and subject to periods of profound melancholy, but nothing worse. Then she took that winter journey to her sister's deathbed, brought home the boy, and, hastened by exposure and chill and grief, I suppose, her mind gave way,—that's all!" And Ivory sighed drearily as he stretched himself on the greensward, and looked off towards the snow-clad New Hampshire hills. "I've meant to write the story of the 'Cochrane craze' sometime, or such part of it as has to do with my family history, and you shall read it if you like. I should set down my child-hood and my boyhood memories, together with such scraps of village hearsay as seem reliable. You were not so much younger than I, but I was in the thick of the excitement, and naturally I heard more than you, having so bitter a reason for being interested. Jacob Cochrane has altogether disappeared from public view, but there's many a family in Maine and New Hampshire, yes, and in the far West, that will feel his influence for years to come."

"I should like very much to read your account. Aunt Abby's version, for instance, is so different from Uncle Bart's that one can scarcely find the truth between the two; and father's bears no relation to that of any of the others."

"Some of us see facts and others see visions," replied Ivory, "and these differences of opinion crop up in the village every day when anything noteworthy is discussed. I came upon a quotation in my reading last evening that described it:

'One said it thundered... another that an angel spake'"

"Do you feel as if your father was dead, Ivory?"

"I can only hope so! That thought brings sadness with it, as one remembers his disappointment and failure, but if he is alive he is a traitor."

There was a long pause and they could see in the distance Humphrey Barker with his clarionet and Pliny Waterhouse with his bass viol driving up to the churchyard fence to hitch their horses. The sun was dipping low and red behind the Town-House Hill on the other side of the river.

"What makes my father dislike the very mention of yours?" asked Waitstill. "I know what they say: that it is because the two men had high words once in a Cochrane meeting, when father tried to interfere with some of the exercises and was put out of doors. It doesn't seem as if that grievance, seventeen or eighteen years ago, would influence his opinion of your mother, or of you."

"It isn't likely that a man of your father's sort would forget or forgive what he considered an injury; and in refusing to have anything to do with the son of a disgraced man and a deranged woman, he is well within his rights."

Ivory's cheeks burned red under the tan, and his hand trembled a little as he plucked bits of clover from the grass and pulled them to pieces absent-mindedly. "How are you getting on at home these days, Waitstill?" he asked, as if to turn his own mind and hers from a too painful subject.

"You have troubles enough of your own without hearing mine, Ivory, and anyway they are not big afflictions, heavy sorrows, like those you have to bear. Mine are just petty, nagging, sordid, cheap little miseries, like gnat-bites;—so petty and so sordid that I can hardly talk to God about them, much less to a human friend. Patty is my only outlet and I need others, yet I find it almost impossible to escape from the narrowness of my life and be of use to any one else." The girl's voice quivered and a single tear-drop on her cheek showed that she was speaking from a full heart. "This afternoon's talk has determined me in one thing," she went on. "I am going to see your mother now and then. I shall have to do it secretly, for your sake, for hers, and for my own, but if I am found out, then I will go openly. There must be times when one can break the lower law, and yet keep the higher. Father's law, in this case, is the lower, and I propose to break it."

"I can't have you getting into trouble, Waitstill," Ivory objected. "You're the one woman I can think of who might help my mother; all the same, I would not make your life harder; not for worlds!"

"It will not be harder, and even if it was I should 'count it all joy' to help a woman bear such sorrow as your mother endures patiently day after day"; and Waitstill rose to her feet and tied on her hat as one who had made up her mind.

It was almost impossible for Ivory to hold his peace then, so full of gratitude was his soul and so great his longing to pour out the feeling that flooded it. He pulled himself together and led the way out of the churchyard. To look at Waitstill again would be to lose his head, but to his troubled heart there came a flood of light, a glory from that lamp that a woman may hold up for a man; a glory that none can take from him, and none can darken; a light by which he may walk and live and die.

XI. A JUNE SUNDAY

IT was a Sunday in June, and almost the whole population of Riverboro and Edgewood was walking or driving in the direction of the meeting-house on Tory Hill.

Church toilettes, you may well believe, were difficult of attainment by Deacon Baxter's daughters, as they had been by his respective helpmates in years gone by. When Waitstill's mother first asked her husband to buy her a new dress, and that was two years after marriage, he simply said: "You look well enough; what do you want to waste money on finery for, these hard times? If other folks are extravagant, that ain't any reason you should be. You ain't obliged to take your neighbors for an example:—take 'em for a warnin'!"

"But, Foxwell, my Sunday dress is worn completely to threads," urged the second Mrs. Baxter.

"That's what women always say; they're all alike; no more idea o' savin' anything than a skunk-blackbird! I can't spare any money for gew-gaws, and you might as well understand it first as last. Go up attic and open the hair trunk by the winder; you'll find plenty there to last you for years to come."

The second Mrs. Baxter visited the attic as commanded, and in turning over the clothes in the old trunk, knew by instinct that they had belonged to her predecessor in office. Some of the dresses were neat, though terribly worn and faded, but all were fortunately far too short and small for a person of her fine proportions. Besides, her very soul shrank from wearing them, and her spirit revolted both from the insult to herself and to the poor dead woman she had succeeded, so she came downstairs to darn and mend and patch again her shabby wardrobe. Waitstill had gone through the same as her mother before her, but in despair, when she was seventeen, she began to cut over the old garments for herself and Patty. Mercifully there were very few of them, and they had long since been discarded. At eighteen she had learned to dye yarns with yellow oak or maple bark and to make purples from elder and sumac berries; she could spin and knit as well as any old "Aunt" of the village, and cut and shape a garment as deftly as the Edgewood tailoress, but the task of making bricks without straw was a hard one, indeed.

She wore a white cotton frock on this particular Sunday. It was starched and ironed with a beautiful gloss, while a touch of distinction was given to her costume by a little black sleeveless "roundabout" made out of the covering of an old silk umbrella. Her flat hat had a single wreath of coarse daisies around the crown, and her mitts were darned in many places, nevertheless you could not entirely spoil her; God had used a liberal hand in making her, and her father's parsimony was a sort of boomerang that flew back chiefly upon himself.

As for Patty, her style of beauty, like Cephas Cole's ell had to be toned down rather than up, to be effective, but circumstances had been cruelly unrelenting in this process of late. Deacon Baxter had given the girls three or four shopworn pieces of faded yellow calico that had been repudiated by the village housewives as not "fast" enough in color to bear the test of proper washing. This had made frocks, aprons, petticoats, and even underclothes, for two full years, and Patty's weekly objurgations when she removed her everlasting yellow dress from the nail where it hung were not such as should have fallen from the lips of a deacon's daughter. Waitstill had taken a piece of the same yellow material, starched and ironed it, cut a curving, circular brim from it, sewed in a pleated crown, and lo! a hat for Patty! What inspired Patty to put on a waist ribbon of deepest wine color, with a little band of the same on the pale yellow hat, no one could say.

"Do you think you shall like that dull red right close to the yellow, Patty?" Waitstill asked anxiously.

"It looks all right on the columbines in the Indian Cellar," replied Patty, turning and twisting the hat on her head. "If we can't get a peek at the Boston fashions, we must just find our styles where we can!"

The various roads to Tory Hill were alive with vehicles on this bright Sunday morning. Uncle Bart and Abel Day, with their respective wives on the back seat of the Cole's double wagon, were passed by Deacon Baxter and his daughters, Waitstill being due at meeting earlier than others by reason of her singing in the choir. The Deacon's one-horse, two-wheeled "shay" could hold three persons, with comfort on its broad seat, and the twenty-year-old mare, although she was always as hollow as a gourd, could generally do the mile, uphill all the way, in half an hour, if urged continually, and the Deacon, be it said, if not good at feeding, was unsurpassed at urging.

Aunt Abby Cole could get only a passing glimpse of Patty in the depths of the "shay," but a glimpse was always enough for her, as her opinion of the girl's charms was considerably affected by the forlorn condition of her son Cephas, whom she suspected of being hopelessly in love with the young person aforesaid, to whom she commonly alluded as "that red-headed baggage."

"Patience Baxter's got the kind of looks that might do well enough at a tavern dance, or a husking, but they're entirely unsuited to the Sabbath day or the meetin'-house," so Aunt Abby remarked to Mrs. Day in the way of backseat confidence. "It's unfortunate that a deacon's daughter should be afflicted with that bold style of beauty! Her hair's all but red; in fact, you might as well call it red, when the sun shines on it: but if she'd ever smack it down with bear's grease she might darken it some; or anyhow she'd make it lay slicker; but it's the kind of hair that just matches that kind of a girl,— sort of up an' comin'! Then her skin's so white and her cheeks so pink and her eyes so snappy that she'd attract attention without half trying though I guess she ain't above makin' an effort."

"She's innocent as a kitten," observed Mrs. Day impartially.

"Oh, yes, she's innocent enough an' I hope she'll keep so! Waitstill's a sight han'somer, if the truth was told; but she's the sort of girl that's made for one man and the rest of em never look at her. The other one's cut out for the crowd, the more the merrier. She's a kind of man-trap, that girl is!—Do urge the horse a little mite, Bartholomew! It makes me kind o' hot to be passed by Deacon Baxter. It's Missionary Sunday, too, when he gen'ally has rheumatism too bad to come out."

"I wonder if he ever puts anything into the plate," said Mrs. Day. "No one ever saw him, that I know of."

"The Deacon keeps the Thou Shalt Not commandments pretty well," was Aunt Abby's terse response. "I guess he don't put nothin' into the plate, but I s'pose we'd ought to be thankful he don't take nothin' out. The Baptists are gettin' ahead faster than they'd ought to, up to the Mills. Our minister ain't no kind of a proselyter, Seems as if he didn't care how folks got to heaven so long as they got there! The other church is havin' a service this afternoon side o' the river, an' I'd kind o' like to go, except it would please 'em too much to have a crowd there to see the immersion. They tell me, but I don't know how true, that that Tillman widder woman that come here from somewheres in Vermont wanted to be baptized to-day, but the other converts declared THEY wouldn't be, if she was!"

"Jed Morrill said they'd have to hold her under water quite a spell to do any good," chuckled Uncle Bart from the front seat.

"Well, I wouldn't repeat it, Bartholomew, on the Sabbath day; not if he did say it. Jed Morrill's responsible for more blasphemious jokes than any man in Edgewood. I don't approve of makin' light of anybody's religious observances if they're ever so foolish," said Aunt Abby somewhat enigmatically. "Our minister keeps remindin' us that the Baptists and Methodists are our brethren, but I wish he'd be a little more anxious to have our S'ceity keep ahead of the others."

"Jed's 'bout right in sizin' up the Widder Tillman," was Mr. Day's timid contribution to the argument. "I ain't a readin' man, but from what folks report I should think she was one o' them critters that set on rocks bewilderin' an' bedevilin' men-folks out o' their senses—SYREENS, I think they call 'em; a reg'lar SYREEN is what that woman is, I guess!"

"There, there, Abel, you wouldn't know a syreen if you found one in your baked beans, so don't take away a woman's character on hearsay." And Mrs. Day, having shut up her husband as was her bounden duty as a wife and a Christian, tied her bonnet strings a little tighter and looked distinctly pleased with herself.

"Abel ain't startin' any new gossip," was Aunt Abby's opinion, as she sprung to his rescue. "One or two more holes in a colander don't make much dif'rence.—Bartholomew, we're certainly goin' to be late this mornin'; we're about the last team on the road"; and Aunt Abby glanced nervously behind. "Elder Boone ain't begun the openin' prayer, though, or we should know it. You can hear him pray a mile away, when the wind's right. I do hate to be late to meetin'. The Elder allers takes notice; the folks in the wing pews allers gapes an' stares, and the choir peeks through the curtain, takin' notes of everything you've got on your back. I hope to the land they'll chord and keep together a little mite better 'n they've done lately, that's all I can say! If the Lord is right in our midst as the Bible says, He can't think much of our singers this summer!"

"They're improvin', now that Pliny Waterhouse plays his fiddle," Mrs. Day remarked pacifically. "There was times in the anthem when they kept together consid'able well last Sunday. They didn't always chord, but there, they chorded some!—we're most there now, Abby, don't fret! Cephas won't ring the last bell till he knows his own folks is crossin' the Common!"

Those were days of conscientious church-going and every pew in the house was crowded. The pulpit was built on pillars that raised it six feet higher than the floor; the top was cushioned and covered with red velvet surmounted by a huge gilt-edged Bible. There was a window in the tower through which Cephas Cole could look into the church, and while tolling the bell could keep watch for the minister. Always exactly on time, he would come in, walk slowly up the right-hand aisle, mount the pulpit stairs, enter and close the door after him. Then Cephas would give one tremendous pull to warn loiterers on the steps; a pull that meant, "Parson's in the pulpit!" and was acted upon accordingly. Opening the big Bible, the minister raised his right hand impressively, and saying, "Let us pray," the whole congregation rose in their pews with a great rustling and bowed their heads devoutly for the invocation.

Next came the hymn, generally at that day one of Isaac Watts's. The singers, fifteen or twenty in number, sat in a raised gallery opposite the pulpit, and there was a rod in front hung with red curtains to hide them when sitting down. Any one was free to join, which perhaps accounted for Aunt Abby's strictures as to time and tune. Jed Morrill, "blasphemious" as he was considered by that acrimonious lady, was the leader, and a good one, too. There would be a great whispering and buzzing when Deacon Sumner with his big fiddle and Pliny Waterhouse with his smaller one would try to get in accord with Humphrey Baker and his clarionet. All went well when Humphrey was there to give the sure key-note, but in his absence Jed Morrill would use his tuning-fork. When the key was finally secured by all concerned, Jed would raise his stick, beat one measure to set the time, and all joined in, or fell in, according to their several abilities. It was not always a perfect thing in the way of a start, but they were well together at the end of the first line, and when, as now, the choir numbered a goodly number of voices, and there were three or four hundred in the pews, nothing more inspiring in its peculiar way was ever heard, than the congregational singing of such splendid hymns as "Old Hundred," "Duke Street," or "Coronation."

Waitstill led the trebles, and Ivory was at the far end of the choir in the basses, but each was conscious of the other's presence. This morning he could hear her noble voice rising a little above, or, perhaps from its quality, separating itself somehow, ever so little, from the others. How full of strength and hope it was, her voice! How steadfast to the pitch; how golden its color; how moving in its crescendos! How the words flowed from her lips; not as if they had been written years ago, but as if they were the expression of her own faith. There were many in the congregation who were stirred, they knew not why, when there chanced to be only a few "carrying the air" and they could really hear Waitstill Baxter singing some dear old hymn, full of sacred memories, like:—

"While Thee I seek, protecting Power,

  Be my vain wishes stilled!

And may this consecrated hour

  With better hopes be filled."

"There may be them in Boston that can sing louder, and they may be able to run up a little higher than Waitstill, but the question is, could any of 'em make Aunt Abby Cole shed tears?" This was Jed Morrill's tribute to his best soprano.

There were Sunday evening prayer-meetings, too, held at "early candlelight," when Waitstill and Lucy Morrill would make a duet of "By cool Siloam's Shady Rill," or the favorite "Naomi," and the two fresh young voices, rising and falling in the tender thirds of the old tunes, melted all hearts to new willingness of sacrifice.

"Father, whate'er of earthly bliss

  Thy sov'reign will denies,

Accepted at Thy Throne of grace

  Let this petition rise!

"Give me a calm, a thankful heart,

  From every murmur free!

The blessing of Thy grace impart

  And let me live to Thee!"

How Ivory loved to hear Waitstill sing these lines! How they eased his burden as they were easing hers, falling on his impatient, longing heart like evening dew on thirsty grass!

XII. THE GREEN-EYED MONSTER

"WHILE Thee I seek, protecting Power," was the first hymn on this particular Sunday morning, and it usually held Patty's rather vagrant attention to the end, though it failed to do so to-day. The Baxters occupied one of the wing pews, a position always to be envied, as one could see the singers without turning around, and also observe everybody in the congregation,—their entrance, garments, behavior, and especially their bonnets,—without being in the least indiscreet, or seeming to have a roving eye.

Lawyer Wilson's pew was the second in front of the Baxters in the same wing, and Patty, seated decorously but unwillingly beside her father, was impatiently awaiting the entrance of the family, knowing that Mark would be with them if he had returned from Boston. Timothy Grant, the parish clerk, had the pew in between, and afforded a most edifying spectacle to the community, as there were seven young Grants of a church-going age, and the ladies of the congregation were always counting them, reckoning how many more were in their cradles at home and trying to guess from Mrs. Grant's lively or chastened countenance whether any new ones had been born since the Sunday before.

Patty settled herself comfortably, and put her foot on the wooden "cricket," raising her buff calico a little on the congregation side, just enough to show an inch or two of petticoat. The petticoat was as modestly long as the frock itself, and disclosing a bit of it was nothing more heinous than a casual exhibition of good needlework. Deacon Baxter furnished only the unbleached muslin for his daughters' undergarments; but twelve little tucks laboriously done by hand, elaborate inch-wide edging, crocheted from white spool cotton, and days of bleaching on the grass in the sun, will make a petticoat that can be shown in church with some justifiable pride.

The Wilsons came up the aisle a moment later than was their usual habit, just after the parson had ascended the pulpit. Mrs. Wilson always entered the pew first and sat in the far end. Patty had looked at her admiringly, and with a certain feeling of proprietorship, for several Sundays. There was obviously no such desirable mother-in-law in the meeting-house. Her changeable silk dress was the latest mode; her shawl of black llama lace expressed wealth in every delicate mesh, and her bonnet had a distinction that could only have emanated from Portland or Boston. Ellen Wilson usually came in next, with as much of a smile to Patty in passing as she dared venture in the Deacon's presence, and after her sidled in her younger sister Selina, commonly called "Silly," and with considerable reason.

Mark had come home! Patty dared not look up, but she felt his approach behind the others, although her eyes sought the floor, and her cheeks hung out signals of abashed but certain welcome. She heard the family settle in their seats somewhat hastily, the click of the pew door and the sound of Lawyer Wilson's cane as he stood it in the corner; then the parson rose to pray and Patty closed her eyes with the rest of the congregation.

Opening them when Elder Boone rose to announce the hymn, they fell—amazed, resentful, uncomprehending—on the spectacle of Mark Wilson finding the place in the book for a strange young woman who sat beside him. Mark himself had on a new suit and wore a seal ring that Patty had never observed before; while the dress, pelisse, and hat of the unknown were of a nature that no girl in Patty's position, and particularly of Patty's disposition, could have regarded without a desire to tear them from her person and stamp them underfoot; or better still, flaunt them herself and show the world how they should be worn!

Mark found the place in the hymn-book for the—creature, shared it with her, and once, when the Grant twins wriggled and Patty secured a better view, once, Mark shifted his hand on the page so that his thumb touched that of his pretty neighbor, who did not remove hers as if she found the proximity either unpleasant or improper. Patty compared her own miserable attire with that of the hated rival in front, and also contrasted Lawyer Wilson's appearance with that of her father; the former, well dressed in the style of a gentleman of the time, in broadcloth, with fine linen, and a tall silk hat carefully placed on the floor of the pew; while Deacon Baxter wore homespun made of wool from his own sheep, spun and woven, dyed and finished, at the fulling-mill in the village, and carried a battered felt hat that had been a matter of ridicule these dozen years. (The Deacon would be buried in two coats, Jed Morrill always said, for he owned just that number, and would be too mean to leave either of 'em behind him!)

The sermon was fifty minutes long, time enough for a deal of thinking. Many a housewife, not wholly orthodox, cut and made over all her children's clothes, in imagination; planned the putting up of her fruit, the making of her preserves and pickles, and arranged her meals for the next week, during the progress of those sermons. Patty watched the parson turn leaf after leaf until the final one was reached. Then came the last hymn, when the people stretched their aching limbs, and rising, turned their backs on the minister and faced the choir. Patty looked at Waitstill and wished that she could put her throbbing head on her sisterly shoulder and cry,—mostly with rage. The benediction was said, and with the final "Amen" the pews were opened and the worshippers crowded into the narrow aisles and moved towards the doors.

Patty's plans were all made. She was out of her pew before the Wilsons could possibly leave theirs, and in her progress down the aisle securely annexed her great admirer, old Dr. Perry, as well as his son Philip. Passing the singing-seats she picked up the humble Cephas and carried him along in her wake, chatting and talking with her little party while her father was at the horse-sheds, making ready to go home between services as was his habit, a cold bite being always set out on the kitchen table according to his orders. By means of these clever manoeuvres Patty made herself the focus of attention when the Wilson party came out on the steps, and vouchsafed Mark only a nonchalant nod, airily flinging a little greeting with the nod,— just a "How d'ye do, Mark? Did you have a good time in Boston?"

Patty and Waitstill, with some of the girls who had come long distances, ate their luncheon in a shady place under the trees behind the meeting-house, for there was an afternoon service to come, a service with another long sermon. They separated after the modest meal to walk about the Common or stray along the road to the Academy, where there was a fine view.

Two or three times during the summer the sisters always went quietly and alone to the Baxter burying-lot, where three grassgrown graves lay beside one another, unmarked save by narrow wooden slabs so short that the initials painted on them were almost hidden by the tufts of clover. The girls had brought roots of pansies and sweet alyssum, and with a knife made holes in the earth and planted them here and there to make the spot a trifle less forbidding. They did not speak to each other during this sacred little ceremony; their hearts were too full when they remembered afresh the absence of headstones, the lack of care, in the place where the three women lay who had ministered to their father, borne him children, and patiently endured his arbitrary and loveless rule. Even Cleve Flanders' grave,—the Edgewood shoemaker, who lay next,—even his resting-place was marked and, with a touch of some one's imagination marked by the old man's own lapstone twenty-five pounds in weight, a monument of his work-a-day life.

Waitstill rose from her feet, brushing the earth from her hands, and Patty did the same. The churchyard was quiet, and they were alone with the dead, mourned and unmourned, loved and unloved.

"I planted one or two pansies on the first one's grave," said Waitstill soberly. "I don't know why we've never done it before. There are no children to take notice of and remember her; it's the least we can do, and, after all, she belongs to the family."

"There is no family, and there never was!" suddenly cried Patty. "Oh! Waity, Waity, we are so alone, you and I! We've only each other in all the world, and I'm not the least bit of help to you, as you are to me! I'm a silly, vain, conceited, ill-behaved thing, but I will be better, I will! You won't ever give me up, will you, Waity, even if I'm not like you? I haven't been good lately!"

"Hush, Patty, hush!" And Waitstill came nearer to her sister with a motherly touch of her hand. "I'll not have you say such things; you that are the helpfullest and the lovingest girl that ever was, and the cleverest, too, and the liveliest, and the best company-keeper!"

"No one thinks so but you!" Patty responded dolefully, although she wiped her eyes as if a bit consoled.

It is safe to say that Patty would never have given Mark Wilson a second thought had he not taken her to drive on that afternoon in early May. The drive, too, would have quickly fled from her somewhat fickle memory had it not been for the kiss. The kiss was, indeed, a decisive factor in the situation, and had shed a rosy, if somewhat fictitious light of romance over the past three weeks. Perhaps even the kiss, had it never been repeated, might have lapsed into its true perspective, in due course of time, had it not been for the sudden appearance of the stranger in the Wilson pew. The moment that Patty's gaze fell upon that fashionably dressed, instantaneously disliked girl, Marquis Wilson's stock rose twenty points in the market. She ceased, in a jiffy, to weigh and consider and criticize the young man, but regarded him with wholly new eyes. His figure was better than she had realized, his smile more interesting, his manners more attractive, his eyelashes longer; in a word, he had suddenly grown desirable. A month ago she could have observed, with idle and alien curiosity, the spectacle of his thumb drawing nearer to another (feminine) thumb, on the page of the Watts and Select Hymn book; now, at the morning service, she had wished nothing so much as to put Mark's thumb back into his pocket where it belonged, and slap the girl's thumb smartly and soundly as it deserved.

The ignorant cause of Patty's distress was a certain Annabel Franklin, the daughter of a cousin of Mrs. Wilson's. Mark had stayed at the Franklin house during his three weeks' visit in Boston, where he had gone on business for his father. The young people had naturally seen much of each other and Mark's inflammable fancy had been so kindled by Annabel's doll-like charms that he had persuaded her to accompany him to his home and get a taste of country life in Maine. Such is man, such is human nature, and such is life, that Mark had no sooner got the whilom object of his affections under his own roof than she began to pall.

Annabel was twenty-three, and to tell the truth she had palled before, more than once. She was so amiable, so well-finished,—with her smooth flaxen hair, her neat nose, her buttonhole of a mouth, and her trim shape,—that she appealed to the opposite sex quite generally and irresistibly as a worthy helpmate. The only trouble was that she began to bore her suitors somewhat too early in the game, and they never got far enough to propose marriage. Flaws in her apparent perfection appeared from day to day and chilled the growth of the various young loves that had budded so auspiciously. She always agreed with everybody and everything in sight, even to the point of changing her mind on the instant, if circumstances seemed to make it advisable. Her instinctive point of view, when she went so far as to hold one, was somewhat cut and dried; in a word, priggish. She kept a young man strictly on his good behavior, that much could be said in her favor; the only criticism that could be made on this estimable trait was that no bold youth was ever tempted to overstep the bounds of discretion when in her presence. No unruly words of love ever rose to his lips; his hand never stole out involuntarily and imprudently to meet her small chilly one; the sight of her waist never even suggested an encircling arm; and as a fellow never desired to kiss her, she was never obliged to warn or rebuke or strike him off her visiting list. Her father had an ample fortune and some one would inevitably turn up who would regard Annabel as an altogether worthy and desirable spouse. That was what she had seemed to Mark Wilson for a full week before he left the Franklin house in Boston, but there were moments now when he regretted, fugitively, that he had ever removed her from her proper sphere. She did not seem to fit in to the conditions of life in Edgewood, and it may even be that her most glaring fault had been to describe Patty Baxter's hair at this very Sunday dinner as "carroty," her dress altogether "dreadful," and her style of beauty "unladylike." Ellen Wilson's feelings were somewhat injured by these criticisms of her intimate friend, and in discussing the matter privately with her brother he was inclined to agree with her.

And thus, so little do we know of the prankishness of the blind god, thus was Annabel Franklin working for her rival's best interests; and instead of reviling her in secret, and treating her with disdain in public, Patty should have welcomed her cordially to all the delights of Riverboro society.

XIII. HAYING-TIME

EVERYBODY in Riverboro, Edgewood, Milliken's Mills, Spruce Swamp, Duck Pond, and Moderation was "haying." There was a perfect frenzy of haying, for it was the Monday after the "Fourth," the precise date in July when the Maine farmer said good-bye to repose, and "hayed" desperately and unceasingly, until every spear of green in his section was mowed down and safely under cover. If a man had grass of his own, he cut it, and if he had none, he assisted in cutting that of some other man, for "to hay," although an unconventional verb, was, and still is, a very active one, and in common circulation, although not used by the grammarians.

Whatever your trade, and whatever your profession, it counted as naught in good weather. The fish-man stopped selling fish, the meat-man ceased to bring meat; the cobbler, as well as the judge, forsook the bench; and even the doctor made fewer visits than usual. The wage for work in the hay-fields was a high one, and every man, boy, and horse in a village was pressed into service.

When Ivory Boynton had finished with his own small crop, he commonly went at once to Lawyer Wilson, who had the largest acreage of hay-land in the township. Ivory was always in great demand, for he was a mighty worker in the field, and a very giant at "pitching," being able to pick up a fair-sized hay-cock at one stroke of the fork and fling it on to the cart as if it were a feather. Lawyer Wilson always took a hand himself if signs of rain appeared, and Mark occasionally visited the scene of action when a crowd in the field made a general jollification, or when there was an impending thunderstorm. In such cases even women and girls joined the workers and all hands bent together to the task of getting a load into the barn and covering the rest.

Deacon Baxter was wont to call Mark Wilson a "worthless, whey-faced, lily-handed whelp," but the description, though picturesque, was decidedly exaggerated. Mark disliked manual labor, but having imbibed enough knowledge of law in his father's office to be an excellent clerk, he much preferred travelling about, settling the details of small cases, collecting rents and bad bills, to any form of work on a farm. This sort of life, on stage-coaches and railway trains, or on long driving trips with his own fast trotter, suited his adventurous disposition and gave him a sense of importance that was very necessary to his peace of mind. He was not especially intimate with Ivory Boynton, who studied law with his father during all vacations and in every available hour of leisure during term time, as did many another young New England schoolmaster. Mark's father's praise of Ivory's legal ability was a little too warm to please his son, as was the commendation of one of the County Court judges on Ivory's preparation of a brief in a certain case in the Wilson office. Ivory had drawn it up at Mr. Wilson's request, merely to show how far he understood the books and cases he was studying, and he had no idea that it differed in any way from the work of any other student; all the same, Mark's own efforts in a like direction had never received any special mention. When he was in the hay-field he also kept as far as possible from Ivory, because there, too, he felt a superiority that made him, for the moment, a trifle discontented. It was no particular pleasure for him to see Ivory plunge his fork deep into the heart of a haycock, take a firm grasp of the handle, thrust forward his foot to steady himself, and then raise the great fragrant heap slowly, and swing it up to the waiting haycart amid the applause of the crowd. Rodman would be there, too, helping the man on top of the load and getting nearly buried each time, as the mass descended upon him, but doing his slender best to distribute and tread it down properly, while his young heart glowed with pride at Cousin Ivory's prowess.

Independence Day had passed, with its usual gayeties for the young people, in none of which the Baxter family had joined, and now, at eleven o'clock on this burning July morning, Waitstill was driving the old mare past the Wilson farm on her way to the river field. Her father was working there, together with the two hired men whom he took on for a fortnight during the height of the season. If mowing, raking, pitching, and carting of the precious crop could only have been done at odd times during the year, or at night, he would not have embittered the month of July by paying out money for labor: but Nature was inexorable in the ripening of hay and Old Foxy was obliged to succumb to the inevitable. Waitstill had a basket packed with luncheon for three and a great demijohn of cool ginger tea under the wagon seat. Other farmers sometimes served hard cider, or rum, but her father's principles were dead against this riotous extravagance. Temperance, in any and all directions, was cheap, and the Deacon was a very temperate man, save in language.

The fields on both sides of the road were full of haymakers and everywhere there was bustle and stir. There would be three or four men, one leading, the others following, slowly swinging their way through a noble piece of grass, and the smell of the mown fields in the sunshine was sweeter than honey in the comb. There were patches of black-eyed Susans in the meadows here and there, while pink and white hardhack grew by the road, with day lilies and blossoming milkweed. The bobolinks were fluting from every tree; there were thrushes in the alder bushes and orioles in the tops of the elms, and Waitstill's heart overflowed with joy at being in such a world of midsummer beauty, though life, during the great heat and incessant work of haying-time, was a little more rigorous than usual. The extra food needed for the hired men always kept her father in a state of mind closely resembling insanity. Coming downstairs to cook breakfast she would find the coffee or tea measured out for the pot. The increased consumption of milk angered him beyond words, because it lessened the supply of butter for sale. Everything that could be made with buttermilk was ordered so to be done, and nothing but water could be used in mixing the raised bread. The corncake must never have an egg; the piecrust must be shortened only with lard, or with a mixture of beef-fat and dripping; and so on, and so on, eternally.

When the girls were respectively seventeen and thirteen, Waitstill had begged a small plot of ground for them to use as they liked, and beginning at that time they had gradually made a little garden, with a couple of fruit trees and a thicket of red, white, and black currants raspberry and blackberry bushes. For several summers now they had sold enough of their own fruit to buy a pair of shoes or gloves, a scarf or a hat, but even this tiny income was beginning to be menaced. The Deacon positively suffered as he looked at that odd corner of earth, not any bigger than his barn floor, and saw what his girls had done with no tools but a spade and a hoe and no help but their own hands. He had no leisure (so he growled) to cultivate and fertilize ground for small fruits, and no money to pay a man to do it, yet here was food grown under his very eye, and it did not belong to him! The girls worked in their garden chiefly at sunrise in spring and early summer, or after supper in the evening; all the same Waitstill had been told by her father the day before that she was not only using ground, but time, that belonged to him, and that he should expect her to provide "pie-filling" out of her garden patch during haying, to help satisfy the ravenous appetites of that couple of "great, gorming, greedy lubbers" that he was hiring this year. He had stopped the peeling of potatoes before boiling because he disapproved of the thickness of the parings he found in the pig's pail, and he stood over Patty at her work in the kitchen until Waitstill was in daily fear of a tempest of some sort.

Coming in from the shed one morning she met her father just issuing from the kitchen where Patty was standing like a young Fury in front of the sink. "Father's been spying at the eggshells I settled the coffee with, and said I'd no business to leave so much good in the shell when I broke an egg. I will not bear it; he makes me feel fairly murderous! You'd better not leave me alone with him when I'm like this. Oh! I know that I'm wicked, but isn't he wicked too, and who was wicked first?"

Patty's heart had been set on earning and saving enough pennies for a white muslin dress and every day rendered the prospect more uncertain; this was a sufficient grievance in itself to keep her temper at the boiling point had there not been various other contributory causes. Waitstill's patience was flagging a trifle, too, under the stress of the hot days and the still hotter, breathless nights. The suspicion crossed her mind now and then that her father's miserliness and fits of temper might be caused by a mental malady over which he now had little or no control, having never mastered himself in all his life. Her power of endurance would be greater, she thought, if only she could be certain that this theory was true, though her slavery would be just as galling.

It would be so easy for her to go away and earn a living; she who had never had a day of illness in her life; she who could sew, knit, spin, weave, and cook. She could make enough money in Biddeford or Portsmouth to support herself, and Patty, too, until the proper work was found for both. But there would be a truly terrible conflict of wills, and such fierce arraignment of her unfilial conduct, such bitter and caustic argument from her father, such disapproval from the parson and the neighbors, that her very soul shrank from the prospect. If she could go alone, and have no responsibility over Patty's future, that would be a little more possible, but she must think wisely for two.

And how could she leave Ivory when there might perhaps come a crisis in his life where she could be useful to him? How could she cut herself off from those Sundays in the choir, those dear fugitive glimpses of him in the road or at prayer-meeting? They were only sips of happiness, where her thirsty heart yearned for long, deep draughts, but they were immeasurably better than nothing. Freedom from her father's heavy yoke, freedom to work, and read, and sing, and study, and grow,—oh! how she longed for this, but at what a cost would she gain it if she had to harbor the guilty conscience of an undutiful and rebellious daughter, and at the same time cut herself off from the sight of the one being she loved best in all the world.

She felt drawn towards Ivory's mother to-day. Three weeks had passed since her talk with Ivory in the churchyard, but there had been no possibility of an hour's escape from home. She was at liberty this afternoon—relatively at liberty; for although her work, as usual, was laid out for her, it could be made up somehow or other before nightfall. She could drive over to the Boynton's place, hitch her horse in the woods near the house, make her visit, yet be in plenty of time to go up to the river field and bring her father home to supper. Patty was over at Mrs. Abel Day's, learning a new crochet stitch and helping her to start a log-cabin quilt. Ivory and Rodman, she new, were both away in the Wilson hay-field; no time would ever be more favorable; so instead of driving up Town-House Hill when she returned to the village she kept on over the bridge.

XIV. UNCLE BART DISCOURSES

UNCLE BART and Cephas were taking their nooning hour under the Nodhead apple tree as Waitstill passed the joiner's shop and went over the bridge.

"Uncle Bart might somehow guess where I am going," she thought, "but even if he did he would never tell any one."

"Where's Waitstill bound this afternoon, I wonder?" drawled Cephas, rising to his feet and looking after the departing team. "That reminds me, I'd better run up to Baxter's and see if any-thing's wanted before I open the store."

"If it makes any dif'rence," said his father dryly, as he filled his pipe, "Patty's over to Mis' Day's spendin' the afternoon. Don't s'pose you want to call on the pig, do you? He's the only one to home."

Cephas made no remark, but gave his trousers a hitch, picked up a chip, opened his jack-knife, and sitting down on the greensward began idly whittling the bit of wood into shape.

"I kind o' wish you'd let me make the new ell two-story, father; 't wouldn't be much work, take it in slack time after hayin'."

"Land o' Liberty! What do you want to do that for, Cephas? You 'bout pestered the life out o' me gittin' me to build the ell in the first place, when we didn't need it no more'n a toad does a pocketbook. Then nothin' would do but you must paint it, though I shan't be able to have the main house painted for another year, so the old wine an' the new bottle side by side looks like the Old Driver, an' makes us a laughin'-stock to the village;—and now you want to change the thing into a two-story! Never heerd such a crazy idee in my life."

"I want to settle down," insisted Cephas doggedly.

"Well, settle; I'm willin'! I told you that, afore you painted the ell. Ain't two rooms, fourteen by fourteen, enough for you to settle down in? If they ain't, I guess your mother'd give you one o' the chambers in the main part."

"She would if I married Phoebe Day, but I don't want to marry Phoebe," argued Cephas. "And mother's gone and made a summer kitchen for herself out in the ell, a'ready. I bet yer she'll never move out if I should want to move in on a 'sudden."

"I told you you was takin' that risk when you cut a door through from the main part," said his father genially. "If you hadn't done that, your mother would 'a' had to gone round outside to git int' the ell and mebbe she'd 'a' stayed to home when it stormed, anyhow. Now your wife'll have her troopin' in an' out, in an' out, the whole 'durin' time."

"I only cut the door through to please so't she'd favor my gittin' married, but I guess 't won't do no good. You see, father, what I was thinkin' of is, a girl would mebbe jump at a two-story, four-roomed ell when she wouldn't look at a smaller place."

"Pends upon whether the girl's the jumpin' kind or not! Hadn't you better git everything fixed up with the one you've picked out, afore you take your good savin's and go to buildin' a bigger place for her?"

"I've asked her once a'ready," Cephas allowed, with a burning face. "I don't s'pose you know the one I mean?"

"No kind of an idee," responded his father, with a quizzical wink that was lost on the young man, as his eyes were fixed upon his whittling. "Does she belong to the village?"

"I ain't goin' to let folks know who I've picked out till I git a little mite forrarder," responded Cephas craftily. "Say, father, it's all right to ask a girl twice, ain't it?

"Certain it is, my son. I never heerd there was any special limit to the number o' times you could ask 'em, and their power o' sayin' 'No' is like the mercy of the Lord; it endureth forever.—You wouldn't consider a widder, Cephas? A widder'd be a good comp'ny-keeper for your mother."

"I hain't put my good savin's into an ell jest to marry a comp'ny-keeper for mother," responded Cephas huffily. "I want to be number one with my girl and start right in on trainin' her up to suit me."

"Well, if trainin' 's your object you'd better take my advice an' keep it dark before marriage, Cephas. It's astonishin' how the female sect despises bein' trained; it don't hardly seem to be in their nature to make any changes in 'emselves after they once gits started."

"How are you goin' to live with 'em, then?" Cephas inquired, looking up with interest coupled with some incredulity.

"Let them do the training," responded his father, peacefully puffing out the words with his pipe between his lips. "Some of 'em's mild and gentle in discipline, like Parson Boone's wife or Mis' Timothy Grant, and others is strict and firm like your mother and Mis' Abel Day. If you happen to git the first kind, why, do as they tell you, and thank the Lord 't ain't any worse. If you git the second kind, jest let 'em put the blinders on you and trot as straight as you know how, without shying nor kickin' over the traces, nor bolting 'cause they've got control o' the bit and 't ain't no use fightin' ag'in' their superior strength.—So fur as you can judge, in the early stages o' the game, my son,—which ain't very fur,—which kind have you picked out?"

Cephas whittled on for some moments without a word, but finally, with a sigh drawn from the very toes of his boots, he responded gloomily,—

"She's awful spunky, the girl is, anybody can see that; but she's a young thing, and I thought bein' married would kind o' tame her down!"

"You can see how much marriage has tamed your mother down," observed Uncle Bart dispassionately; "howsomever, though your mother can't be called tame, she's got her good p'ints, for she's always to be counted on. The great thing in life, as I take it, Cephas, is to know exactly what to expect. Your mother's gen'ally credited with an onsartin temper, but folks does her great injustice in so thinking for in a long experience I've seldom come across a temper less onsartin than your mother's. You know exactly where to find her every mornin' at sun-up and every night at sundown. There ain't nothin' you can do to put her out o' temper, cause she's all out aforehand. You can jest go about your reg'lar business 'thout any fear of disturbin' her any further than she's disturbed a'ready, which is consid'rable. I don't mind it a mite nowadays, though, after forty years of it. It would kind o' gall me to keep a stiddy watch of a female's disposition day by day, wonderin' when she was goin' to have a tantrum. A tantrum once a year's an awful upsettin' kind of a thing in a family, my son, but a tantrum every twenty-four hours is jest part o' the day's work." There was a moment's silence during which Uncle Bart puffed his pipe and Cephas whittled, after which the old man continued: "Then, if you happen to marry a temper like your mother's, Cephas, look what a pow'ful worker you gen'ally get! Look at the way they sweep an' dust an' scrub an' clean! Watch 'em when they go at the dish-washin', an' how they whack the rollin'-pin, an' maul the eggs, an' heave the wood int' the stove, an' slat the flies out o' the house! The mild and gentle ones enough, will be settin' in the kitchen rocker read-in' the almanac when there ain't no wood in the kitchen box, no doughnuts in the crock, no pies on the swing shelf in the cellar, an' the young ones goin' round without a second shift to their backs!"

Cephas's mind was far away during this philosophical dissertation on the ways of women. He could see only a sunny head fairly rioting with curls; a pair of eyes that held his like magnets, although they never gave him a glance of love; a smile that lighted the world far better than the sun; a dimple into which his heart fell headlong whenever he looked at it!

"You're right, father; 'tain't no use kickin' ag'in 'em," he said as he rose to his feet preparatory to opening the Baxter store. "When I said that 'bout trainin' up a girl to suit me, I kind o' forgot the one I've picked out. I'm considerin' several, but the one I favor most-well, I believe she'd fire up at the first sight o' training and that's the gospel truth."

"Considerin' several, be you, Cephas?" laughed Uncle Bart. "Well, all I hope is, that the one you favor most—the girl you've asked once a'ready—is considerin' you!"

Cephas went to the pump, and wetting a large handkerchief put it in the crown of his straw hat and sauntered out into the burning heat of the open road between his father's shop and Deacon Baxter's store.

"I shan't ask her the next time till this hot spell's over," he thought, "and I won't do it in that dodgasted old store ag'in, neither; I ain't so tongue-tied outdoors an' I kind o' think I'd be more in the sperit of it after sundown, some night after supper!"

XV. IVORY'S MOTHER

WAITSTILL found a cool and shady place in which to hitch the old mare, loosening her check-rein and putting a sprig of alder in her headstall to assist her in brushing off the flies.

One could reach the Boynton house only by going up a long grass-grown lane that led from the high-road. It was a lonely place, and Aaron Boynton had bought it when he moved from Saco, simply because he secured it at a remarkable bargain, the owner having lost his wife and gone to live in Massachusetts. Ivory would have sold it long ago had circumstances been different, for it was at too great a distance from the schoolhouse and from Lawyer Wilson's office to be at all convenient, but he dreaded to remove his mother from the environment to which she was accustomed, and doubted very much whether she would be able to care for a house to which she had not been wonted before her mind became affected. Here in this safe, secluded corner, amid familiar and thoroughly known conditions, she moved placidly about her daily tasks, performing them with the same care and precision that she had used from the beginning of her married life. All the heavy work was done for her by Ivory and Rodman; the boy in particular being the fleetest-footed, the most willing, and the neatest of helpers; washing dishes, sweeping and dusting, laying the table, as deftly and quietly as a girl. Mrs. Boynton made her own simple dresses of gray calico in summer, or dark linsey-woolsey in winter by the same pattern that she had used when she first came to Edgewood: in fact there were positively no external changes anywhere to be seen, tragic and terrible as had been those that had wrought havoc in her mind.

Waitstill's heart beat faster as she neared the Boynton house. She had never so much as seen Ivory's mother for years. How would she be met? Who would begin the conversation, and what direction would it take? What if Mrs. Boynton should refuse to talk to her at all? She walked slowly along the lane until she saw a slender, gray-clad figure stooping over a flower-bed in front of the cottage. The woman raised her head with a fawn-like gesture that had something in it of timidity rather than fear, picked some loose bits of green from the ground, and, quietly turning her back upon the on coming stranger, disappeared through the open front door.

There could be no retreat on her own part now, thought Waitstill. She wished for a moment that she had made this first visit under Ivory's protection, but her idea had been to gain Mrs. Boynton's confidence and have a quiet friendly talk, such a one as would be impossible in the presence of a third person. Approaching the steps, she called through the doorway in her clear voice: "Ivory asked me to come and see you one day, Mrs. Boynton. I am Waitstill Baxter, the little girl on Town House Hill that you used to know."

Mrs. Boynton came from an inner room and stood on the threshold. The name "Waitstill" had always had a charm for her ears, from the time she first heard it years ago, until it fell from Ivory's lips this summer; and again it caught her fancy.

"'WAITSTILL!'" she repeated softly; "'WAITSTILL!' Does Ivory know you?"

"We've known each other for ever so long; ever since we went to the brick school together when we were girl and boy. And when I was a child my stepmother brought me over here once on an errand and Ivory showed me a humming-bird's nest in that lilac bush by the door."

Mrs. Boynton smiled "Come and look!" she whispered. "There is always a humming-bird's nest in our lilac. How did you remember?"

The two women approached the bush and Mrs. Boynton carefully parted the leaves to show the dainty morsel of a home thatched with soft gray-green and lined with down. "The birds have flown now," she said. "They were like little jewels when they darted off in the sunshine."

Her voice was faint and sweet, as if it came from far away, and her eyes looked, not as if they were seeing you, but seeing something through you. Her pale hair was turned back from her paler face, where the veins showed like blue rivers, and her smile was like the flitting of a moonbeam. She was standing very close to Waitstill, closer than she had been to any woman for many years, and she studied her a little, wistfully, yet courteously, as if her attention was attracted by something fresh and winning. She looked at the color, ebbing and flowing in the girl's cheeks; at her brows and lashes; at her neck, as white as swan's-down; and finally put out her hand with a sudden impulse and touched the knot of wavy bronze hair under the brimmed hat.

"I had a daughter once," she said. "My second baby was a girl, but she lived only a few weeks. I need her very much, for I am a great care to Ivory. He is son and daughter both, now that Mr. Boynton is away from home.—You did not see any one in the road as you turned in from the bars, I suppose?"

"No," answered Waitstill, surprised and confused, "but I didn't really notice; I was thinking of a cool place for my horse to stand."

"I sit out here in these warm afternoons," Mrs. Boynton continued, shading her eyes and looking across the fields, "because I can see so far down the lane. I have the supper-table set for my husband already, and there is a surprise for him, a saucer of wild strawberries I picked for him this morning. If he does not come, I always take away the plate and cup before Ivory gets here; it seems to make him unhappy."

"He doesn't like it when you are disappointed, I suppose," Waitstill ventured. "I have brought my knitting, Mrs. Boynton, so that I needn't keep you idle if you wish to work. May I sit down a few minutes? And here is a cottage cheese for Ivory and Rodman, and a jar of plums for you, preserved from my own garden."

Mrs. Boynton's eyes searched the face of this visitor from a world she had almost forgotten and finding nothing but tenderness there, said with just a trace of bewilderment: "Thank you yes, do sit down; my workbasket is just inside the door. Take that rocking-chair; I don't have another one out here because I have never been in the habit of seeing visitors."

"I hope I am not intruding," stammered Waitstill, seating herself and beginning her knitting, to see if it would lessen the sense of strain between them.

"Not at all. I always loved young and beautiful people, and so did my husband. If he comes while you are here, do not go away, but sit with him while I get his supper. If Elder Cochrane should be with him, you would see two wonderful men. They went away together to do some missionary work in Maine and New Hampshire and perhaps they will come back together. I do not welcome callers because they always ask so many difficult questions, but you are different and have asked me none at all."

"I should not think of asking questions, Mrs. Boynton."

"Not that I should mind answering them," continued Ivory's mother, "except that it tires my head very much to think. You must not imagine I am ill; it is only that I have a very bad memory, and when people ask me to remember something, or to give an answer quickly, it confuses me the more. Even now I have forgotten why you came, and where you live; but I have not forgotten your beautiful name."

"Ivory thought you might be lonely, and I wanted so much to know you that I could not keep away any longer, for I am lonely and unhappy too. I am always watching and hoping for what has never come yet. I have no mother, you have lost your daughter; I thought—I thought—perhaps we could be a comfort to each other!" And Waitstill rose from her chair and put out her hand to help Mrs. Boynton down the steps, she looked so frail, so transparent, so prematurely aged. "I could not come very often—but if I could only smooth your hair sometimes when your head aches, or do some cooking for you, or read to you, or any little thing like that, as I would fer my own mother—if I could, I should be so glad!"

Waitstill stood a head higher than Ivory's mother and the glowing health of her, the steadiness of her voice, the warmth of her hand-clasp must have made her seem like a strong refuge to this storm-tossed derelict. The deep furrow between Lois Boynton's eyes relaxed a trifle, the blood in her veins ran a little more swiftly under the touch of the young hand that held hers so closely. Suddenly a light came into her face and her lip quivered.

"Perhaps I have been remembering wrong all these years," she said. "It is my great trouble, remembering wrong. Perhaps my baby did not die as I thought; perhaps she lived and grew up; perhaps" (her pale cheek burned and her eyes shone like stars) "perhaps she has come back!"

Waitstill could not speak; she put her arm round the trembling figure, holding her as she was wont to hold Patty, and with the same protective instinct. The embrace was electric in its effect and set altogether new currents of emotion in circulation. Something in Lois Boynton's perturbed mind seemed to beat its wings against the barriers that had heretofore opposed it, and, freeing itself, mounted into clearer air and went singing to the sky. She rested her cheek on the girl's breast with a little sob. "Oh! let me go on remembering wrong," she sighed, from that safe shelter. "Let me go on remembering wrong! It makes me so happy!"

Waitstill gently led her to the rocking-chair and sat down beside her on the lowest step, stroking her thin hand. Mrs. Boynton's eyes were closed, her breath came and went quickly, but presently she began to speak hurriedly, as if she were relieving a surcharged heart.

"There is something troubling me," she began, "and it would ease my mind if I could tell it to some one who could help. Your hand is so warm and so firm! Oh, hold mine closely and let me draw in strength as long as you can spare it; it is flowing, flowing from your hand into mine, flowing like wine.... My thoughts at night are not like my thoughts by day, these last weeks.... I wake suddenly and feel that my husband has been away a long time and will never come back.... Often, at night, too, I am in sore trouble about something else, something I have never told Ivory, the first thing I have ever hidden from my dear son, but I think I could tell you, if only I could be sure about it."

"Tell me if it will help you; I will try to understand"

"Tell me if it will help you; I will try to understand," said Waitstill brokenly.

"Ivory says Rodman is the child of my dead sister. Some one must have told him so; could it have been I? It haunts me day and night, for unless I am remembering wrong again, I never had a sister. I can call to mind neither sister nor brother."

"You went to New Hampshire one winter," Waitstill reminded her gently, as if she were talking to a child. "It was bitter cold for you to take such a hard journey. Your sister died, and you brought her little boy, Rodman, back, but you were so ill that a stranger had to take care of you on the stage-coach and drive you to Edgewood next day in his own sleigh. It is no wonder you have forgotten something of what happened, for Dr. Perry hardly brought you through the brain fever that followed that journey."

"I seem to think, now, that it is not so!" said Mrs. Boynton, opening her eyes and looking at Waitstill despairingly. "I must grope and grope in the dark until I find out what is true, and then tell Ivory. God will punish false speaking! His heart is closed against lies and evil-doing!"

"He will never punish you if your tired mind remembers wrong," said Waitstill. "He knows, none better, how you have tried to find Him and hold Him, through many a tangled path. I will come as often as I can and we will try to frighten away these worrying thoughts."

"If you will only come now and then and hold my hand," said Ivory's mother,—"hold my hand so that your strength will flow into my weakness, perhaps I shall puzzle it all out, and God will help me to remember right before I die."

"Everything that I have power to give away shall be given to you," promised Waitstill. "Now that I know you, and you trust me, you shall never be left so alone again,—not for long, at any rate. When I stay away you will remember that I cannot help it, won't you?"

"Yes, I shall think of you till I see you again I shall watch the long lane more than ever now. Ivory sometimes takes the path across the fields but my dear husband will come by the old road, and now there will be you to look for!"

XVI. LOCKED OUT

AT the Baxters the late supper was over and the girls had not sat at the table with their father, having eaten earlier, by themselves. The hired men had gone home to sleep. Patty had retired to the solitude of her bedroom almost at dusk, quite worn out with the heat, and Waitstill sat under the peach tree in the corner of her own little garden, tatting, and thinking of her interview with Ivory's mother. She sat there until nearly eight o'clock, trying vainly to put together the puzzling details of Lois Boynton's conversation, wondering whether the perplexities that vexed her mind were real or fancied, but warmed to the heart by the affection that the older woman seemed instinctively to feel for her. "She did not know me, yet she cared for me at once," thought Waitstill tenderly and proudly; "and I for her, too, at the first glance."

She heard her father lock the barn and shed and knew that he would be going upstairs immediately, so she quickly went through the side yard and lifted the latch of the kitchen door. It was fastened. She went to the front door and that, too, was bolted, although it had been standing open all the evening, so that if a breeze should spring up, it might blow through the house. Her father supposed, of course, that she was in bed, and she dreaded to bring him downstairs for fear of his anger; still there was no help for it and she rapped smartly at the side door. There was no answer and she rapped again, vexed with her own carelessness. Patty's face appeared promptly behind her screen of mosquito netting in the second story, but before she could exchange a word with her sister, Deacon Baxter opened the blinds of his bedroom window and put his head out.

"You can try sleepin' outdoors, or in the barn to-night," he called. "I didn't say anything to you at supper-time because I wanted to see where you was intendin' to prowl this evenin'."

"I haven't been 'prowling' anywhere, father," answered Waitstill; "I've been out in the garden cooling off; it's only eight o'clock."

"Well, you can cool off some more," he shouted, his temper now fully aroused; "or go back where you was this afternoon and see if they'll take you in there! I know all about your deceitful tricks! I come home to grind the scythes and found the house and barn empty Cephas said you'd driven up Saco Hill and I took his horse and followed you and saw where you went Long's you couldn't have a feller callin' on you here to home, you thought you'd call on him, did yer, you bold-faced hussy?"

"I am nothing of the sort," the girl answered him quietly; "Ivory Boynton was not at his house, he was in the hay-field. You know it, and you know that I knew it. I went to see a sick, unhappy woman who has no neighbors. I ought to have gone long before. I am not ashamed of it, and I don't regret it. If you ask unreasonable things of me, you must expect to be disobeyed once in a while.

"Must expect to be disobeyed, must I?" the old man cried, his face positively terrifying in its ugliness. "We'll see about that! If you wa'n't callin' on a young man, you were callin' on a crazy woman, and I won't have it, I tell you, do you hear? I won't have a daughter o' mine consortin' with any o' that Boynton crew. Perhaps a night outdoors will teach you who's master in this house, you imperdent, shameless girl! We'll try it, anyway!" And with that he banged down the window and disappeared, gibbering and jabbering impotent words that she could hear but not understand.

Waitstill was almost stunned by the suddenness of this catastrophe. She stood with her feet rooted to the earth for several minutes and then walked slowly away out of sight of the house. There was a chair beside the grindstone under the Porter apple tree and she sank into it, crossed her arms on the back, and bowing her head on them, burst into a fit of weeping as tempestuous and passionate as it was silent, for although her body fairly shook with sobs no sound escaped.

The minutes passed, perhaps an hour; she did not take account of time. The moon went behind clouds, the night grew misty and the stars faded one by one. There would be rain to-morrow and there was a great deal of hay cut, so she thought in a vagrant sort of way.

Meanwhile Patty upstairs was in a state of suppressed excitement and terror. It was a quarter of an hour before her father settled himself in bed; then an age, it seemed to her, before she heard his heavy breathing. When she thought it quite safe, she slipped on a print wrapper, took her shoes in her hand, and crept noiselessly downstairs, out through the kitchen and into the shed. Lifting the heavy bar that held the big doors in place she closed them softly behind her, stepped out, and looked about her in the darkness. Her quick eye espied in the distance, near the barn, the bowed figure in the chair, and she flew through the wet grass without a thought of her bare feet till she reached her sister's side and held her in a close embrace.

"My darling, my own, own, poor darling!" she cried softly, the tears running down her cheeks. "How wicked, how unjust to serve my dearest sister so! Don't cry, my blessing, don't cry; you frighten me! I'll take care of you, dear! Next time I'll interfere; I'll scratch and bite; yes, I'll strangle anybody that dares to shame you and lock you out of the house! You, the dearest, the patientest, the best!"

Waitstill wiped her eyes. "Let us go farther away where we can talk," she whispered.

"Where had we better sleep?" Patty asked. "On the hay, I think, though we shall stifle with the heat"; and Patty moved towards the barn.

"No, you must go back to the house at once, Patty dear; father might wake and call you, and that would make matters worse. It's beginning to drizzle, or I should stay out in the air. Oh! I wonder if father's mind is going, and if this is the beginning of the end! If he is in his sober senses, he could not be so strange, so suspicious, so unjust."

"He could be anything, say anything, do anything," exclaimed Patty. "Perhaps he is not responsible and perhaps he is; it doesn't make much difference to us. Come along, blessed darling! I'll tuck you in, and then I'll creep back to the house, if you say I must. I'll go down and make the kitchen fire in the morning; you stay out here and see what happens. A good deal will happen, I'm thinking, if father speaks to me of you! I shouldn't be surprised to see the fur flying in all directions; I'll seize the first moment to bring you out a cup of coffee and we'll consult about what to do. I may tell you now, I'm all for running away!"

Waitstill's first burst of wretchedness had subsided and she had recovered her balance. "I'm afraid we must wait a little longer, Patty," she advised. "Don't mention my name to father, but see how he acts in the morning. He was so wild, so unlike himself, that I almost hope he may forget what he said and sleep it off. Yes, we must just wait."

"No doubt he'll be far calmer in the morning if he remembers that, if he turns you out, he faces the prospect of three meals a day cooked by me," said Patty. "That's what he thinks he would face, but as a matter of fact I shall tell him that where you sleep I sleep, and where you eat I eat, and when you stop cooking I stop! He won't part with two unpaid servants in a hurry, not at the beginning of haying." And Patty, giving Waitstill a last hug and a dozen tearful kisses, stole reluctantly back to the house by the same route through which he had left it.

Patty was right. She found the fire lighted when she went down into the kitchen next morning, and without a word she hurried breakfast on to the table as fast as she could cook and serve it. Waitstill was safe in the barn chamber, she knew, and would be there quietly while her father was feeding the horse and milking the cows; or perhaps she might go up in the woods and wait until she saw him driving away.

The Deacon ate his breakfast in silence, looking and acting very much as usual, for he was generally dumb at meals. When he left the house, however, and climbed into the wagon, he turned around and said in his ordinary gruff manner: "Bring the lunch up to the field yourself to-day, Patience. Tell your sister I hope she's come to her senses in the course of the night. You've got to learn, both of you, that my 'say-so' must be law in this house. You can fuss and you can fume, if it amuses you any, but 't won't do no good. Don't encourage Waitstill in any whinin' nor blubberin'. Jest tell her to come in and go to work and I'll overlook what she done this time. And don't you give me any more of your eye-snappin' and lip-poutin' and head-in-the-air imperdence! You're under age, and if you don't look out, you'll get something that's good for what ails you! You two girls jest aid an' abet one another that's what you do, aid an' abet one another, an if you carry it any further I'll find some way o' separatin' you, do you hear?"

Patty spoke never a word, nor fluttered an eyelash. She had a proper spirit, but now her heart was cold with a new fear, and she felt, with Waitstill, that her father must be obeyed and his temper kept within bounds, until God provided them a way of escape.

She ran out to the barn chamber and, not finding Waitstill, looked across the field and saw her coming through the path from the woods. Patty waved her hand, and ran to meet her sister, joy at the mere fact of her existence, of being able to see her again, and of hearing her dear voice, almost choking her in its intensity. When they reached the house she helped her upstairs as if she were a child, brought her cool water to wash away the dust of the haymow, laid out some clean clothes for her, and finally put her on the lounge in the darkened sitting-room.

"I won't let anybody come near the house," she said, "and you must have a cup of tea and a good sleep before I tell you all that father said. Just comfort yourself with the thought that he is going to 'overlook it' this time! After I carry up his luncheon, I shall stop at the store and ask Cephas to come out on the river bank for a few minutes. Then I shall proceed to say what I think of him for telling father where you went yesterday afternoon."

"Don't blame Cephas!" Waitstill remonstrated. "Can't you see just how it happened? He and Uncle Bart were sitting in front of the shop when I drove by. When father came home and found the house empty and the horse not in the stall, of course he asked where I was, and Cephas probably said he had seen me drive up Saco Hill. He had no reason to think that there was any harm in that."

"If he had any sense he might know that he shouldn't tell anything to father except what happens in the store," Patty insisted. "Were you frightened out in the barn alone last night, poor dear?"

"I was too unhappy to think of fear and I was chiefly nervous about you, all alone in the house with father."

"I didn't like it very much, myself! I buttoned my bedroom door and sat by the window all night, shivering and bristling at the least sound. Everybody calls me a coward, but I'm not! Courage isn't not being frightened; it's not screeching when you are frightened. Now, what happened at the Boyntons'?"

"Patty, Ivory's mother is the most pathetic creature I ever saw!" And Waitstill sat up on the sofa, her long braids of hair hanging over her shoulders, her pale face showing the traces of her heavy weeping. "I never pitied any one so much in my whole life! To go up that long, long lane; to come upon that dreary house hidden away in the trees; to feel the loneliness and the silence; and then to know that she is living there like a hermit-thrush in a forest, without a woman to care for her, it is heart-breaking!"

"How does the house look,—dreadful?"

"No: everything is as neat as wax. She isn't 'crazy,' Patty, as we understand the word. Her mind is beclouded somehow and it almost seems as if the cloud might lift at any moment. She goes about like somebody in a dream, sewing or knitting or cooking. It is only when she talks, and you notice that her eyes really see nothing, but are looking beyond you, that you know there is anything wrong."

"If she appears so like other people, why don't the neighbors go to see her once in a while?"

"Callers make her unhappy, she says, and Ivory told me that he dared not encourage any company in the house for fear of exciting her, and making her an object of gossip, besides. He knows her ways perfectly and that she is safe and content with her fancies when she is alone, which is seldom, after all."

"What does she talk about?" asked Patty.

"Her husband mostly. She is expecting him to come back daily. We knew that before, of course, but no one can realize it till they see her setting the table for him and putting a saucer of wild strawberries by his plate; going about the kitchen softly, like a gentle ghost."

"It gives me the shudders!" said Patty. "I couldn't bear it! If she never sees strangers, what in the world did she make of you? How did you begin?"

"I told her I had known Ivory ever since we were school children. She was rather strange and indifferent at first, and then she seemed to take a fancy to me."

"That's queer!" said Patty, smiling fondly and giving Waitstill's hair the hasty brush of a kiss.

"She told me she had had a girl baby, born two or three years after Ivory, and that she had always thought it died when it was a few weeks old. Then suddenly she came closer to me—

"Oh! Waity, weren't you terrified?"

"No, not in the least. Neither would you have been if you had been there. She put her arms round me and all at once I understood that the poor thing mistook me just for a moment for her own daughter come back to life. It was a sudden fancy and I don't think it lasted, but I didn't know how to deal with it, or contradict it, so I simply tried to soothe her and let her ease her heart by talking to me. She said when I left her: 'Where is your house? I hope it is near! Do come again and sit with me. Strength flows into my weakness when you hold my hand!' I somehow feel, Patty, that she needs a woman friend even more than a doctor. And now, what am I to do? How can I forsake her; and yet here is this new difficulty with father?"

"I shouldn't forsake her; go there when you can, but be more careful about it. You told father that you didn't regret what you had done, and that when he ordered you to do unreasonable things, you should disobey him. After all, you are not a black slave. Father will never think of that particular thing again, perhaps, any more than he ever alluded to my driving to Saco with Mrs. Day after you had told him it was necessary for one of us to go there occasionally. He knows that if he is too hard on us, Dr. Perry or Uncle Bart would take him in hand. They would have done it long ago if we had ever given any one even a hint of what we have to endure. You will be all right, because you only want to do kind, neighborly things. I am the one that will always have to suffer, because I can't prove that it's a Christian duty to deceive father and steal off to a dance or a frolic. Yet I might as well be a nun in a convent for all the fun I get! I want a white book-muslin dress; I want a pair of thin shoes with buckles; I want a white hat with a wreath of yellow roses; I want a volume of Byron's poems; and oh! nobody knows—nobody but the Lord could understand—how I want a string of gold beads."

"Patty, Patty! To hear you chatter anybody would imagine you thought of nothing but frivolities. I wish you wouldn't do yourself such injustice; even when nobody hears you but me, it is wrong."

"Sometimes when you think I'm talking nonsense it's really the gospel truth," said Patty. "I'm not a grand, splendid character, Waitstill, and it's no use your deceiving yourself about me; if you do, you'll be disappointed."

"Go and parboil the beans and get them into the pot, Patty. Pick up some of the windfalls and make a green-apple pie, and I'll be with you in the kitchen myself before long. I never expect to be disappointed in you, Patty, only continually surprised and pleased."

"I thought I'd begin making some soft soap to-day," said Patty mischievously, as she left the room. "We have enough grease saved up. We don't really need it yet, but it makes such a disgusting smell that I'd rather like father to have it with his dinner. It's not much of a punishment for our sleepless night."

AUTUMN
XVII. A BRACE OF LOVERS

HAYING was over, and the close, sticky dog-days, too, and August was slipping into September. There had been plenty of rain all the season and the countryside was looking as fresh and green as an emerald. The hillsides were already clothed with a verdant growth of new grass and

"The red pennons of the cardinal flowers

Hung motionless upon their upright staves."

How they gleamed in the meadow grasses and along the brooksides like brilliant flecks of flame, giving a new beauty to the nosegays that Waitstill carried or sent to Mrs. Boynton every week.

To the eye of the casual observer, life in the two little villages by the river's brink went on as peacefully as ever, but there were subtle changes taking place nevertheless. Cephas Cole had "asked" the second time and again had been refused by Patty, so that even a very idiot for hopefulness could not urge his father to put another story on the ell.

"If it turns out to be Phoebe Day," thought Cephas dolefully, "two rooms is plenty good enough, an' I shan't block up the door that leads from the main part, neither, as I thought likely I should. If so be it's got to be Phoebe, not Patty, I shan't care whether mother troops out 'n' in or not." And Cephas dealt out rice and tea and coffee with so languid an air, and made such frequent mistakes in weighing the sugar, that he drew upon himself many a sharp rebuke from the Deacon.

"Of course I'd club him over the head with a salt fish twice a day under ord'nary circumstances," Cephas confided to his father with a valiant air that he never wore in Deacon Baxter's presence; "but I've got a reason, known to nobody but myself, for wantin' to stan' well with the old man for a spell longer. If ever I quit wantin' to stan' well with him, he'll get his comeuppance, short an sudden!"

"Speakin' o' standin' well with folks, Phil Perry's kind o' makin' up to Patience Baxter, ain't he, Cephas?" asked Uncle Bart guardedly. "Mebbe you wouldn't notice it, hevin' no partic'lar int'rest, but your mother's kind o got the idee into her head lately, an' she's turrible far-sighted."

"I guess it's so!" Cephas responded gloomily. "It's nip an' tuck 'tween him an' Mark Wilson. That girl draws 'em as molasses does flies! She does it 'thout liftin' a finger, too, no more 'n the molasses does. She just sets still an' IS! An' all the time she's nothin' but a flighty little red-headed spitfire that don't know a good husband when she sees one. The feller that gits her will live to regret it, that's my opinion!" And Cephas thought to himself: "Good Lord, don't I wish I was regrettin' it this very minute!"

"I s'pose a girl like Phoebe Day'd be consid'able less trouble to live with?" ventured Uncle Bart.

"I never could take any fancy to that tow hair o' hern! I like the color well enough when I'm peeling it off a corn cob, but I don't like it on a girl's head," objected Cephas hypercritically. "An' her eyes hain't got enough blue in 'em to be blue: they're jest like skim-milk. An' she keeps her mouth open a little mite all the time, jest as if there wa'n't no good draught through, an' she was a-tryin' to git air. An' 't was me that begun callin' her 'Feeble Phoebe in school, an' the scholars'll never forgit it; they'd throw it up to me the whole 'durin' time if I should go to work an' keep company with her!"

"Mebbe they've forgot by this time," Uncle Bart responded hopefully; "though 't is an awful resk when you think o' Companion Pike! Samuel he was baptized and Samuel he continued to be, 'till he married the Widder Bixby from Waterboro. Bein' as how there wa'n't nothin' partic'ly attractive 'bout him,—though he was as nice a feller as ever lived,—somebody asked her why she married him, an' she said her cat hed jest died an' she wanted a companion. The boys never let go o' that story! Samuel Pike he ceased to be thirty year ago, an' Companion Pike he's remained up to this instant minute!"

"He ain't lived up to his name much," remarked Cephas. "He's to home for his meals, but I guess his wife never sees him between times."

"If the cat hed lived mebbe she'd 'a' been better comp'ny on the whole," chuckled Uncle Bart. "Companion was allers kind o' dreamy an' absent-minded from a boy. I remember askin' him what his wife's Christian name was (she bein' a stranger to Riverboro) an' he said he didn't know! Said he called her Mis' Bixby afore he married her an' Mis' Pike afterwards!"

"Well, there 's something turrible queer 'bout this marryin' business," and Cephas drew a sigh from the heels of his boots. "It seems's if a man hedn't no natcheral drawin' towards a girl with a good farm 'n' stock that was willin' to have him! Seems jest as if it set him ag'in' her somehow! And yet, if you've got to sing out o' the same book with a girl your whole lifetime, it does seem's if you'd ought to have a kind of a fancy for her at the start, anyhow!"

"You may feel dif'rent as time goes on, Cephas, an' come to see Feeble—I would say Phoebe—as your mother does. 'The best fire don't flare up the soonest,' you know." But old Uncle Bart saw that his son's heart was heavy and forbore to press the subject.

Annabel Franklin had returned to Boston after a month's visit and to her surprise had returned as disengaged as she came. Mark Wilson, thoroughly bored by her vacuities of mind, longed now for more intercourse with Patty Baxter, Patty, so gay and unexpected; so lively to talk with, so piquing to the fancy, so skittish and difficult to manage, so temptingly pretty, with a beauty all her own, and never two days alike.

There were many lions in the way and these only added to the zest of pursuit. With all the other girls of the village opportunities multiplied, but he could scarcely get ten minutes alone with Patty. The Deacon's orders were absolute in regard to young men. His daughters were never to drive or walk alone with them, never go to dances or "routs" of any sort, and never receive them at the house; this last mandate being quite unnecessary, as no youth in his right mind would have gone a-courtin' under the Deacon's forbidding gaze. And still there were sudden, delicious chances to be seized now and then if one had his eyes open and his wits about him. There was the walk to or from the singing-school, when a sentimental couple could drop a few feet, at least, behind the rest and exchange a word or two in comparative privacy; there were the church "circles" and prayer-meetings, and the intervals between Sunday services when Mark could detach Patty a moment from the group on the meeting-house steps. More valuable than all these, a complete schedule of Patty's various movements here and there, together with a profound study of Deacon Baxter's habits, which were ordinarily as punctual as they were disagreeable, permitted Mark many stolen interviews, as sweet as they were brief. There was never a second kiss, however, in these casual meetings and partings. The first, in springtime, had found Patty a child, surprised, unprepared. She was a woman now; for it does not take years to achieve that miracle; months will do it, or days, or even hours. Her summer's experience with Cephas Cole had wonderfully broadened her powers, giving her an assurance sadly lacking before, as well as a knowledge of detail, a certain finished skill in the management of a lover, which she could ably use on any one who happened to come along. And, at the moment, any one who happened to come along served the purpose admirably, Philip Perry as well as Marquis Wilson.

Young Perry's interest in Patty, as we have seen, began with his alienation from Ellen Wilson, the first object of his affections, and it was not at the outset at all of a sentimental nature. Philip was a pillar of the church, and Ellen had proved so entirely lacking in the religious sense, so self-satisfied as to her standing with the heavenly powers, that Philip dared not expose himself longer to her society, lest he find himself "unequally yoked together with an unbeliever," thus defying the scriptural admonition as to marriage.

Patty, though somewhat lacking in the qualities that go to the making of trustworthy saints, was not, like Ellen, wholly given over to the fleshpots and would prove a valuable convert, Philip thought; one who would reflect great credit upon him if he succeeded in inducing her to subscribe to the stern creed of the day.

Philip was a very strenuous and slightly gloomy believer, dwelling considerably on the wrath of God and the doctrine of eternal punishment. There was an old "pennyroyal" hymn much in use which describes the general tenor of his meditation:—

"My thoughts on awful subjects roll,

Damnation and the dead.

What horrors seize the guilty soul

Upon a dying bed."

(No wonder that Jacob Cochrane's lively songs, cheerful, hopeful, militant, and bracing, fell with a pleasing sound upon the ear of the believer of that epoch.) The love of God had, indeed, entered Philip's soul, but in some mysterious way had been ossified after it got there. He had intensely black hair, dark skin, and a liver that disposed him constitutionally to an ardent belief in the necessity of hell for most of his neighbors, and the hope of spending his own glorious immortality in a small, properly restricted, and prudently managed heaven. He was eloquent at prayer-meeting and Patty's only objection to him there was in his disposition to allude to himself as a "rebel worm," with frequent references to his "vile body." Otherwise, and when not engaged in theological discussion, Patty liked Philip very much. His own father, although an orthodox member of the fold in good and regular standing, had "doctored" Phil conscientiously for his liver from his youth up, hoping in time to incite in him a sunnier view of life, for the doctor was somewhat skilled in adapting his remedies to spiritual maladies. Jed Morrill had always said that when old Mrs. Buxton, the champion convert of Jacob Cochrane, was at her worst,—keeping her whole family awake nights by her hysterical fears for their future,—Dr. Perry had given her a twelfth of a grain of tartar emetic, five times a day until she had entire mental relief and her anxiety concerning the salvation of her husband and children was set completely at rest.

The good doctor noted with secret pleasure his son's growing fondness for the society of his prime favorite, Miss Patience Baxter. "He'll begin by trying to save her soul," he thought; "Phil always begins that way, but when Patty gets him in hand he'll remember the existence of his heart, an organ he has never taken into consideration. A love affair with a pretty girl, good but not too pious, will help Phil considerable, however it turns out."

There is no doubt but that Phil was taking his chances and that under Patty's tutelage he was growing mellower. As for Patty, she was only amusing herself, and frisking, like a young lamb, in pastures where she had never strayed before. Her fancy flew from Mark to Phil and from Phil back to Mark again, for at the moment she was just a vessel of emotion, ready to empty herself on she knew not what. Temperamentally, she would take advantage of currents rather than steer at any time, and it would be the strongest current that would finally bear her away. Her idea had always been that she could play with fire without burning her own fingers, and that the flames she kindled were so innocent and mild that no one could be harmed by them. She had fancied, up to now, that she could control, urge on, or cool down a man's feeling forever and a day, if she chose, and remain mistress of the situation. Now, after some weeks of weighing and balancing her two swains, she found herself confronting a choice, once and for all. Each of them seemed to be approaching the state of mind where he was likely to say, somewhat violently: "Take me or leave me, one or the other!" But she did not wish to take them, and still less did she wish to leave them, with no other lover in sight but Cephas Cole, who was almost, though not quite, worse than none.

If matters, by lack of masculine patience and self-control, did come to a crisis, what should she say definitely to either of her suitors? Her father despised Mark Wilson a trifle more than any young man on the river, and while he could have no objection to Phil Perry's character or position in the world, his hatred of old Dr. Perry amounted to a disease. When the doctor had closed the eyes of the third Mrs. Baxter, he had made some plain and unwelcome statements that would rankle in the Deacon's breast as long as he lived. Patty knew, therefore, that the chance of her father's blessing falling upon her union with either of her present lovers was more than uncertain, and of what use was an engagement, if there could not be a marriage?

If Patty's mind inclined to a somewhat speedy departure from her father's household, she can hardly be blamed, but she felt that she could not carry any of her indecisions and fears to her sister for settlement. Who could look in Waitstill's clear, steadfast eyes and say: "I can't make up my mind which to marry"? Not Patty. She felt, instinctively, that Waitstill's heart, if it moved at all, would rush out like a great river to lose itself in the ocean, and losing itself forget the narrow banks through which it had flowed before. Patty knew that her own love was at the moment nothing more than the note of a child's penny flute, and that Waitstill was perhaps vibrating secretly with a deeper, richer music than could ever come to her. Still, music of some sort she meant to feel. "Even if they make me decide one way or another before I am ready," she said to herself, "I'll never say 'yes' till I'm more in love than I am now!"

There were other reasons why she did not want to ask Waitstill's advice. Not only did she shrink from the loving scrutiny of her sister's eyes, and the gentle probing of her questions, which would fix her own motives on a pinpoint and hold them up unbecomingly to the light; but she had a foolish, generous loyalty that urged her to keep Waitstill quite aloof from her own little private perplexities.

"She will only worry herself sick," thought Patty. "She won't let me marry without asking father's permission, and she'd think she ought not to aid me in deceiving him, and the tempest would be twice as dreadful if it fell upon us both! Now, if anything happens, I can tell father that I did it all myself and that Waitstill knew nothing about it whatever. Then, oh, joy! if father is too terrible, I shall be a married woman and I can always say: 'I will not permit such cruelty! Waitstill is dependent upon you no longer, she shall come at once to my husband and me!'"

This latter phrase almost intoxicated Patty, so that there were moments when she could have run up to Milliken's Mills and purchased herself a husband at any cost, had her slender savings permitted the best in the market; and the more impersonal the husband the more delightedly Patty rolled the phrase under her tongue.

"I can never be 'published' in church," she thought, "and perhaps nobody will ever care enough about me to brave father's displeasure and insist on running away with me. I do wish somebody would care 'frightfully' about me, enough for that; enough to help me make up my mind; so that I could just drive up to father's store some day and say: 'Good afternoon, father! I knew you'd never let me marry—'" (there was always a dash here, in Patty's imaginary discourses, a dash that could be filled in with any Christian name according to her mood of the moment) 'so I just married him anyway; and you needn't be angry with my sister, for she knew nothing about it. My husband and I are sorry if you are displeased, but there's no help for it; and my husband's home will always be open to Waitstill, whatever happens.'"

Patty, with all her latent love of finery and ease, did not weigh the worldly circumstances of the two men, though the reflection that she would have more amusement with Mark than with Philip may have crossed her mind. She trusted Philip, and respected his steady-going, serious view of life; it pleased her vanity, too, to feel how her nonsense and fun lightened his temperamental gravity, playing in and out and over it like a butterfly in a smoke bush. She would be safe with Philip always, but safety had no special charm for one of her age, who had never been in peril. Mark's superior knowledge of the world, moreover, his careless, buoyant manner of carrying himself, his gay, boyish audacity, all had a very distinct charm for her;—and yet—

But there would be no "and yet" a little later. Patty's heart would blaze quickly enough when sufficient heat was applied to it, and Mark was falling more and more deeply in love every day. As Patty vacillated, his purpose strengthened; the more she weighed, the more he ceased to weigh, the difficulties of the situation; the more she unfolded herself to him, the more he loved and the more he respected her. She began by delighting his senses; she ended by winning all that there was in him, and creating continually the qualities he lacked, after the manner of true women even when they are very young and foolish.

XVIII. A STATE O' MAINE PROPHET

SUMMER was dying hard, for although it had passed, by the calendar, Mother Nature was still keeping up her customary attitude.

There had been a soft rain in the night and every spear of grass was brilliantly green and tipped with crystal. The smoke bushes in the garden plot, and the asparagus bed beyond them, looked misty as the sun rose higher, drying the soaked earth and dripping branches. Spiders' webs, marvels of lace, dotted the short grass under the apple trees. Every flower that had a fragrance was pouring it gratefully into the air; every bird with a joyous note in its voice gave it more joyously from a bursting throat; and the river laughed and rippled in the distance at the foot of Town House Hill. Then dawn grew into full morning and streams of blue smoke rose here and there from the Edgewood chimneys. The world was alive, and so beautiful that Waitstill felt like going down on her knees in gratitude for having been born into it and given a chance of serving it in any humble way whatsoever.

Wherever there was a barn, in Riverboro or Edgewood, one could have heard the three-legged stools being lifted from the pegs, and then would begin the music of the milk-pails; first the resonant sound of the stream on the bottom of the tin pail, then the soft delicious purring of the cascade into the full bucket, while the cows serenely chewed their cuds and whisked away the flies with swinging tails. Deacon Baxter was taking his cows to a pasture far over the hill, the feed having grown too short in his own fields. Patty was washing dishes in the kitchen and Waitstill was in the dairy-house at the butter-making, one of her chief delights. She worked with speed and with beautiful sureness, patting, squeezing, rolling the golden mass, like the true artist she was, then turning the sweet-scented waxen balls out of the mould on to the big stone-china platter that stood waiting. She had been up early and for the last hour she had toiled with devouring eagerness that she might have a little time to herself. It was hers now, for Patty would be busy with the beds after she finished the dishes, so she drew a folded paper from her pocket, the first communication she had ever received in Ivory's handwriting, and sat down to read it.

MY DEAR WAITSTILL:—

Rodman will take this packet and leave it with you when he finds opportunity. It is not in any real sense a letter, so I am in no danger of incurring your father's displeasure. You will probably have heard new rumors concerning my father during the past few days, for Peter Morrill has been to Enfield, New Hampshire, where he says letters have been received stating that my father died in Cortland, Ohio, more than five years ago. I shall do what I can to substantiate this fresh report as I have always done with all the previous ones, but I have little hope of securing reliable information at this distance, and after this length of time. I do not know when I can ever start on a personal quest myself, for even had I the money I could not leave home until Rodman is much older, and fitted for greater responsibility. Oh! Waitstill, how you have helped my poor, dear mother! Would that I were free to tell you how I value your friendship! It is something more than mere friendship! What you are doing is like throwing a life-line to a sinking human being. Two or three times, of late, mother has forgotten to set out the supper things for my father. Her ten years' incessant waiting for him seems to have subsided a little, and in its place she watches for you. [Ivory had written "watches for her daughter" but carefully erased the last two words.] You come but seldom, but her heart feeds on the sight of you. What she needed, it seems, was the magical touch of youth and health and strength and sympathy, the qualities you possess in such great measure.

If I had proof of my father's death I think now, perhaps, that I might try to break it gently to my mother, as if it were fresh news, and see if possibly I might thus remove her principal hallucination. You see now, do you not, how sane she is in many, indeed in most ways,—how sweet and lovable, even how sensible?

To help you better to understand the influence that has robbed me of both father and mother and made me and mine the subject of town and tavern gossip for years past, I have written for you just a sketch of the "Cochrane craze"; the romantic story of a man who swayed the wills of his fellow-creatures in a truly marvellous manner. Some local historian of his time will doubtless give him more space; my wish is to have you know something more of the circumstances that have made me a prisoner in life instead of a free man; but prisoner as I am at the moment, I am sustained just now by a new courage. I read in my copy of Ovid last night: "The best of weapons is the undaunted heart." This will help you, too, in your hard life, for yours is the most undaunted heart in all the world.

IVORY BOYNTON

The chronicle of Jacob Cochrane's career in the little villages near the Saco River has no such interest for the general reader as it had for Waitstill Baxter. She hung upon every word that Ivory had written and realized more clearly than ever before the shadow that had followed him since early boyhood; the same shadow that had fallen across his mother's mind and left, continual twilight there.

No one really knew, it seemed, why or from whence Jacob Cochrane had come to Edgewood. He simply appeared at the old tavern, a stranger, with satchel in hand, to seek entertainment. Uncle Bart had often described this scene to Waitstill, for he was one of those sitting about the great open fire at the time. The man easily slipped into the group and soon took the lead in conversation, delighting all with his agreeable personality, his nimble tongue and graceful speech. At supper-time the hostess and the rest of the family took their places at the long table, as was the custom, and he astonished them by his knowledge not only of town history, but of village matters they had supposed unknown to any one.

When the stranger had finished his supper and returned to the bar-room, he had to pass through a long entry, and the landlady, whispering to her daughter, said:—

"Betsy, you go up to the chamber closet and get the silver and bring it down. This man is going to sleep there and I am afraid of him. He must be a fortune-teller, and the Lord only knows what else!"

In going to the chamber the daughter had to pass through the bar-room. As she was moving quietly through, hoping to escape the notice of the newcomer, he turned in his chair, and looking her full in the face, suddenly said:—

"Madam, you needn't touch your silver. I don't want it. I am a gentleman."

Whereupon the bewildered Betsy scuttled back to her mother and told her the strange guest was indeed a fortune-teller.

Of Cochrane's initial appearance as a preacher Ivory had told Waitstill in their talk in the churchyard early in the summer. It was at a child's funeral that the new prophet created his first sensation and there, too, that Aaron and Lois Boynton first came under his spell. The whole countryside had been just then wrought up to a state of religious excitement by revival meetings and Cochrane gained the benefit of this definite preparation for his work. He claimed that all his sayings were from divine inspiration and that those who embraced his doctrine received direct communication from the Almighty. He disdained formal creeds and all manner of church organizations, declaring sectarian names to be marks of the beast and all church members to be in Babylon. He introduced re-baptism as a symbolic cleansing from sectarian stains, and after some months advanced a proposition that his flock hold all things in common. He put a sudden end to the solemn "deaconing-out" and droning of psalm tunes and grafted on to his form of worship lively singing and marching accompanied by clapping of hands and whirling in circles; during the progress of which the most hysterical converts, or the most fully "Cochranized," would swoon upon the floor; or, in obeying their leader's instructions to "become as little children," would sometimes go through the most extraordinary and unmeaning antics.

It was not until he had converted hundreds to the new faith that he added more startling revelations to his gospel. He was in turn bold, mystical, eloquent, audacious, persuasive, autocratic; and even when his self-styled communications from the "Almighty" controverted all that his hearers had formerly held to be right, he still magnetized or hypnotized them into an unwilling assent to his beliefs. There was finally a proclamation to the effect that marriage vows were to be annulled when advisable and that complete spiritual liberty was to follow; a liberty in which a new affinity might be sought, and a spiritual union begun upon earth, a union as nearly approximate to God's standards as faulty human beings could manage to attain.

Some of the faithful fell away at this time, being unable to accept the full doctrine, but retained their faith in Cochrane's original power to convert sinners and save them from the wrath of God. Storm-clouds began to gather in the sky however, as the delusion spread, month by month and local ministers everywhere sought to minimize the influence of the dangerous orator, who rose superior to every attack and carried himself like some magnificent martyr-at-will among the crowds that now criticized him here or there in private and in public.

"What a picture of splendid audacity he must have been," wrote Ivory, "when he entered the orthodox meeting-house at a huge gathering where he knew that the speakers were to denounce his teachings. Old Parson Buzzell gave out his text from the high pulpit: Mark XIII, 37, 'AND WHAT I SAY UNTO YOU I SAY UNTO ALL, WATCH!' Just here Cochrane stepped in at the open door of the church and heard the warning, meant, he knew, for himself, and seizing the moment of silence following the reading of the text, he cried in his splendid sonorous voice, without so much as stirring from his place within the door-frame: "'Behold I stand at the door and knock. If any man hear my voice I will come in to him and will sup with him,—I come to preach the everlasting gospel to every one that heareth, and all that I want here is my bigness on the floor.'"

"I cannot find," continued Ivory on another page, "that my father or mother ever engaged in any of the foolish and childish practices which disgraced the meetings of some of Cochrane's most fanatical followers and converts. By my mother's conversations (some of which I have repeated to you, but which may be full of errors, because of her confusion of mind), I believe she must have had a difference of opinion with my father on some of these views, but I have no means of knowing this to a certainty; nor do I know that the question of choosing spiritual consorts' ever came between or divided them. This part of the delusion always fills me with such unspeakable disgust that I have never liked to seek additional light from any of the older men and women who might revel in giving it. That my mother did not sympathize with my father's going out to preach Cochrane's gospel through the country, this I know, and she was so truly religious, so burning with zeal, that had she fully believed in my father's mission she would have spurred him on, instead of endeavoring to detain him."

"You know the retribution that overtook Cochrane at last," wrote Ivory again, when he had shown the man's early victories and his enormous influence. "There began to be indignant protests against his doctrines by lawyers and doctors, as well as by ministers; not from all sides however; for remember, in extenuation of my father's and my mother's espousal of this strange belief, that many of the strongest and wisest men, as well as the purest and finest women in York county came under this man's spell for a time and believed in him implicitly, some of them even unto the end.

"Finally there was Cochrane's arrest and examination, the order for him to appear at the Supreme Court, his failure to do so, his recapture and trial, and his sentence of four years imprisonment on several counts, in all of which he was proved guilty. Cochrane had all along said that the Anointed of the Lord would never be allowed to remain in jail, but he was mistaken, for he stayed in the State's Prison at Charlestown, Massachusetts, for the full duration of his sentence. Here (I am again trying to plead the cause of my father and mother), here he received much sympathy and some few visitors, one of whom walked all the way from Edgewood to Boston, a hundred and fifteen miles, with a petition for pardon, a petition which was delivered, and refused, at the Boston State House. Cochrane issued from prison a broken and humiliated man, but if report says true, is still living, far out of sight and knowledge, somewhere in New Hampshire. He once sent my father an epitaph of his own selection, asking him to have it carved upon his gravestone should he die suddenly when away from his friends. My mother often repeats it, not realizing how far from the point it sounds to us who never knew him in his glory, but only in his downfall.

"'He spread his arms full wide abroad

   His works are ever before his God,

  His name on earth shall long remain,

   Through envious sinners fret in vain.'"

"We are certain," concluded Ivory, "that my father preached with Cochrane in Limington, Limerick, and Parsonsfield; he also wrote from Enfield and Effingham in New Hampshire; after that, all is silence. Various reports place him in Boston, in New York, even as far west as Ohio, whether as Cochranite evangelist or what not, alas! we can never know. I despair of ever tracing his steps. I only hope that he died before he wandered too widely, either from his belief in God or his fidelity to my mother's long-suffering love."

Waitstill read the letter twice through and replaced it in her dress to read again at night. It seemed the only tangible evidence of Ivory's love that she had ever received and she warmed her heart with what she felt that he had put between the lines.

"Would that I were free to tell you how I value your friendship!" "My mother's heart feeds on the sight of you!" "I want you to know something of the circumstances that have made me a prisoner in life, instead of a free man." "Yours is the most undaunted heart in all the world!" These sentences Waitstill rehearsed again and again and they rang in her ears like music, converting all the tasks of her long day into a deep and silent joy.

XIX. AT THE BRICK STORE

THERE were two grand places for gossip in the community; the old tavern on the Edgewood side of the bridge and the brick store in Riverboro. The company at the Edgewood Tavern would be a trifle different in character, more picturesque, imposing, and eclectic because of the transient guests that gave it change and variety. Here might be found a judge or lawyer on his way to court; a sheriff with a handcuffed prisoner; a farmer or two, stopping on the road to market with a cartful of produce; and an occasional teamster, peddler, and stage-driver. On winter nights champion story-tellers like Jed Morrill and Rish Bixby would drop in there and hang their woollen neck-comforters on the pegs along the wall-side, where there were already hats, topcoats, and fur mufflers, as well as stacks of whips, canes, and ox-goads standing in the corners. They would then enter the room, rubbing their hands genially, and, nodding to Companion Pike, Cephas Cole, Phil Perry and others, ensconce themselves snugly in the group by the great open fireplace. The landlord was always glad to see them enter, for their stories, though old to him, were new to many of the assembled company and had a remarkable greet on the consumption of liquid refreshment.

On summer evenings gossip was languid in the village, and if any occurred at all it would be on the loafer's bench at one or the other side of the bridge. When cooler weather came the group of local wits gathered in Riverboro, either at Uncle Bart's joiner's shop or at the brick store, according to fancy. The latter place was perhaps the favorite for Riverboro talkers. It was a large, two-story, square, brick building with a big-mouthed chimney and an open fire. When every house in the two villages had six feet of snow around it, roads would always be broken to the brick store, and a crowd of ten or fifteen men would be gathered there talking, listening, betting, smoking, chewing, bragging, playing checkers, singing, and "swapping stories."

Some of the men had been through the War of 1812 and could display wounds received on the field of valor; others were still prouder of scars won in encounters with the Indians, and there was one old codger, a Revolutionary veteran, Bill Dunham by name, who would add bloody tales of his encounters with the "Husshons." His courage had been so extraordinary and his slaughter so colossal that his hearers marvelled that there was a Hessian left to tell his side of the story, and Bill himself doubted if such were the case.

"'T is an awful sin to have on your soul," Bill would say from his place in a dark corner, where he would sit with his hat pulled down over his eyes till the psychological moment came for the "Husshons" to be trotted out. "'T is an awful sin to have on your soul,—the extummination of a race o' men; even if they wa'n't nothin' more 'n so many ignorant cockroaches. Them was the great days for fightin'! The Husshons was the biggest men I ever seen on the field, most of 'em standin' six feet eight in their stockin's,—but Lord! how we walloped 'em! Once we had a cannon mounted an' loaded for 'em that was so large we had to draw the ball into it with a yoke of oxen!"

Bill paused from force of habit, just as he had paused for the last twenty years. There had been times when roars of incredulous laughter had greeted this boast, but most of this particular group had heard the yarn more than once and let it pass with a smile and a wink, remembering the night that Abel Day had asked old Bill how they got the oxen out of the cannon on that most memorable occasion.

"Oh!" said Bill, "that was easy enough; we jest unyoked 'em an' turned 'em out o' the primin'-hole!"

It was only early October, but there had been a killing frost, and Ezra Simms, who kept the brick store, flung some shavings and small wood on the hearth and lighted a blaze, just to induce a little trade and start conversation on what threatened to be a dull evening. Peter Morrill, Jed's eldest brother, had lately returned from a long trip through the state and into New Hampshire, and his adventures by field and flood were always worth listening to. He went about the country mending clocks, and many an old time-piece still bears his name, with the date of repairing, written in pencil on the inside of its door.

There was never any lack of subjects at the brick store, the idiosyncrasies of the neighbors being the most prolific source of anecdote and comment. Of scandal about women there was little, though there would be occasional harmless pleasantries concerning village love affairs; prophecies of what couple would be next "published" in the black-walnut frame up at the meeting-house; a genial comment on the number and chances of Patience Baxter's various beaux; and whenever all else failed, the latest story of Deacon Baxter's parsimony, in which the village traced the influence of heredity.

"He can't hardly help it, inheritin' it on both sides," was Abel Day's opinion. "The Baxters was allers snug, from time 'memorial, and Foxy's the snuggest of 'em. When I look at his ugly mug an' hear his snarlin' voice, I thinks to myself, he's goin' the same way his father did. When old Levi Baxter was left a widder-man in that house o' his'n up river, he grew wuss an' wuss, if you remember, till he wa'n't hardly human at the last; and I don't believe Foxy even went up to his own father's funeral."

"'T would 'a' served old Levi right if nobody else had gone," said Rish Bixby. "When his wife died he refused to come into the house till the last minute. He stayed to work in the barn until all the folks had assembled, and even the men were all settin' down on benches in the kitchen. The parson sent me out for him, and I'm blest if the old skunk didn't come in through the crowd with his sleeves rolled up,—went to the sink and washed, and then set down in the room where the coffin was, as cool as a cowcumber."

"I remember that funeral well," corroborated Abel Day. "An' Mis' Day heerd Levi say to his daughter, as soon as they'd put poor old Mrs. Baxter int' the grave: 'Come on, Marthy; there 's no use cryin' over spilt milk; we'd better go home an' husk out the rest o' that corn.' Old Foxy could have inherited plenty o' meanness from his father, that's certain, an' he's added to his inheritance right along, like the thrifty man he is. I hate to think o' them two fine girls wearin' their fingers to the bone for his benefit."

"Oh, well! 't won't last forever," said Rish Bixby. "They're the handsomest couple o' girls on the river an' they'll get husbands afore many years. Patience'll have one pretty soon, by the looks. She never budges an inch but Mark Wilson or Phil Perry are follerin' behind, with Cephas Cole watchin' his chance right along, too. Waitstill don't seem to have no beaux; what with flyin' around to keep up with the Deacon, an' bein' a mother to Patience, her hands is full, I guess."

"If things was a little mite dif'rent all round, I could prognosticate who Waitstill could keep house for," was Peter Morrill's opinion.

"You mean Ivory Boynton? Well, if the Deacon was asked he'd never give his consent, that's certain; an' Ivory ain't in no position to keep a wife anyways. What was it you heerd 'bout Aaron Boynton up to New Hampshire, Peter?" asked Abel Day.

"Consid'able, one way an' another; an' none of it would 'a' been any comfort to Ivory. I guess Aaron 'n' Jake Cochrane was both of 'em more interested in savin' the sisters' souls than the brothers'! Aaron was a fine-appearin' man, and so was Jake for that matter, 'n' they both had the gift o' gab. There's nothin' like a limber tongue if you want to please the women-folks! If report says true, Aaron died of a fever out in Ohio somewheres; Cortland's the place, I b'lieve. Seems's if he hid his trail all the way from New Hampshire somehow, for as a usual thing, a man o' book-larnin' like him would be remembered wherever he went. Wouldn't you call Aaron Boynton a turrible larned man, Timothy?"

Timothy Grant, the parish clerk, had just entered the store on an errand, but being directly addressed, and judging that the subject under discussion was a discreet one, and that it was too early in the evening for drinking to begin, he joined the group by the fireside. He had preached in Vermont for several years as an itinerant Methodist minister before settling down to farming in Edgewood, only giving up his profession because his quiver was so full of little Grants that a wandering life was difficult and undesirable. When Uncle Bart Cole had remarked that Mis' Grant had a little of everything in the way of baby-stock now,—black, red, an' yaller-haired, dark and light complected, fat an' lean, tall an' short, twins an' singles,—Jed Morrill had observed dryly: "Yes, Mis' Grant kind o' reminds me of charity."

"How's that?" inquired Uncle Bart.

"She beareth all things," chuckled Jed.

"Aaron Boynton was, indeed, a man of most adhesive larnin'," agreed Timothy, who had the reputation of the largest and most unusual vocabulary in Edgewood. "Next to Jacob Cochrane I should say Aaron had more grandeloquence as an orator than any man we've ever had in these parts. It don't seem's if Ivory was goin' to take after his father that way. The little feller, now, is smart's a whip, an' could talk the tail off a brass monkey."

"Yes, but Rodman ain't no kin to the Boyntons," Abel reminded him. "He inhails from the other side o' the house."

"That's so; well, Ivory does, for certain, an' takes after his mother, right enough, for she hain't spoken a dozen words in as many years, I guess. Ivory's got a sight o' book-knowledge, though, an' they do say he could talk Greek an' Latin both, if we had any of 'em in the community to converse with. I've never paid no intention to the dead languages, bein' so ocker-pied with other studies."

"Why do they call 'em the dead languages, Tim?" asked Rish Bixby.

"Because all them that ever spoke 'em has perished off the face o' the land," Timothy answered oracularly. "Dead an' gone they be, lock, stock, an' barrel; yet there was a time when Latins an' Crustaceans an' Hebrews an' Prooshians an' Australians an' Simesians was chatterin' away in their own tongues, an' so pow'ful that they was wallopin' the whole earth, you might say."

"I bet yer they never tried to wallop these here United States," interpolated Bill Dunham from the dark corner by the molasses hogs-head.

"Is Ivory in here?" The door opened and Rodman Boynton appeared on the threshold.

"No, sonny, Ivory ain't been in this evening," replied Ezra Simms. "I hope there ain't nothin' the matter over to your house?"

"No, nothing particular," the boy answered hesitatingly; "only Aunt Boynton don't seem so well as common and I can't find Ivory anywhere."

"Come along with me; I'll help you look for him an' then I'll go as fur as the lane with yer if we don't find him." And kindly Rish Bixby took the boy's hand and left the store.

"Mis' Boynton had a spell, I guess!" suggested the storekeeper, peering through the door into the darkness. "'T ain't like Ivory to be out nights and leave her to Rod."

"She don't have no spells," said Abel Day. "Uncle Bart sees consid'able of Ivory an' he says his mother is as quiet as a lamb.—Couldn't you git no kind of a certif'cate of Aaron's death out o' that Enfield feller, Peter? Seems's if that poor woman'd oughter be stopped watchin' for a dead man; tuckerin' herself all out, an' keepin' Ivory an' the boy all nerved up."

"I've told Ivory everything I could gether up in the way of information, and give him the names of the folks in Ohio that had writ back to New Hampshire. I didn't dialate on Aaron's goin's-on in Effingham an' Portsmouth, cause I dassay 't was nothin' but scandal. Them as hates the Cochranites'll never allow there's any good in 'em, whereas I've met some as is servin' the Lord good an' constant, an' indulgin' in no kind of foolishness an' deviltry whatsoever."

"Speakin' o' Husshons," said Bill Dunham from his corner, "I remember—"

"We wa'n't alludin' to no Husshons," retorted Timothy Grant. "We was dealin' with the misfortunes of Aaron Boynton, who never fit valoriously on the field o' battle, but perished out in Ohio of scarlit fever, if what they say in Enfield is true."

"'Tis an easy death," remarked Bill argumentatively. "Scarlit fever don't seem like nothin' to me! Many's the time I've been close enough to fire at the eyeball of a Husshon, an' run the resk o' bein' blown to smithereens!—calm and cool I alters was, too! Scarlit fever is an easy death from a warrior's p'int o' view!"

"Speakin' of easy death," continued Timothy, "you know I'm a great one for words, bein' something of a scholar in my small way. Mebbe you noticed that Elder Boone used a strange word in his sermon last Sunday? Now an' then, when there's too many yawnin' to once in the congregation, Parson'll out with a reg'lar jaw-breaker to wake 'em up. The word as near as I could ketch it was 'youthinasia.' I kep' holt of it till noontime an' then I run home an' looked through all the y's in the dictionary without findin' it. Mebbe it's Hebrew, I thinks, for Hebrew's like his mother's tongue to Parson, so I went right up to him at afternoon meetin' an' says to him: 'What's the exact meanin' of "youthinasia"? There ain't no sech word in the Y's in my Webster,' says I. 'Look in the E's, Timothy; "euthanasia"' says he, 'means easy death'; an' now, don't it beat all that Bill Dunham should have brought that expression of 'easy death' into this evenin's talk?"

"I know youth an' I know Ashy," said Abel Day, "but blessed if I know why they should mean easy death when they yoke 'em together." "That's because you ain't never paid no 'tention to entomology," said Timothy. "Aaron Boynton was master o' more 'ologies than you could shake a stick at, but he used to say I beat him on entomology. Words air cur'ous things sometimes, as I know, hevin' had consid'able leisure time to read when I was joggin' 'bout the country an' bein' brought into contack with men o' learnin'. The way I worked it out, not wishin' to ask Parson any more questions, bein' something of a scholar myself, is this: The youth in Ashy is a peculiar kind o' youth, 'n' their religion disposes 'em to lay no kind o' stress on huming life. When anything goes wrong with 'em an' they get a set-back in war, or business, or affairs with women-folks, they want to die right off; so they take a sword an' stan' it straight up wherever they happen to be, in the shed or the barn, or the henhouse, an' they p'int the sharp end right to their waist-line, where the bowels an' other vital organisms is lowcated; an' then they fall on to it. It runs 'em right through to the back an' kills 'em like a shot, and that's the way I cal'late the youth in Ashy dies, if my entomology is correct, as it gen'ally is."

"Don't seem an easy death to me," argued Okra, "but I ain't no scholar. What college did thou attend to, Tim?"

"I don't hold no diaploma," responded Timothy, "though I attended to Wareham Academy quite a spell, the same time as your sister was goin' to Wareham Seminary where eddication is still bein' disseminated though of an awful poor kind, compared to the old times."

"It's live an' larn," said the storekeeper respectfully. "I never thought of a Seminary bein' a place of dissemination before, but you can see the two words is near kin."

"You can't alters tell by the sound," said Timothy instructively. "Sometimes two words'll start from the same root, an' branch out diff'rent, like 'critter' an' 'hypocritter.' A 'hypocritter' must natcherally start by bein' a 'critter,' but a critter ain't obliged to be a 'hypocritter' 'thout he wants to."

"I should hope not," interpolated Abel Day, piously. "Entomology must be an awful interest-in' study, though I never thought of observin' words myself, kept to avoid vulgar language an' profanity."

"Husshon's a cur'ous word for a man," inter-jected Bill Dunham with a last despairing effort. "I remember seein' a Husshon once that—"

"Perhaps you ain't one to observe closely, Abel," said Timothy, not taking note of any interruption, simply using the time to direct a stream of tobacco juice to an incredible distance, but landing it neatly in the exact spot he had intended. "It's a trade by itself, you might say, observin' is, an' there's another sing'lar corraption! The Whigs in foreign parts, so they say, build stone towers to observe the evil machinations of the Tories, an' so the word 'observatory' come into general use! All entomology; nothin' but entomology."

"I don't see where in thunder you picked up so much larnin', Timothy!" It was Abel Day's exclamation, but every one agreed with him.

XX. THE ROD THAT BLOSSOMED

IVORY BOYNTON had taken the horse and gone to the village on an errand, a rare thing for him to do after dark, so Rod was thinking, as he sat in the living-room learning his Sunday-School lesson on the same evening that the men were gossiping at the brick store. His aunt had required him, from the time when he was proficient enough to do so, to read at least a part of a chapter in the Bible every night. Beginning with Genesis he had reached Leviticus and had made up his mind that the Bible was a much more difficult book than "Scottish Chiefs," not withstanding the fact that Ivory helped him over most of the hard places. At the present juncture he was vastly interested in the subject of "rods" as unfolded in the book of Exodus, which was being studied by his Sunday-School class. What added to the excitement was the fact that his uncle's Christian name, Aaron, kept appearing in the chronicle, as frequently as that of the great lawgiver Moses himself; and there were many verses about the wonder-working rods of Moses and Aaron that had a strange effect upon the boy's ear, when he read them aloud, as he loved to do whenever he was left alone for a time. When his aunt was in the room his instinct kept him from doing this, for the mere mention of the name of Aaron, he feared, might sadden his aunt and provoke in her that dangerous vein of reminiscence that made Ivory so anxious.

"It kind o' makes me nervous to be named 'Rod,' Aunt Boynton," said the boy, looking up from the Bible. "All the rods in these Exodus chapters do such dreadful things! They become serpents, and one of them swallows up all the others: and Moses smites the waters with a rod and they become blood, and the people can't drink the water and the fish die! Then they stretch a rod across the streams and ponds and bring a plague of frogs over the land, with swarms of flies and horrible insects."

"That was to show God's power to Pharaoh, and melt his hard heart to obedience and reverence," explained Mrs. Boynton, who had known the Bible from cover to cover in her youth and could still give chapter and verse for hundreds of her favorite passages.

"It took an awful lot of melting, Pharaoh's heart!" exclaimed the boy. "Pharaoh must have been worse than Deacon Baxter! I wonder if they ever tried to make him good by being kind to him! I've read and read, but I can't find they used anything on him but plagues and famines and boils and pestilences and thunder and hail and fire!—Have I got a middle name, Aunt Boynton, for I don't like Rod very much?"

"I never heard that you had a middle name; you must ask Ivory," said his aunt abstractedly.

"Did my father name me Rod, or my mother?'

"I don't really know; perhaps it was your mother, but don't ask questions, please."

"I forgot, Aunt Boynton! Yes, I think perhaps my mother named me. Mothers 'most always name their babies, don't they? My mother wasn't like you; she looked just like the picture of Pocahontas in my History. She never knew about these Bible rods, I guess."

"When you go a little further you will find pleasanter things about rods," said his aunt, knitting, knitting, intensely, as was her habit, and talking as if her mind were a thousand miles away. "You know they were just little branches of trees, and it was only God's power that made them wonderful in any way."

"Oh! I thought they were like the singing-teacher's stick he keeps time with."

"No; if you look at your Concordance you'll finds it gives you a chapter in Numbers where there's something beautiful about rods. I have forgotten the place; it has been many years since I looked at it. Find it and read it aloud to me." The boy searched his Concordance and readily found the reference in the seventeenth chapter of Numbers.

"Stand near me and read," said Mrs. Boynton. "I like to hear the Bible read aloud!"

Rodman took his Bible and read, slowly and haltingly, but with clearness and understanding:

1. AND THE LORD SPAKE UNTO MOSES, SAYING,

2. SPEAK UNTO THE CHILDREN OF ISRAEL, AND TAKE OF EVERY ONE OF THEM A ROD ACCORDING TO THE HOUSE OF THEIR FATHERS, OF ALL THEIR PRINCES ACCORDING TO THE HOUSE OF THEIR FATHERS TWELVE RODS: WRITE THOU EVERY MAN'S NAME UPON HIS ROD.

Through the boy's mind there darted the flash of a thought, a sad thought. He himself was a Rod on whom no man's name seemed to be written, orphan that he was, with no knowledge of his parents!

Suddenly he hesitated, for he had caught sight of the name of Aaron in the verse that he was about to read, and did not wish to pronounce it in his aunt's hearing.

"This chapter is most too hard for me to read out loud, Aunt Boynton," he stammered. "Can I study it by myself and read it to Ivory first?" "Go on, go on, you read very sweetly; I can not remember what comes and I wish to hear it."

The boy continued, but without raising his eyes from the Bible.

3. AND THOU SHALT WRITE AARON'S NAME UPON THE ROD OF LEVI: FOR ONE ROD SHALL BE FOR THE HEAD OF THE HOUSE OF THEIR FATHERS.

4. AND THOU SHALT LAY THEM UP IN THE TABERNACLE OF THE CONGREGATION BEFORE THE TESTIMONY, WHERE I WILL MEET WITH YOU.

5. AND IT SHALL COME TO PASS THAT THE MAN'S ROD, WHOM I SHALL CHOOSE, SHALL BLOSSOM: AND I WILL MAKE TO CEASE FROM ME THE MURMURINGS OF THE CHILDREN OF ISRAEL, WHEREBY THEY MURMUR AGAINST YOU.

Rodman had read on, absorbed in the story and the picture it presented to his imagination. He liked the idea of all the princes having a rod according to the house of their fathers; he liked to think of the little branches being laid on the altar in the tabernacle, and above all he thought of the longing of each of the princes to have his own rod chosen for the blossoming.

6. AND MOSES SPOKE UNTO THE CHILDREN OF ISRAEL, AND EVERY ONE OF THEIR PRINCES GAVE HIM A ROD A PIECE, FOR EACH PRINCE ONE, ACCORDING TO THEIR FATHER'S HOUSES, EVEN TWELVE RODS; AND THE ROD OF AARON WAS AMONG THEIR RODS.

Oh! how the boy hoped that Aaron's branch would be the one chosen to blossom! He felt that his aunt would be pleased, too; but he read on steadily, with eyes that glowed and breath that came and went in a very palpitation of interest.

7. AND MOSES LAID UP THE RODS BEFORE THE LORD IN THE TABERNACLE OF WITNESS.

8. AND IT CAME TO PASS, THAT ON THE MORROW MOSES WENT INTO THE TABERNACLE OF WITNESS; AND, BEHOLD, THE ROD OF AARON WAS BUDDED AND BROUGHT FORTH BUDS, AND BLOOMED BLOSSOMS, AND YIELDED ALMONDS.

It was Aaron's rod, then, and was an almond branch! How beautiful, for the blossoms would have been pink; and how the people must have marvelled to see the lovely blooming thing on the dark altar; first budding, then blossoming, then bearing nuts! And what was the rod chosen for? He hurried on to the next verse.

9. AND MOSES BROUGHT OUT ALL THE RODS FROM BEFORE THE LORD UNTO ALL THE CHILDREN OF ISRAEL: AND THEY LOOKED, AND TOOK EVERY MAN HIS ROD.

10. AND THE LORD SAID UNTO MOSES, BRING AARON'S ROD AGAIN BEFORE THE TESTIMONY TO BE KEPT FOR A TOKEN AGAINST THE REBELS; AND THOU SHALT QUITE TAKE AWAY THEIR MURMURINGS FROM ME, THAT THEY DIE NOT.

"Oh! Aunt Boynton!" cried the boy, "I love my name after I've heard about the almond rod! Aren't you proud that it's Uncle's name that was written on the one that blossomed?"

He turned swiftly to find that his aunt's knitting had slipped on the floor; her nerveless hands drooped by her side as if there were no life in them, and her head had fallen against the back of her chair. The boy was paralyzed with fear at the sight of her closed eyes and the deathly pallor of her face. He had never seen her like this before, and Ivory was away. He flew for a bottle of spirit, always kept in the kitchen cupboard for emergencies, and throwing wood on the fire in passing, he swung the crane so that the tea-kettle was over the flame. He knew only the humble remedies that he had seen used here or there in illness, and tried them timidly, praying every moment that he might hear Ivory's step. He warmed a soapstone in the embers, and taking off Mrs. Boynton's shoes, put it under her cold feet. He chafed her hands and gently poured a spoonful of brandy between her pale lips. Then sprinkling camphor on a handkerchief he held it to her nostrils and to his joy she stirred in her chair; before many minutes her lids fluttered, her lips moved, and she put her hand to her heart.

"Are you better, Aunt dear?" Rod asked in a very wavering and tearful voice.

She did not answer; she only opened her eyes and looked at him. At length she whispered faintly, "I want Ivory; I want my son."

"He's out, Aunt dear. Shall I help you to bed the way Ivory does? If you'll let me, then I'll run to the bridge 'cross lots, like lightning, and bring him back."

She assented, and leaning heavily on his slender shoulder, walked feebly into her bedroom off the living-room. Rod was as gentle as a mother and he was familiar with all the little offices that could be of any comfort; the soapstone warmed again for her feet, the bringing of her nightgown from the closet, and when she was in bed, another spoonful of brandy in hot milk; then the camphor by her side, an extra homespun blanket over her, and the door left open so that she could see the open fire that he made into a cheerful huddles contrived so that it would not snap and throw out dangerous sparks in his absence.

All the while he was doing this Mrs. Boynton lay quietly in the bed talking to herself fitfully, in the faint murmuring tone that was habitual to her. He could distinguish scarcely anything, only enough to guess that her mind was still on the Bible story that he was reading to her when she fainted. "THE ROD OF AARON WAS AMONG THE OTHER RODS," he heard her say; and, a moment later, "BRING AARON'S ROD AGAIN BEFORE THE TESTIMONY."

Was it his uncle's name that had so affected her, wondered the boy, almost sick with remorse, although he had tried his best to evade her command to read the chapter aloud? What would Ivory, his hero, his pattern and example, say? It had always seen Rod's pride to carry his little share of every burden that fell to Ivory, to be faithful and helpful in every task given to him. He could walk through fire without flinching, he thought, if Ivory told him to, and he only prayed that he might not be held responsible for this new calamity.

"I want Ivory!" came in a feeble voice from the bedroom.

"Does your side ache worse?" Rod asked, tip-toeing to the door.

"No, I am quite free from pain."

"Would you be afraid to stay alone just for a while if I lock both doors and run to find Ivory and bring him back?"

"No, I will sleep," she whispered, closing her eyes. "Bring him quickly before I forget what I want to say to him."

Rod sped down the lane and over the fields to the brick store where Ivory usually bought his groceries. His cousin was not there, but one of the men came out and offered to take his horse and drive over the bridge to see if he were at one of the neighbors' on that side of the river. Not a word did Rod breathe of his aunt's illness; he simply said that she was lonesome for Ivory, and so he came to find him. In five minutes they saw the Boynton horse hitched to a tree by the road-side, and in a trice Rod called him and, thanking Mr. Bixby, got into Ivory's wagon to wait for him. He tried his best to explain the situation as they drove along, but finally concluded by saying: "Aunt really made me read the chapter to her, Ivory. I tried not to when I saw Uncle's name in most every verse, but I couldn't help it."

"Of course you couldn't! Now you jump out and hitch the horse while I run in and see that nothing has happened while she's been left alone. Perhaps you'll have to go for Dr. Perry."

Ivory went in with fear and trembling, for there was no sound save the ticking of the tall clock. The fire burned low upon the hearth, and the door was open into his mother's room. He lifted a candle that Rod had left ready on the table and stole softly to her bedside. She was sleeping like a child, but exhaustion showed itself in every line of her face. He felt her hands and feet and found the soapstone in the bed; saw the brandy bottle and the remains of a cup of milk on the light-stand; noted the handkerchief, still strong of camphor on the counterpane, and the blanket spread carefully over her knees, and then turned approvingly to meet Rod stealing into the room on tiptoe, his eyes big with fear.

"We won't wake her, Rod. I'll watch a while, then sleep on the sitting-room lounge."

"Let me watch, Ivory! I'd feel better if you'd let me, honest I would!"

The boy's face was drawn with anxiety. Ivory's attention was attracted by the wistful eyes and the beauty of the forehead under the dark hair. He seemed something more than the child of yesterday—a care and responsibility and expense, for all his loving obedience; he seemed all at once different to-night; older, more dependable, more trustworthy; in fact, a positive comfort and help in time of trouble.

"I did the best I knew how; was anything wrong?" asked the boy, as Ivory stood regarding him with a friendly smile.

"Nothing wrong, Rod! Dr. Perry couldn't have done any better with what you had on hand. I don't know how I should get along without you, boy!" Here Ivory patted Rod's shoulder. "You're not a child any longer, Rod; you're a man and a brother, that's what you are; and to prove it I'll take the first watch and call you up at one o'clock to take the second, so that I can be ready for my school work to-morrow! How does that suit you?"

"Tip-top!" said the boy, flushing with pride. "I'll lie down with my clothes on; it's only nine o'clock and I'll get four hours' sleep; that's a lot more than Napoleon used to have!"

He carried the Bible upstairs and just before he blew out his candle he looked again at the chapter in Numbers, thinking he would show it to Ivory privately next day. Again the story enchanted him, and again, like a child, he put his own name and his living self among the rods in the tabernacle.

"Ivory would be the prince of our house," he thought. "Oh! how I'd like to be Ivory's rod and have it be the one that was chosen to blossom and keep the rebels from murmuring!"

XXI. LOIS BURIES HER DEAD

THE replies that Ivory had received from his letters of inquiry concerning his father's movements since leaving Maine, and his possible death in the West, left no reasonable room for doubt. Traces of Aaron Boynton in New Hampshire, in Massachusetts, in New York, and finally in Ohio, all pointed in one direction, and although there were gaps and discrepancies in the account of his doings, the fact of his death seemed to be established by two apparently reliable witnesses.

That he was not unaccompanied in his earliest migrations seemed clear, but the woman mentioned as his wife disappeared suddenly from the reports, and the story of his last days was the story of a broken-down, melancholy, unfriended man, dependent for the last offices on strangers. He left no messages and no papers, said Ivory's correspondent, and never made mention of any family connections whatsoever. He had no property and no means of defraying the expenses of his illness after he was stricken with the fever. No letters were found among his poor effects and no article that could prove his identity, unless it were a small gold locket, which bore no initials or marks of any kind, but which contained two locks of fair and brown hair, intertwined. The tiny trinket was enclosed in the letter, as of no value, unless some one recognized it as a keepsake. Ivory read the correspondence with a heavy heart, inasmuch as it corroborated all his worst fears. He had sometimes secretly hoped that his father might return and explain the reason of his silence; or in lieu of that, that there might come to light the story of a pilgrimage, fanatical, perhaps, but innocent of evil intention, one that could be related to his wife and his former friends, and then buried forever with the death that had ended it.

Neither of these hopes could now ever be realized, nor his father's memory made other than a cause for endless regret, sorrow, and shame. His father, who had begun life so handsomely, with rare gifts of mind and personality, a wife of unusual beauty and intelligence, and while still young in years, a considerable success in his chosen profession. His poor father! What could have been the reasons for so complete a downfall?

Ivory asked Dr. Perry's advice about showing one or two of the briefer letters and the locket to his mother. After her fainting fit and the exhaustion that followed it, Ivory begged her to see the old doctor, but without avail. Finally, after days of pleading he took her hands in his and said: "I do everything a mortal man can do to be a good son to you, mother; won't you do this to please me, and trust that I know what is best?" Whereupon she gave a trembling assent, as if she were agreeing to something indescribably painful, and indeed this sight of a former friend seemed to frighten her strangely.

After Dr. Perry had talked with her for a half-hour and examined her sufficiently to make at least a reasonable guess as to her mental and physical condition, he advised Ivory to break the news of her husband's death to her.

"If you can get her to comprehend it," he said, "it is bound to be a relief from this terrible suspense."

"Will there be any danger of making her worse? Mightn't the shock Cause too violent emotion?" asked Ivory anxiously.

"I don't think she is any longer capable of violent emotion," the doctor answered. "Her mind is certainly clearer than it was three years ago, but her body is nearly burned away by the mental conflict. There is scarcely any part of her but is weary; weary unto death, poor soul. One cannot look at her patient, lovely face without longing to lift some part of her burden. Make a trial, Ivory; it's a justifiable experiment and I think it will succeed. I must not come any oftener myself than is absolutely necessary; she seemed afraid of me."

The experiment did succeed. Lois Boynton listened breathlessly, with parted lips, and with apparent comprehension, to the story Ivory told her. Over and over again he told her gently the story of her husband's death, trying to make it sink into her mind clearly, so that there should be no consequent bewilderment She was calm and silent, though her face showed that she was deeply moved. She broke down only when Ivory showed her the locket.

"I gave it to my husband when you were born, my son!" she sobbed. "After all, it seems no surprise to me that your father is dead. He said he would come back when the Mayflowers bloomed, and when I saw the autumn leaves I knew that six months must have gone and he would never stay away from us for six months without writing. That is the reason I have seldom watched for him these last weeks. I must have known that it was no use!"

She rose from her rocking-chair and moved feebly towards her bedroom. "Can you spare me the rest of the day, Ivory?" she faltered, as she leaned on her son and made her slow progress from the kitchen. "I must bury the body of my grief and I want to be alone at first... If only I could see Waitstill! We have both thought this was coming: she has a woman's instinct... she is younger and stronger than I am, and she said it was braver not to watch and pine and fret as I have done... but to have faith in God that He would send me a sign when He was ready.... She said if I could manage to be braver you would be happier too... ." Here she sank on to her bed exhausted, but still kept up her murmuring faintly and feebly, between long intervals of silence.

"Do you think Waitstill could come to-morrow?" she asked. "I am so much braver when she is here with me.... After supper I will put away your father's cup and plate once and for all, Ivory, and your eyes need never fill with tears again, as they have, sometimes, when you have seen me watching.... You needn't worry about me; I am remembering better these days, and the bells that ring in my ears are not so loud. If only the pain in my side were less and I were not so pressed for breath, I should be quite strong and could see everything clearly at last. ... There is something else that remains to be remembered. I have almost caught it once and it must come to me again before long.... Put the locket under my pillow, Ivory; close the door, please, and leave me to myself.... I can't make it quite clear, my feeling about it, but it seems just as if I were going to bury your father and I want to be alone."

XXII. HARVEST-TIME

NEW ENGLAND'S annual pageant of autumn was being unfolded day by day in all its accustomed splendor, and the feast and riot of color, the almost unimaginable glory, was the common property of the whole countryside, rich and poor, to be shared alike if perchance all eyes were equally alive to the wonder and the beauty.

Scarlet days and days of gold followed fast one upon the other; Saco Water flowing between quiet woodlands that were turning red and russet and brown, and now plunging through rocky banks all blazing with crimson.

Waitstill Baxter went as often as she could to the Boynton farm, though never when Ivory was at home, and the affection between the younger and the older woman grew closer and closer, so that it almost broke Waitstill's heart to leave the fragile creature, when her presence seemed to bring such complete peace and joy.

"No one ever clung to me so before," she often thought as she was hurrying across the fields after one of her half-hour visits. "But the end must come before long. Ivory does not realize it yet, nor Rodman, but it seems as if she could never survive the long winter. Thanksgiving Day is drawing nearer and nearer, and how little I am able to do for a single creature, to prove to God that I am grateful for my existence! I could, if only I were free, make such a merry day for Patty and Mark and their young friends. Oh! what joy if father were a man who would let me set a bountiful table in our great kitchen; would sit at the head and say grace, and we could bow our heads over the cloth, a united family! Or, if I had done my duty in my home and could go to that other where I am so needed—go with my father's blessing! If only I could live in that sad little house and brighten it! I would trim the rooms with evergreen and creeping-Jenny; I would put scarlet alder berries and white ever-lastings and blue fringed gentians in the vases! I would put the last bright autumn leaves near Mrs. Boynton's bed and set out a tray with a damask napkin and the best of my cooking; then I would go out to the back door where the woodbine hangs like a red waterfall and blow the dinner-horn for my men down in the harvest-field! All the woman in me is wasting, wasting! Oh! my dear, dear man, how I long for him! Oh! my own dear man, my helpmate, shall I ever live by his side? I love him, I want him, I need him! And my dear little unmothered, unfathered boy, how happy I could make him! How I should love to cook and sew for them all and wrap them in comfort! How I should love to smooth my dear mother's last days,—for she is my mother, in spirit, in affection, in desire, and in being Ivory's!"

Waitstill's longing, her discouragement, her helplessness, overcame her wholly, and she flung herself down under a tree in the pasture in a very passion of sobbing, a luxury in which she could seldom afford to indulge herself. The luxury was short-lived, for in five minutes she heard Rodman's voice, and heard him running to meet her as he often did when she came to their house or went away from it, dogging her footsteps or Patty's whenever or wherever he could waylay them.

"Why, my dear, dear Waity, did you tumble and hurt yourself?" the boy cried.

"Yes, dreadfully, but I'm better now, so walk along with me and tell me the news, Rod."

"There isn't much news. Ivory told you I'd left school and am studying at home? He helps me evenings and I'm 'way ahead of the class."

"No, Ivory didn't tell me. I haven't seen him lately."

"I said if the big brother kept school, the little brother ought to keep house," laughed the boy.

"He says I can hire out as a cook pretty soon! Aunt Boynton's 'most always up to get dinner and supper, but I can make lots of things now,— things that Aunt Boynton can eat, too."

"Oh, I cannot bear to have you and Ivory cooking for yourselves!" exclaimed Waitstill, the tears starting again from her eyes. "I must come over the next time when you are at home, Rod, and I can help you make something nice for supper.

"We get along pretty well," said Rodman contentedly. "I love book-learning like Ivory and I'm going to be a schoolmaster or a preacher when Ivory's a lawyer. Do you think Patty'd like a schoolmaster or a preacher best, and do you think I'd be too young to marry her by and by, if she would wait for me?"

"I didn't think you had any idea of marrying Patty," laughed Waitstill through her tears. "Is this something new?"

"It's not exactly new," said Rod, jumping along like a squirrel in the path. "Nobody could look at Patty and not think about marrying her. I'd love to marry you, too, but you re too big and grand for a boy. Of course, I'm not going to ask Patty yet. Ivory said once you should never ask a girl until you can keep her like a queen; then after a minute he said: 'Well, maybe not quite like a queen, Rod, for that would mean longer than a man could wait. Shall we say until he could keep her like the dearest lady in the land?' That 's the way he said it.—You do cry dreadfully easy to-day, Waity; I'm sure you barked your leg or skinned your knee when you fell down.—Don't you think the 'dearest lady in the land' is a nice-sounding sentence?"

"I do, indeed!" cried Waitstill to herself as she turned the words over and over trying to feed her hungry heart with them.

"I love to hear Ivory talk; it's like the stories in the books. We have our best times in the barn, for I'm helping with the milking, now. Our yellow cow's name is Molly and the red cow used to be Dolly, but we changed her to Golly, 'cause she's so troublesome. Molly's an easy cow to milk and I can get almost all there is, though Ivory comes after me and takes the strippings. Golly swishes her tail and kicks the minute she hears us coming; then she stands stiff-legged and grits her teeth and holds on to her milk HARD, and Ivory has to pat and smooth and coax her every single time. Ivory says she's got a kind of an attachment inside of her that she shuts down when he begins to milk."

"We had a cross old cow like that, once," said Waitstill absently, loving to hear the boy's chatter and the eternal quotations from his beloved hero.

"We have great fun cooking, too," continued Rod. "When Aunt Boynton was first sick she stayed in bed more, and Ivory and I hadn't got used to things. One morning we bound up each other's burns. Ivory had three fingers and I two, done up in buttery rags to take the fire out. Ivory called us 'Soldiers dressing their Wounds after the Battle.' Sausages spatter dreadfully, don't they? And when you turn a pancake it flops on top of the stove. Can you flop one straight, Waity?"

"Yes, I can, straight as a die; that's what girls are made for. Now run along home to your big brother, and do put on some warmer clothes under your coat; the weather's getting colder."

"Aunt Boynton hasn't patched our thick ones yet, but she will soon, and if she doesn't, Ivory'll take this Saturday evening and do them himself; he said so."

"He shall not!" cried Waitstill passionately. "It is not seemly for Ivory to sew and mend, and I will not allow it. You shall bring me those things that need patching without telling any one, do you hear, and I will meet you on the edge of the pasture Saturday afternoon and give them back to you. You are not to speak of it to any one, you understand, or perhaps I shall pound you to a jelly. You'd make a sweet rosy jelly to eat with turkey for Thanksgiving dinner, you dear, comforting little boy!"

Rodman ran towards home and Waitstill hurried along, scarcely noticing the beauties of the woods and fields and waysides, all glowing masses of goldenrod and purple frost flowers. The stone walls were covered with wild-grape and feathery clematis vines. Everywhere in sight the cornfields lay yellow in the afternoon sun and ox carts heavily loaded with full golden ears were going home to the barns to be ready for husking.

A sudden breeze among the orchard boughs as she neared the house was followed by a shower of russets, and everywhere the red Baldwins gleamed on the apple-tree boughs, while the wind-falls were being gathered and taken to the cider mills. There was a grove of maples on the top of Town-House Hill and the Baxters' dooryard was a blaze of brilliant color. To see Patty standing under a little rock maple, her brown linsey-woolsey in I one with the landscape, and the hood of her brown cape pulled over her bright head, was a welcome for anybody. She looked flushed and excited as she ran up to her sister and said, "Waity, darling, you've been crying! Has father been scolding you?"

"No, dear, but my heart is aching to-day so that I can scarcely bear it. A wave of discouragement came over me as I was walking through the woods, and I gave up to it a bit. I remembered how soon it will be Thanksgiving Day, and I'll so like to make it happier for you and a few others that I love."

Patty could have given a shrewd guess as to the chief cause of the heartache, but she forebore to ask any questions. "Cheer up, Waity," she cried. "You never can tell; we may have a thankful Thanksgiving, after all! Who knows what may happen? I'm 'strung up' this afternoon and in a fighting mood. I've felt like a new piece of snappy white elastic all day; it's the air, just like wine, so cool and stinging and full of courage! Oh, yes, we won't give up hope yet awhile, Waity, not until we're snowed in!"

"Put your arms round me and give me a good hug, Patty! Love me hard, HARD, for, oh! I need it badly just now!"

And the two girls clung together for a moment and then went into the house with hands close-locked and a kind of sad, desperate courage in their young hearts. What would either of them have done, each of them thought, had she been forced to endure alone the life that went on day after day in Deacon Baxter's dreary house?

XXIII. AUNT ABBY'S WINDOW

MRS. ABEL DAY had come to spend the afternoon with Aunt Abby Cole and they were seated at the two sitting-room windows, sweeping the landscape with eagle eyes in the intervals of making patchwork.

"The foliage has been a little mite too rich this season," remarked Aunt Abby. "I b'lieve I'm glad to see it thinin' out some, so 't we can have some kind of an idee of what's goin' on in the village."

"There's plenty goin' on," Mrs. Day answered unctuously; "some of it aboveboard an' some underneath it."

"An' that's jest where it's aggravatin' to have the leaves so thick and the trees so high between you and other folks' houses. Trees are good for shade, it's true, but there's a limit to all things. There was a time when I could see 'bout every-thing that went on up to Baxters', and down to Bart's shop, and, by goin' up attic, consid'able many things that happened on the bridge. Bart vows he never planted that plum tree at the back door of his shop; says the children must have hove out plum stones when they was settin' on the steps and the tree come up of its own accord. He says he didn't take any notice of it till it got quite a start and then 't was such a healthy young bush he couldn't bear to root it out. I tell him it's kind o' queer it should happen to come up jest where it spoils my view of his premises. Men folks are so exasperatin' that sometimes I wish there was somebody different for us to marry, but there ain't,—so there we be!"

"They are an awful trial," admitted Mrs. Day. "Abel never sympathizes with my head-aches. I told him a-Sunday I didn't believe he'd mind if I died the next day, an' all he said was: 'Why don't you try it an' see, Lyddy?' He thinks that's humorous."

"I know; that's the way Bartholomew talks; I guess they all do. You can see the bridge better 'n I can, Lyddy; has Mark Wilson drove over sence you've been settin' there? He's like one o' them ostriches that hides their heads in the sand when the bird-catchers are comin' along, thinkin' 'cause they can't see anything they'll never BE seen! He knows folks would never tell tales to Deacon Baxter, whatever the girls done; they hate him too bad. Lawyer Wilson lives so far away, he can't keep any watch o' Mark, an' Mis' Wilson's so cityfied an' purse-proud nobody ever goes to her with any news, bad or good; so them that's the most concerned is as blind as bats. Mark's consid'able stiddier'n he used to be, but you needn't tell me he has any notion of bringin' one o' that Baxter tribe into his family. He's only amusin' himself."

"Patty'll be Mrs. Wilson or nothin'," was Mrs. Day's response. "Both o' them girls is silk purses an' you can't make sows' ears of 'em. We ain't neither of us hardly fair to Patty, an' I s'pose it 's because she didn't set any proper value on Cephas."

"Oh, she's good enough for Mark, I guess, though I ain't so sure of his intentions as you be. She's nobody's fool, Patty ain't, I allow that, though she did treat Cephas like the dirt in the road. I'm thankful he's come to his senses an' found out the diff'rence between dross an' gold."

"It's very good of you to put it that way, Abby," Mrs. Day responded gratefully, for it was Phoebe, her own offspring, who was alluded to as the most precious of metals. "I suppose we'd better have the publishing notice put up in the frame before Sunday? There'll be a great crowd out that day and at Thanksgiving service the next Thursday too!"

"Cephas says he don't care how soon folks hears the news, now all's settled," said his mother. "I guess he's kind of anxious that the village should know jest how little truth there is in the gossip 'bout him bein' all upset over Patience Baxter. He said they took consid'able notice of him an' Phoebe settin' together at the Harvest Festival last evenin'. He thought the Baxter girls would be there for certain, but I s'pose Old Foxy wouldn't let 'em go up to the Mills in the evenin', nor spend a quarter on their tickets."

"Mark could have invited Patty an' paid for her ticket, I should think; or passed her in free, for that matter, when the Wilsons got up the entertainment; but, of course, the Deacon never allows his girls to go anywheres with men-folks."

"Not in public; so they meet 'em side o' the river or round the corner of Bart's shop, or anywhere they can, when the Deacon's back's turned. If you tied a handkerchief over Waitstill's eyes she could find her way blindfold to Ivory Boynton's house, but she's good as gold, Waitstill is; she'll stay where her duty calls her, every time! If any misfortune or scandal should come near them two girls, the Deacon will have no-body but himself to thank for it, that's one sure thing!"

"Young folks can't be young but once," sighed Mrs. Day. "I thought we had as handsome a turn-out at the entertainment last evenin' as any village on the Saco River could 'a' furnished: an' my Phoebe an' your Cephas, if I do say so as shouldn't, was about the best-dressed an' best-appearin' couple there was present. Also, I guess likely, they're startin' out with as good prospects as any bride an' groom that's walked up the middle aisle o' the meetin'-house for many a year.... How'd you like that Boston singer that the Wilsons brought here, Abby?—Wait a minute, is Cephas, or the Deacon, tendin' store this after-noon?"

"The Deacon; Cephas is paintin' up to the Mills."

"Well, Mark Wilson's horse an' buggy is meanderin' slowly down Aunt Betty-Jack's hill, an' Mark is studyin' the road as if he was lookin' for a four-leafed clover."

"He'll hitch at the tavern, or the Edgewood store, an' wait his chance to get a word with Patience," said Aunt Abby. "He knows when she takes milk to the Morrills', or butter to the parsonage; also when she eats an' drinks an' winks her eye an' ketches her breath an' lifts her foot. Now he's disappeared an' we'll wait.. .. Why, as to that Boston singer,—an' by the way, they say Ellen Wilson's goin' to take lessons of her this winter,—she kind o' bewildered me, Lyddy! Of course, I ain't never been to any cities, so I don't feel altogether free to criticise; but what did you think of her, when she run up so high there, one time? I don't know how high she went, but I guess there wa'n't no higher to go!"

"It made me kind o' nervous," allowed Mrs. Day.

"Nervous! Bart' an' I broke out in a cold sweat! He said she couldn't hold a candle to Waitstill Baxter. But it's that little fly-away Wilson girl that'll get the lessons, an' Waitstill will have to use her voice callin' the Deacon home to dinner. Things ain't divided any too well in this world, Lyddy."

"Waitstill's got the voice, but she lacks the trainin'. The Boston singer knows her business, I'll say that for her," said Mrs. Day.

"She's got good stayin' power," agreed Aunt Abby. "Did you notice how she held on to that high note when she'd clumb where she wanted to git? She's got breath enough to run a gristmill, that girl has! And how'd she come down, when she got good and ready to start? Why, she zig-zagged an' saw-toothed the whole way! It kind o' made my flesh creep!"

"I guess part o' the trouble's with us country folks," Mrs. Day responded, "for folks said she sung runs and trills better'n any woman up to Boston."

"Runs an' trills," ejaculated Abby scornfully. "I was talkin' 'bout singin' not runnin'. My niece Ella up to Parsonfield has taken three terms on the pianner an' I've heerd her practise. Scales has got to be done, no doubt, but they'd ought to be done to home, where they belong; a concert ain't no place for 'em... . There, what did I tell yer? Patience Baxter's crossin' the bridge with a pail in her hand. She's got that everlastin' yeller-brown, linsey-woolsey on, an' a white 'cloud' wrapped around her head with con'sid'able red hair showin' as usual. You can always see her fur's you can a sunrise! And there goes Rod Boynton, chasin' behind as usual. Those Baxter girls make a perfect fool o' that boy, but I don't s'pose Lois Boynton's got wit enough to make much fuss over the poor little creeter!"

Mark Wilson could certainly see Patty Baxter as far as he could a sunrise, although he was not intimately acquainted with that natural phenomenon. He took a circuitous route from his watch-tower, and, knowing well the point from which there could be no espionage from Deacon Baxter's store windows, joined Patty in the road, took the pail from her hand, and walked up the hill beside her. Of course, the village could see them, but, as Aunt Abby had intimated, there wasn't a man, woman, or child on either side of the river who wouldn't have taken the part of the Baxter girls against their father.

XXIV. PHOEBE TRIUMPHS

MEANTIME Feeble Phoebe Day was driving her father's horse up to the Mills to bring Cephas Cole home. It was a thrilling moment, a sort of outward and visible sign of an inward and spiritual tie, for their banns were to be published the next day, so what did it matter if the community, nay, if the whole universe, speculated as to why she was drawing her beloved back from his daily toil? It had been an eventful autumn for Cephas. After a third request for the hand of Miss Patience Baxter, and a refusal of even more than common decision and energy, Cephas turned about face and employed the entire month of September in a determined assault upon the affections of Miss Lucy Morrill, but with no better avail. His heart was not ardently involved in this second wooing, but winter was approaching, he had moved his mother out of her summer quarters back to the main house, and he doggedly began papering the ell and furnishing the kitchen without disclosing to his respected parents the identity of the lady for whose comfort he was so hospitably preparing.

Cephas's belief in the holy state of matrimony as being the only one proper for a man, really ought to have commended him to the opposite (and ungrateful) sex more than it did, and Lucy Morrill held as respectful an opinion of the institution and its manifold advantages as Cephas himself, but she was in a very unsettled frame of mind and not at all susceptible to wooing. She had a strong preference for Philip Perry, and held an opinion, not altogether unfounded in human experience, that in course of time, when quite deserted by Patty Baxter, his heart might possibly be caught on the rebound. It was only a chance, but Lucy would almost have preferred remaining unmarried, even to the withering age of twenty-five, rather than not be at liberty to accept Philip Perry in case she should be asked.

Cephas therefore, by the middle of October, could be picturesquely and alliteratively described as being raw from repeated rejections. His bruised heart and his despised ell literally cried out for the appreciation so long and blindly withheld. Now all at once Phoebe disclosed a second virtue; her first and only one, hitherto, in the eyes of Cephas, having been an ability to get on with his mother, a feat in which many had made an effort and few indeed had succeeded. Phoebe, it seems, had always secretly admired, respected, and loved Cephas Cole! Never since her pale and somewhat glassy blue eye had opened on life had she beheld a being she could so adore if encouraged in the attitude.

The moment this unusual and unexpected poultice was really applied to Cephas's wounds, they began to heal. In the course of a month the most ordinary observer could have perceived a physical change in him. He cringed no more, but held his head higher; his back straightened; his voice developed a gruff, assertive note, like that of a stern Roman father; he let his moustache grow, and sometimes, in his most reckless moments, twiddled the end of it. Finally he swaggered; but that was only after Phoebe had accepted him and told him that if a girl traversed the entire length of the Saco River (which she presumed to be the longest in the world, the Amazon not being familiar to her), she could not hope to find his equal as a husband.

And then congratulations began to pour in! Was ever marriage so fortuitous! The Coles' farm joined that of the Days and the union between the two only children would cement the friendship between the families. The fact that Uncle Bart was a joiner, Cephas a painter, and Abel Day a mason and bricklayer made the alliance almost providential in its business opportunities. Phoebe's Massachusetts aunt sent a complete outfit of gilt-edged china, a clock, and a mahogany chamber set. Aunt Abby relinquished to the young couple a bedroom and a spare chamber in the "main part," while the Days supplied live-geese feathers and table and bed-linen with positive prodigality. Aunt Abby trod the air like one inspired. "Balmy" is the only adjective that could describe her.

"If only I could 'a' looked ahead," smiled Uncle Bart quizzically to himself, "I'd 'a' had thirteen sons and daughters an' married off one of 'em every year. That would 'a' made Abby's good temper kind o' permanent."

Cephas was content, too. There was a good deal in being settled and having "the whole doggoned business" off your hands. Phoebe looked a very different creature to him in these latter days. Her eyes were just as pale, of course, but they were brighter, and they radiated love for him, an expression in the female eye that he had thus far been singularly unfortunate in securing. She still held her mouth slightly open, but Cephas thought that it might be permissible, perhaps after three months of wedded bliss, to request her to be more careful in closing it. He believed, too, that she would make an effort to do so just to please him; whereas a man's life or property would not be safe for a single instant if he asked Miss Patience Baxter to close her mouth, not if he had been married to her for thirty times three months!

Cephas did not think of Patty any longer with bitterness, in these days, being of the opinion that she was punished enough in observing his own growing popularity and prosperity.

"If she should see that mahogany chamber set going into the ell I guess she'd be glad enough to change her tune!" thought Cephas, exultingly; and then there suddenly shot through his mind the passing fancy—"I wonder if she would!" He promptly banished the infamous suggestion however, reinforcing his virtue with the reflection that the chamber set was Phoebe's, anyway, and the marriage day appointed, and the invitations given out, and the wedding-cake being baked, a loaf at a time, by his mother and Mrs. Day.

As a matter of fact Patty would have had no eyes for Phoebe's magnificent mahogany, even had the cart that carried it passed her on the hill where she and Mark Wilson were walking. Her promise to marry him was a few weeks old now, and his arm encircled her slender waist under the brown homespun cape. That in itself was a new sensation and gave her the delicious sense of belonging to somebody who valued her highly, and assured her of his sentiments clearly and frequently, both by word and deed. Life, dull gray life, was going to change its hue for her presently, and not long after, she hoped, for Waitstill, too! It needed only a brighter, a more dauntless courage; a little faith that nettles, when firmly grasped, hurt the hand less, and a fairer future would dawn for both of them. The Deacon was a sharper nettle than she had ever meddled with before, but in these days, when the actual contact had not yet occurred, she felt sure of herself and longed for the moment when her pluck should be tested and proved.

The "publishing" of Cephas and his third choice, their dull walk up the aisle of the meeting-house before an admiring throng, on the Sunday when Phoebe would "appear bride," all this seemed very tame as compared with the dreams of this ardent and adventurous pair of lovers who had gone about for days harboring secrets greater and more daring, they thought, than had ever been breathed before within the hearing of Saco Water.

XXV. LOVE'S YOUNG DREAMS

IT was not an afternoon for day-dreams, for there was a chill in the air and a gray sky. Only a week before the hills along the river might have been the walls of the New Jerusalem, shining like red gold; now the glory had departed and it was a naked world, with empty nests hanging to boughs that not long ago had been green with summer. The old elm by the tavern, that had been wrapped in a bright trail of scarlet woodbine, was stripped almost bare of its autumn beauty. Here and there a maple showed a remnant of crimson, and a stalwart oak had some rags of russet still clinging to its gaunt boughs. The hickory trees flung out a few yellow flags from the ends of their twigs, but the forests wore a tattered and dishevelled look, and the withered leaves that lay in dried heaps upon the frozen ground, driven hither and thither by every gust of the north wind, gave the unthinking heart a throb of foreboding. Yet the glad summer labor of those same leaves was finished according to the law that governed them, and the fruit was theirs and the seed for the coming year. No breeze had been strong enough to shake them from the tree till they were ready to forsake it. Now they had severed the bond that had held them so tightly and fluttered down to give the earth all their season's earnings. On every hillside, in every valley and glen, the leaves that had made the summer landscape beautiful, lay contentedly:

"Where the rain might rain upon them,

Where the sun might shine upon them,

Where the wind might sigh upon them,

And the snow might die upon them."

Brown, withered, dead, buried in snow they might be, yet they were ministering to all the leaves of the next spring-time, bequeathing to them in turn the beauty that had been theirs; the leafy canopies for countless song birds, the grateful shade for man and beast.

Young love thought little of Nature's miracles, and hearts that beat high and fast were warm enough to forget the bleak wind and gathering clouds. If there were naked trees, were there not full barrels of apples in every cellar? If there was nothing but stubble in the frozen fields, why, there was plenty of wheat and corn at the mill all ready for grinding. The cold air made one long for a cheery home and fireside, the crackle of a hearth-log, the bubbling of a steaming kettle; and Patty and Mark clung together as they walked along, making bright images of a life together, snug, warm, and happy.

Patty was a capricious creature, but all her changes were sudden and endearing ones, captivating those who loved her more than a monotonous and unchanging virtue. Any little shower, with Patty, always ended with a rainbow that made the landscape more enchanting than before. Of late her little coquetries and petulances had disappeared as if by magic. She had been melted somehow from irresponsible girlhood into womanhood, and that, too, by the ardent affection of a very ordinary young man who had no great gift save that of loving Patty greatly. The love had served its purpose, in another way, too, for under its influence Mark's own manhood had broadened and deepened. He longed to bind Patty to him for good and all, to capture the bright bird whose fluttering wings and burnished plumage so captured his senses and stirred his heart, but his longings had changed with the quality of his love and he glowed at the thought of delivering the girl from her dreary surroundings and giving her the tenderness, the ease and comfort, the innocent gayety, that her nature craved.

"You won't fail me, Patty darling?" he was saying at this moment. "Now that our plans are finally made, with never a weak point any where as far as I can see, my heart is so set upon carrying them out that every hour of waiting seems an age!"

"No, I won't fail, Mark; but I never know the day that father will go to town until the night before. I can always hear him making his preparations in the barn and the shed, and ordering Waitstill here and there. He is as excited as if he was going to Boston instead of Milltown."

"The night before will do. I will watch the house every evening till you hang a white signal from your window."

"It won't be white," said Patty, who would be mischievous on her deathbed; "my Sunday-go-to-meetin' petticoat is too grand, and everything else that we have is yellow."

"I shall see it, whatever color it is, you can be sure of that!" said Mark gallantly. "Then it's decided that next morning I'll wait at the tavern from sunrise, and whenever your father and Waitstill have driven up Saco Hill, I'll come and pick you up and we'll be off like a streak of lightning across the hills to New Hampshire. How lucky that Riverboro is only thirty miles from the state line!—It looks like snow, and how I wish it would be something more than a flurry; a regular whizzing, whirring storm that would pack the roads and let us slip over them with our sleigh-bells ringing!"

"I should like that, for they would be our only wedding-bells. Oh! Mark! What if Waitstill shouldn't go, after all: though I heard father tell her that he needed her to buy things for the store, and that they wouldn't be back till after nightfall. Just to think of being married without Waitstill!"

"You can do without Waitstill on this one occasion, better than you can without me," laughed Mark, pinching Patty's cheek. "I've given the town clerk due notice and I have a friend to meet me at his office. He is going to lend me his horse for the drive home, and we shall change back the next week. That will give us a fresh horse each way, and we'll fly like the wind, snow or no snow, When we come down Guide Board Hill that night, Patty, we shall be man and wife; isn't that wonderful?"

"We shall be man and wife in New Hampshire, but not in Maine, you say," Patty reminded him dolefully. "It does seem dreadful that we can't be married in our own state, and have to go dangling about with this secret on our minds, day and night; but it can't be helped! You'll try not to even think of me as your wife till we go to Portsmouth to live, won't you?"

"You're asking too much when you say I'm not to think of you as my wife, for I shall think of nothing else, but I've given you my solemn promise," said Mark stoutly, "and I'll keep it as sure as I live. We'll be legally married by the laws of New Hampshire, but we won't think of it as a marriage till I tell your father and mine, and we drive away once more together. That time it will be in the sight of everybody, with our heads in the air. I've got the little house in Portsmouth all ready, Patty: it's small, but it's in a nice part of the town. Portsmouth is a pretty place, but it'll be a great deal prettier when it has Mrs. Mark Wilson living in it. We can be married over again in Maine, afterwards, if your heart is set upon it. I'm willing to marry you in every state of the Union, so far as I am concerned."

"I think you've been so kind and good and thoughtful, Mark dear," said Patty, more fondly and meltingly than she had ever spoken to him before, "and so clever too! I do respect you for getting that good position in Portsmouth and being able to set up for yourself at your age. I shouldn't wonder a bit if you were a judge some day, and then what a proud girl I shall be!"

Patty's praise was bestowed none too frequently, and it sounded very sweet in the young man's ears.

"I do believe I can get on, with you to help me, Patty," he said, pressing her arm more closely to his side, and looking down ardently into her radiant face. "You're a great deal cleverer than I am, but I have a faculty for the business of the law, so my father says, and a faculty for money-making, too. And even if we have to begin in a small way, my salary will be a certainty, and we'll work up together. I can see you in a yellow satin dress, stiff enough to stand alone!"

"It must be white satin, if you please, not yellow! After having used a hundred and ten yards of shop-worn yellow calico on myself within two years, I never want to wear that color again. If only I could come to you better provided," she sighed, with the suggestion of tears in her voice. "If I'd been a common servant I could have saved something from my wages to be married on; I haven't even got anything to be married IN!"

"I'll get you anything you want in Portland to-morrow."

"Certainly not; I'd rather be married in rags than have you spend your money upon me beforehand!"

"Remember to have a box of your belongings packed and slipped under the shed somewhere. You can't be certain what your father will say or do when the time comes for telling him, and I want you to be ready to leave on a moment's notice."

"I will; I'll do everything you say, Mark, but are you sure that we have thought of every other way? I do so hate being underhanded."

"Every other way! I am more than willing to ask your father, but we know he would treat me with contempt, for he can't bear the sight of me! He would probably lock you up and feed you on bread and water. That being the state of things, how can I tell our plans to my own father? He never would look with favor on my running away with you; and mother is, by nature, set upon doing things handsomely and in proper order. Father would say our elopement would be putting us both wrong before the community, and he'd advise me to wait. 'You are both young'—I can hear him announcing his convictions now, as clearly as if he was standing here in the road—'You are both young and you can well afford to wait until something turns up.' As if we hadn't waited and waited from all eternity!"

"Yes, we have been engaged to be married for at least five weeks," said Patty, with an upward glance peculiar to her own sparkling face,—one that always intoxicated Mark. "I am seventeen and a half; your father couldn't expect a confirmed old maid like me to waste any more time. But I never would do this—this—sudden, unrespectable thing, if there was any other way. Everything depends on my keeping it secret from Waitstill, but she doesn't suspect anything yet. She thinks of me as nothing but a child still. Do you suppose Ellen would go with us, just to give me a little comfort?"

"She might," said Mark, after reflecting a moment. "She is very devoted to you, and perhaps she could keep a secret; she never has, but there's always a first time. You can't go on adding to the party, though, as if it was a candy-pull! We cannot take Lucy Morrill and Phoebe Day and Cephas Cole, because it would be too hard on the horse; and besides, I might get embarrassed at the town clerk's office and marry the wrong girl; or you might swop me off for Cephas! But I'll tell Ellen if you say so; she's got plenty of grit."

"Don't joke about it, Mark, don't. I shouldn't miss Waitstill so much if I had Ellen, and how happy I shall be if she approves of me for a sister and thinks your mother and father will like me in time."

"There never was a creature born into the world that wouldn't love you, Patty!"

"I don't know; look at Aunt Abby Cole!" said Patty pensively. "Well, it does not seem as if a marriage that isn't good in Riverboro was really decent! How tiresome of Maine to want all those days of public notice; people must so often want to get married in a minute. If I think about anything too long I always get out of the notion."

"I know you do; that's what I'm afraid of!"—and Mark's voice showed decided nervousness. "You won't get out of the notion of marrying me, will you, Patty dear?"

"Marrying you is more than a 'notion,' Mark," said Patty soberly. "I'm only a little past seventeen, but I'm far older because of the difficulties I've had. I don't wonder you speak of my 'notions.' I was as light as a feather in all my dealings with you at first."

"So was I with you! I hadn't grown up, Patty."

"Then I came to know you better and see how you sympathized with Waitstill's troubles and mine. I couldn't love anybody, I couldn't marry anybody, who didn't feel that things at our house can't go on as they are! Father has had a good long trial! Three wives and two daughters have done their best to live with him, and failed. I am not willing to die for him, as my mother did, nor have Waitstill killed if I can help it. Sometimes he is like a man who has lost his senses and sometimes he is only grim and quiet and cruel. If he takes our marriage without a terrible scene, Mark, perhaps it will encourage Waitstill to break her chains as I have mine."

"There's sure to be an awful row," Mark said, as one who had forecasted all the probabilities. "It wouldn't make any difference if you married the Prince of Wales; nothing would suit your father but selecting the man and making all the arrangements; and then he would never choose any one who wouldn't tend the store and work on the farm for him without wages."

"Waitstill will never run away; she isn't like me. She will sit and sit there, slaving and suffering, till doomsday; for the one that loves her isn't free like you!"

"You mean Ivory Boynton? I believe he worships the ground she walks on. I like him better than I used, and I understand him better. Oh! but I'm a lucky young dog to have a kind, liberal father and a bit of money put by to do with as I choose. If I hadn't, I'd be eating my heart out like Ivory!"

"No, you wouldn't eat your heart out; you'd always get what you wanted somehow, and you wouldn't wait for it either; and I'm just the same. I'm not built for giving up, and enduring, and sacrificing. I'm naturally just a tuft of thistle-down, Mark; but living beside Waitstill all these years I've grown ashamed to be so light, blowing about hither and thither. I kept looking at her and borrowing some of her strength, just enough to make me worthy to be her sister. Waitstill is like a bit of Plymouth Rock, only it's a lovely bit on the land side, with earth in the crevices, and flowers blooming all over it and hiding the granite. Oh! if only she will forgive us, Mark, I won't mind what father says or does."

"She will forgive us, Patty darling; don't fret, and cry, and make your pretty eyes all red. I'll do nothing in all this to make either of you girls ashamed of me, and I'll keep your father and mine ever before my mind to prevent my being foolish or reckless; for, you know, Patty, I'm heels over head in love with you, and it's only for your sake I'm taking all these pains and agreeing to do without my own wedded wife for weeks to come!"

"Does the town clerk, or does the justice of the peace give a wedding-ring, just like the minister?" Patty asked. "I shouldn't feel married without a ring."

"The ring is all ready, and has 'M.W. to P.B.' engraved in it, with the place for the date waiting; and here is the engagement ring if you'll wear it when you're alone, Patty. My mother gave it to me when she thought there would be something between Annabel Franklin and me. The moment I looked at it—you see it's a topaz stone—and noticed the yellow fire in it, I said to myself: 'It is like no one but Patty Baxter, and if she won't wear it, no other girl shall!' It's the color of the tip ends of your curls and it's just like the light in your eyes when you're making fun!"

"It's heavenly!" cried Patty. "It looks as if it had been made of the yellow autumn leaves, and oh! how I love the sparkle of it! But never will I take your mother's ring or wear it, Mark, till I've proved myself her loving, dutiful daughter. I'll do the one wrong thing of running away with you and concealing our marriage, but not another if I can help it."

"Very well," sighed Mark, replacing the ring in his pocket with rather a crestfallen air. "But the first thing you know you'll be too good for me, Patty! You used to be a regular will-o'-the-wisp, all nonsense and fun, forever laughing and teasing, so that a fellow could never be sure of you for two minutes together."

"It's all there underneath," said Patty, putting her hand on his arm and turning her wistful face up to his. "It will come again; the girl in me isn't dead; she isn't even asleep; but she's all sobered down. She can't laugh just now, she can only smile; and the tears are waiting underneath, ready to spring out if any one says the wrong word. This Patty is frightened and anxious and her heart beats too fast from morning till night. She hasn't any mother, and she cannot say a word to her dear sister, and she's going away to be married to you, that's almost a stranger, and she isn't eighteen, and doesn't know what's coming to her, nor what it means to be married. She dreads her father's anger, and she cannot rest till she knows whether your family will love her and take her in; and, oh! she's a miserable, worried girl, not a bit like the old Patty."

Mark held her close and smoothed the curls under the loose brown hood. "Don't you fret, Patty darling! I'm not the boy I was last week. Every word you say makes me more of a man. At first I would have run away just for the joke; anything to get you away from the other fellows and prove I was the best man, but now' I'm sobered down, too. I'll do nothing rash; I'll be as staid as the judge you want me to be twenty years later. You've made me over, Patty, and if my love for you wasn't the right sort at first, it is now. I wish the road to New Hampshire was full of lions and I could fight my way through them just to show you how strong I feel!"

"There'll be lions enough," smiled Patty through her tears, "though they won't have manes and tails; but I can imagine how father will roar, and how my courage will ooze out of the heels of my boots!"

"Just let me catch the Deacon roaring at my wife!" exclaimed Mark with a swelling chest. "Now, run along, Patty dear, for I don't want you scolded on my account. There's sure to be only a day or two of waiting now, and I shall soon see the signal waving from your window. I'll sound Ellen and see if she's brave enough to be one of the eloping party. Good-night! Good-night! Oh! How I hope our going away will be to-morrow, my dearest, dearest Patty!"

WINTER
XXVI. A WEDDING-RING

THE snow had come. It had begun to fall softly and steadily at the beginning of the week, and now for days it had covered the ground deeper and deeper, drifting about the little red brick house on the hilltop, banking up against the barn, and shrouding the sheds and the smaller buildings. There had been two cold, still nights; the windows were covered with silvery landscapes whose delicate foliage made every pane of glass a leafy bower, while a dazzling crust bediamonded the hillsides, so that no eye could rest on them long without becoming snow-blinded.

Town-House Hill was not as well travelled as many others, and Deacon Baxter had often to break his own road down to the store, without waiting for the help of the village snow-plough to make things easier for him. Many a path had Waitstill broken in her time, and it was by no means one of her most distasteful tasks—that of shovelling into the drifts of heaped-up whiteness, tossing them to one side or the other, and cutting a narrow, clean-edged track that would pack down into the hardness of marble.

There were many "chores" to be done these cold mornings before any household could draw a breath of comfort. The Baxters kept but one cow in winter, killed the pig,—not to eat, but to sell,—and reduced the flock of hens and turkeys; but Waitstill was always as busy in the barn as in her own proper domain. Her heart yearned for all the dumb creatures about the place, intervening between them and her father's scanty care; and when the thermometer descended far below zero she would be found stuffing hay into the holes and cracks of the barn and hen-house, giving the horse and cow fresh beddings of straw and a mouthful of extra food between the slender meals provided by the Deacon.

It was three o'clock in the afternoon and a fire in the Baxters' kitchen since six in the morning had produced a fairly temperate climate in that one room, though the entries and chambers might have been used for refrigerators, as the Deacon was as parsimonious in the use of fuel as in all other things, and if his daughters had not been hardy young creatures, trained from their very birth to discomforts and exposures of every sort, they would have died long ago.

The Baxter kitchen and glittered in all its accustomed cleanliness and order. Scrubbing and polishing were cheap amusements, and nobody grudged them to Waitstill. No tables in Riverboro were whiter, no tins more lustrous, no pewter brighter, no brick hearths ruddier than hers. The beans and brown bread and Indian pudding were basking in the warmth of the old brick oven, and what with the crackle and sparkle of the fire, the gleam of the blue willow-ware on the cupboard shelves, and the scarlet geraniums blooming on the sunny shelf above the sink, there were few pleasanter place to be found in the village than that same Baxter kitchen. Yet Waitstill was ill at ease this afternoon; she hardly knew why. Her father had just put the horse into the pung and driven up to Milliken's Mills for some grain, and Patty was down at the store instructing Bill Morrill (Cephas Cole's successor) in his novel task of waiting on customers and learning the whereabouts of things; no easy task in the bewildering variety of stock in a country store; where pins, treacle, gingham, Epsom salts, Indian meal, shoestrings, shovels, brooms, sulphur, tobacco, suspenders, rum, and indigo may be demanded in rapid succession.

Patty was quiet and docile these days, though her color was more brilliant than usual and her eyes had all their accustomed sparkle. She went about her work steadily, neither ranting nor railing at fate, nor bewailing her lot, but even in this Waitstill felt a sense of change and difference too subtle to be put in words. She had noted Patty's summer flirtations, but regarded them indulgently, very much as if they had been the irresponsible friskings of a lamb in a meadow. Waitstill had more than the usual reserve in these matters, for in New England at that time, though the soul was a subject of daily conversation, the heart was felt to be rather an indelicate topic, to be alluded to as seldom as possible. Waitstill certainly would never have examined Patty closely as to the state of her affections, intimate as she was with her sister's thoughts and opinions about life; she simply bided her time until Patty should confide in her. She had wished now and then that Patty's capricious fancy might settle on Philip Perry, although, indeed, when she considered it seriously, it seemed like an alliance between a butterfly and an owl. Cephas Cole she regarded as quite beneath Patty's rightful ambitions, and as for Mark Wilson, she had grown up in the belief, held in the village generally, that he would marry money and position, and drift out of Riverboro into a gayer, larger world. Her devotion to her sister was so ardent, and her admiration so sincere, that she could not think it possible that Patty would love anywhere in vain; nevertheless, she had an instinct that her affections were crystallizing somewhere or other, and when that happened, the uncertain and eccentric temper of her father would raise a thousand obstacles.

While these thoughts coursed more or less vagrantly through Waitstill's mind, she suddenly determined to get her cloak and hood and run over to see Mrs. Boynton. Ivory had been away a good deal in the woods since early November chopping trees and helping to make new roads. He could not go long distances, like the other men, as he felt constrained to come home every day or two to look after his mother and Rodman, but the work was too lucrative to be altogether refused. With Waitstill's help, he had at last overcome his mother's aversion to old Mrs. Mason, their nearest neighbor; and she, being now a widow with very slender resources, went to the Boyntons' several times each week to put the forlorn household a little on its feet.

It was all uphill and down to Ivory's farm, Waitstill reflected, and she could take her sled and slide half the way, going and coming, or she could cut across the frozen fields on the crust. She caught up her shawl from a hook on the kitchen door, and, throwing it over her head and shoulders to shield herself from the chill blasts on the stairway, ran up to her bedroom to make herself ready for the walk.

She slipped on a quilted petticoat and warmer dress, braided her hair freshly, while her breath went out in a white cloud to meet the freezing air; snatched her wraps from her closet, and was just going down the stairs when she remembered that an hour before, having to bind up a cut finger for her father, she had searched Patty's bureau drawer for an old handkerchief, and had left things in disorder while she ran to answer the Deacon's impatient call and stamp upon the kitchen floor.

"Hurry up and don't make me stan' here all winter!" he had shouted. "If you ever kept things in proper order, you wouldn't have to hunt all over the house for a piece of rag when you need it!"

Patty was very dainty about her few patched and darned belongings; also very exact in the adjustment of her bits of ribbon, her collars of crocheted thread, her adored coral pendants, and her pile of neat cotton handkerchiefs, hem-stitched by her own hands. Waitstill, accordingly, with an exclamation at her own unwonted carelessness, darted into her sister's room to replace in perfect order the articles she had disarranged in her haste. She knew them all, these poor little trinkets,—humble, pathetic evidences of Patty's feminine vanity and desire to make her bright beauty a trifle brighter.

Suddenly her hand and her eye fell at the same moment on something hidden in a far corner under a white "fascinator," one of those head-coverings of filmy wool, dotted with beads, worn by the girls of the period. She drew the glittering, unfamiliar object forward, and then lifted it wonderingly in her hand. It was a string of burnished gold beads, the avowed desire of Patty's heart; a string of beads with a brilliant little stone in the fastening. And, as if that were not mystery enough, there was something slipped over the clasped necklace and hanging from it, as Waitstill held it up to the light—a circlet of plain gold, a wedding-ring!

Waitstill stood motionless in the cold with such a throng of bewildering thoughts, misgivings, imaginings, rushing through her head that they were like a flock of birds beating their wings against her ears. The imaginings were not those of absolute dread or terror, for she knew her Patty. If she had seen the necklace alone she would have been anxious, indeed, for it would have meant that the girl, urged on by ungoverned desire for the ornament, had accepted present from one who should not have given it to her secretly; but the wedding-ring meant some-thing different for Patty,—something more, something certain, something unescapable, for good or ill. A wedding-ring could stand for nothing but marriage. Could Patty be married? How, when, and where could so great a thing happen without her knowledge? It seemed impossible. How had such a child surmounted the difficulties in the path? Had she been led away by the attractions of some stranger? No, there had been none in the village. There was only one man who had the worldly wisdom or the means to carry Patty off under the very eye of her watchful sister; only one with the reckless courage to defy her father; and that was Mark Wilson. His name did not bring absolute confidence to Waitstill's mind. He was gay and young and thoughtless; how had he managed to do this wild thing?—and had he done all decently and wisely, with consideration for the girl's good name? The thought of all the risks lying in the train of Patty's youth and inexperience brought a wail of anguish from Waitstill's lips, and, dropping the beads and closing the drawer, she stumbled blindly down the stairway to the kitchen, intent upon one thought only—to find her sister, to look in her eyes, feel the touch of her hand, and assure herself of her safety.

She gave a dazed look at the tall clock, and was beginning to put on her cloak when the door opened and Patty entered the kitchen by way of the shed; the usual Patty, rosy, buoyant, alert, with a kind of childlike innocence that could hardly be associated with the possession of wedding-rings.

"Are you going out, Waity? Wrap up well, for it's freezing cold. Waity, Waity, dear! What's the matter?" she cried, coming closer to her sister in alarm.

Waitstill's face had lost its clear color, and her eyes had the look of some dumb animal that has been struck and wounded. She sank into the flag-bottomed rocker by the window, and leaning back her head, uttered no word, but closed her eyes and gave one long, shivering sigh and a dry sob that seemed drawn from the very bottom of her heart.

XXVII. THE CONFESSIONAL

"WAITY, I know what it is; you have found out about me! Who has been wicked enough to tell you before I could do so—tell me, who?"

"Oh, Patty, Patty!" cried Waitstill, who could no longer hold back her tears. "How could you deceive me so? How could you shut me out of your heart and keep a secret like this from me, who have tried to be mother and sister in one to you ever since the day you were born? God has sent me much to bear, but nothing so bitter as this—to have my sister take the greatest step of her life without my knowledge or counsel!"

"Stop, dear, stop, and let me tell you!"

"All is told, and not by you as it should have been. We've never had anything separate from each other in all our lives, and when I looked in your bureau drawer for a bit of soft cotton—it was nothing more than I have done a hundred times—you can guess now what I stumbled upon; a wedding-ring for a hand I have held ever since it was a baby's. My sister has a husband, and I am not even sure of his name!"

"Waity, Waity, don't take it so to heart!" and Patty flung herself on her knees beside Waitstill's chair. "Not till you hear everything! When I tell you all, you will dry your eyes and smile and be happy about me, and you will know that in the whole world there is no one else in my love or my life but you and my—my husband."

"Who is the husband?" asked Waitstill dryly, as she wiped her eyes and leaned her elbow on the table.

"Who could it be but Mark? Has there ever been any one but Mark?"

"I should have said that there were several, in these past few months."

Waitstill's tone showed clearly that she was still grieved and hurt beyond her power to conceal. "I have never thought of marrying any one but Mark, and not even of marrying him till a little while ago," said Patty. "Now do not draw away from me and look out of the window as if we were not sisters, or you will break my heart. Turn your eyes to mine and believe in me, Waity, while I tell you everything, as I have so longed to do all these nights and days. Mark and I have loved each other for a long, long time. It was only play at first, but we were young and foolish and did not understand what was really happening between us."

"You are both of you only a few months older than when you were 'young and foolish,'" objected Waitstill.

"Yes, we are—years and years! Five weeks ago I promised Mark that I would marry him; but how was I ever to keep my word publicly? You have noticed how insultingly father treats him of late, passing him by without a word when he meets him in the street? You remember, too, that he has never gone to Lawyer Wilson for advice, or put any business in his hands since spring?"

"The Wilsons are among father's aversions, that is all you can say; it is no use to try and explain them or rebel against them," Waitstill answered wearily.

"That is all very well, and might be borne like many another cross; but I wanted to marry this particular 'aversion,'" argued Patty. "Would you have helped me to marry Mark secretly if I had confided in you?"

"Never in the world—never!"

"I knew it," exclaimed Patty triumphantly. "We both said so! And what was Mark to do? He was more than willing to come up here and ask for me like a man, but he knew that he would be ordered off the premises as if he were a thief. That would have angered Mr. and Mrs. Wilson, and made matters worse. We talked and talked until we were hoarse; we thought and thought until we nearly had brain fever from thinking, but there seemed to be no way but to take the bull by the horns."

"You are both so young, you could well have bided awhile."

"We could have bided until we were gray, nothing would have changed father; and just lately I couldn't make Mark bide," confessed Patty ingenuously. "He has been in a rage about father's treatment of you and me. He knows we haven't the right food to eat, nothing fit to wear, and not an hour of peace or freedom. He has even heard the men at the store say that our very lives might be in danger if we crossed father's will, or angered him beyond a certain point. You can't blame a man who loves a girl, if he wants to take her away from such a wretched life. His love would be good for nothing if he did not long to rescue her!"

"I would never have left you behind to bear your slavery alone, while I slipped away to happiness and comfort—not for any man alive would I I have done it!" This speech, so unlike Waitstill in its ungenerous reproach, was repented of as soon as it left her tongue. "Oh, I did not mean that, my darling!" she cried. "I would have welcomed any change for you, and thanked God for it, if only it could have come honorably and aboveboard."

"But, don't you see, Waity, how my marriage helps everything? That is what makes me happiest; that now I shall have a home and it can be yours. Father has plenty of money and can get a housekeeper. He is only sixty-five, and as hale and hearty as a man can be. You have served your time, and surely you need not be his drudge for the rest of your life. Mark and I thought you would spend half the year with us."

Waitstill waived this point as too impossible for discussion. "When and where were you married, Patty?" she asked.

"In Allentown, New Hampshire, last Monday, the day you and father went to Saco. Ellen went with us. You needn't suppose it was much fun for me! Girls that think running away to be married is nothing but a lark, do not have to deceive a sister like you, nor have a father such as mine to reckon with afterwards."

"You thought of all that before, didn't you, child?"

"Nobody that hasn't already run away to be married once or twice could tell how it was going to feel! Never did I pass so unhappy a day! If Mark was not everything that is kind and gentle, he would have tipped me out of the sleigh into a snowbank and left me by the roadside to freeze. I might have been murdered instead of only married, by the way I behaved; but Mark and Ellen understood. Then, the very next day, Mark's father sent him up to Bridgton on business, and he had to go to Allentown first to return a friend's horse, so he couldn't break the news to father at once, as he intended."

"Does a New Hampshire marriage hold good in Maine?" asked Waitstill, still intent on the bare facts at the bottom of the romance.

"Well, of course," stammered Patty, some-what confused, "Maine has her own way of doing things, and wouldn't be likely to fancy New Hampshire's. But nothing can make it wicked or anything but according to law. Besides, Mark considered all the difficulties. He is wonderfully clever, and he has a clerkship in a Portsmouth law office waiting for him; and that's where we are going to live, in New Hampshire, where we were married, and my darling sister will come soon and stay months and months with us."

"When is Mark coming back to arrange all this?"

"Late to-night or early to-morrow morning. Where did you go after you were married?"

"Where did I go?" echoed Patty, in a childish burst of tears. "Where could I go? It took all day to be married—all day long, working and driving hard from sunrise to seven o'clock in the evening. Then when we reached the bridge, Mark dropped me, and I walked up home in the dark, and went to bed without any supper, for fear that you and father would come back and catch me at it and ask why I was so late."

"My poor, foolish dear!" sighed Waitstill.

Patty's tears flowed faster at the first sound of sympathy in Waitstill's voice, for self-pity is very enfeebling. She fairly sobbed as she continued:—

"So my only wedding-journey was the freezing drive back from Allentown, with Ellen crying all the way and wishing that she hadn't gone with us. Mark and I both say we'll never be married again so long as we live!"

"Where have you seen your husband from that day to this?"

"I haven't laid eyes on him!" said Patty, with a fresh burst of woe. "I have a certificate-thing, and a wedding-ring and a beautiful frock and hat that Mark bought in Boston, but no real husband. I'm no more married than ever I was! Don't you remember I said that Mark was sent away on Tuesday morning? And this is Thursday. I've had three letters from him; but I don't know, till we see how father takes it, when we can tell the Wilsons and start for Portsmouth. We shan't really call ourselves married till we get to Portsmouth; we promised each other that from the first. It isn't much like being a bride, never to see your bridegroom; to have a father who will fly into a passion when he hears that you are married; not to know whether your new family will like or despise you; and to have your only sister angered with you for the first time in her life!"

Waitstill's heart melted, and she lifted Patty's tear-stained face to hers and kissed it. "Well, dear, I would not have had you do this for the world, but it is done, and Mark seems to have been as wise as a man can be when he does an unwise thing. You are married, and you love each other. That's the comforting thing to me."

"We do," sobbed Patty. "No two people ever loved each other better than we; but it's been all spoiled for fear of father."

"I must say I dread to have him hear the news"; and Waitstill knitted her brows anxiously. "I hope it may be soon, and I think I ought to be here when he is told. Mark will never under-stand or bear with him, and there may be trouble that I could avert."

"I'll be here, too, and I'm not afraid!" And Patty raised her head defiantly. "Father can unmarry us, that's why we acted in this miserable, secret, underhanded way. Somehow, though I haven't seen Mark since we went to Allentown, I am braver than I was last week, for now I've got somebody to take my part. I've a good mind to go upstairs and put on my gold beads and my wedding-ring, just to get used to them and to feel a little more married.—No: I can't, after all, for there is father driving up the hill now, and he may come into the house. What brings him home at this hour?"

"I was expecting him every moment"; and Waitstill rose and stirred the fire. "He took the pung and went to the Mills for grain."

"He hasn't anything in the back of the pung—and, oh, Waity! he is standing up now and whipping the horse with all his might. I never saw him drive like that before: what can be the matter? He can't have seen my wedding-ring, and only three people in all the world know about my being married."

Waitstill turned from the window, her heart beating a little faster. "What three people know, three hundred are likely to know sooner or later. It may be a false alarm, but father is in a fury about something. He must not be told the news until he is in a better humor!"

XXVIII. PATTY IS SHOWN THE DOOR

DEACON BAXTER drove into the barn, and flinging a blanket over the wheezing horse, closed the door behind him and hurried into the house without even thinking to lay down his whip.

Opening the kitchen door and stopping outside long enough to kick the snow from his heavy boots, he strode into the kitchen and confronted the two girls. He looked at them sharply before he spoke, scanning their flushed faces and tear-stained eyes; then he broke out savagely:—

"Oh! you're both here; that's lucky. Now stan' up and answer to me. What's this I hear at the Mills about Patience,—common talk outside the store?"

The time had come, then, and by some strange fatality, when Mark was too far away to be of service.

"Tell me what you heard, father, and I can give you a better answer," Patty replied, hedging to gain time, and shaking inwardly.

"Bill Morrill says his brother that works in New Hampshire reports you as ridin' through the streets of Allentown last Monday with a young man."

There seemed but one reply to this, so Patty answered tremblingly: "He says what's true; I was there."

"WHAT!" And it was plain from the Deacon's voice that he had really disbelieved the rumor. A whirlwind of rage swept through him and shook him from head to foot.

"Do you mean to stan' there an' own up to me that you was thirty miles away from home with a young man?" he shouted.

"If you ask me a plain question, I've got to tell you the truth, father: I was."

"How dare you carry on like that and drag my name into scandal, you worthless trollop, you? Who went along with you? I'll skin the hide off him, whoever 't was!"

Patty remained mute at this threat, but Waitstill caught her hand and whispered: "Tell him all, dear; it's got to come out. Be brave, and I'll stand by you."

"Why are you interferin' and puttin' in your meddlesome oar?" the Deacon said, turning to Waitstill. "The girl would never 'a' been there if you'd attended to your business. She's nothin' but a fool of a young filly, an' you're an old cart-horse. It was your job to look out for her as your mother told you to. Anybody might 'a' guessed she needed watchin'!"

"You shall not call my sister an old cart-horse! I'll not permit it!" cried Patty, plucking up courage in her sister's defence, and as usual comporting herself a trifle more like a spitfire than a true heroine of tragedy.

"Hush, Patty! Let him call me anything that he likes; it makes no difference at such a time."

"Waitstill knew nothing of my going away till this afternoon," continued Patty. "I kept it secret from her on purpose, because I was afraid she would not approve. I went with Mark Wilson, and—and—I married him in New Hampshire because we couldn't do it at home without every-body's knowledge. Now you know all."

"Do you mean to tell me you've gone an' married that reckless, wuthless, horse-trottin', card-playin' sneak of a Wilson boy that's courted every girl in town? Married the son of a man that has quarrelled with me and insulted me in public? By the Lord Harry, I'll crack this whip over your shoulders once before I'm done with you! If I'd used it years ago you might have been an honest woman to-day, instead of a—"

Foxwell Baxter had wholly lost control of himself, and the temper, that had never been governed or held in check, lashed itself into a fury that made him for the moment unaccountable for his words or actions.

"Put down that whip, Father, or I'll take it from you."

Waitstill took a step forward in front of Patty. "Put down that whip, father, or I'll take it from you and break it across my knee!" Her eyes blazed and she held her head high. "You've made me do the work of a man, and, thank God, I've got the muscle of one. Don't lift a finger to Patty, or I'll defend her, I promise you! The dinner-horn is in the side entry and two blasts will bring Uncle Bart up the hill, but I'd rather not call him unless you force me to."

The Deacon's grasp on the whip relaxed, and he fell back a little in sheer astonishment at the bravado of the girl, ordinarily so quiet and self-contained. He was speechless for a second, and then recovered breath enough to shout to the terrified Patty: "I won't use the whip till I hear whether you've got any excuse for your scandalous behavior. Hear me tell you one thing: this little pleasure-trip o' yourn won't do you no good, for I'll break the marriage! I won't have a Wilson in my family if I have to empty a shot-gun into him; but your lies and your low streets are so beyond reason I can't believe my ears. What's your excuse, I say?"

"Stop a minute, Patty, before you answer, and let me say a few things that ought to have been said before now," interposed Waitstill. "If Patty has done wrong, father, you've no one but yourself to thank for it, and it's only by God's grace that nothing worse has happened to her. What could you expect from a young thing like that, with her merry heart turned into a lump in her breast every day by your cruelty? Did she deceive you? Well, you've made her afraid of you ever since she was a baby in the cradle, drawing the covers over her little head when she heard your step. Whatever crop you sow is bound to come up, father; that's Nature's law, and God's, as well."

"You hold your tongue, you,—readin' the law to your elders an' betters," said the old man, choking with wrath. "My business is with this wuthless sister o' yourn, not with you!—You've got your coat and hood on, miss, so you jest clear out o' the house; an' if you're too slow about it, I'll help you along. I've no kind of an idea you're rightly married, for that young Wilson sneak couldn't pay so high for you as all that; but if it amuses you to call him your husband, go an' find him an' stay with him. This is an honest house, an' no place for such as you!"

Patty had a good share of the Baxter temper, not under such control as Waitstill's, and the blood mounted into her face.

"You shall not speak to me so!" she said intrepidly, while keeping a discreet eye on the whip. "I'm not a—a—caterpillar to be stepped on, I'm a married woman, as right as a New Hampshire justice can make me, with a wedding-ring and a certificate to show, if need be. And you shall not call my husband names! Time will tell what he is going to be, and that's a son-in-law any true father would be proud to own!"

"Why are you set against this match, father?" argued Waitstill, striving to make him hear reason. "Patty has married into one of the best families in the village. Mark is gay and thought-less, but never has he been seen the worse for liquor, and never has he done a thing for which a wife need hang her head. It is something for a young fellow of four-and-twenty to be able to provide for a wife and keep her in comfort; and when all is said and done, it is a true love-match."

Patty seized this inopportune moment to forget her father's presence, and the tragic nature of the occasion, and, in her usual impetuous fashion, flung her arms around Waitstill's neck and gave her the hug of a young bear.

"My own dear sister," she said. "I don't mind anything, so long as you stand up for us."

"Don't make her go to-night, father," pleaded Waitstill. "Don't send your own child out into the cold. Remember her husband is away from home."

"She can find another up at the Mills as good as he is, or better. Off with you, I say, you trumpery little baggage, you!"

"Go, then, dear, it is better so; Uncle Bart will keep you overnight; run up and get your things"; and Waitstill sank into a chair, realizing the hopelessness of the situation.

"She'll not take anything from my house. It's her husband's business to find her in clothes."

"They'll be better ones than ever you found me," was Patty's response.

No heroics for her; no fainting fits at being disowned; no hysterics at being turned out of house and home; no prayers for mercy, but a quick retort for every gibe from her father; and her defiant attitude enraged the Deacon the more.

"I won't speak again," he said, in a tone that could not be mistaken. "Into the street you go, with the clothes you stand up in, or I'll do what I said I'd do."

"Go, Patty, it's the only thing to be done. Don't tremble, for nobody shall touch a hair of your head. I can trust you to find shelter to-night, and Mark will take care of you to-morrow."

Patty buttoned her shabby coat and tied on her hood as she walked from the kitchen through the sitting-room towards the side door, her heart heaving with shame and anger, and above all with a child's sense of helplessness at being parted from her sister.

"Don't tell the neighbors any more lies than you can help," called her father after her retreating form; "an' if any of 'em dare to come up here an' give me any of their imperdence, they'll be treated same as you. Come back here, Waitstill, and don't go to slobberin' any good-byes over her. She ain't likely to get out o' the village for some time if she's expectin' Mark Wilson to take her away."

"I shall certainly go to the door with my sister," said Waitstill coldly, suiting the action to the word, and following Patty out on the steps. "Shall you tell Uncle Bart everything, dear, and ask him to let you sleep at his house?"

Both girls were trembling with excitement; Waitstill pale as a ghost, Patty flushed and tearful, with defiant eyes and lips that quivered rebelliously.

"I s'pose so," she answered dolefully; "though Aunt Abby hates me, on account of Cephas. I'd rather go to Dr. Perry's, but I don't like to meet Phil. There doesn't seem to be any good place for me, but it's only for a night. And you'll not let father prevent your seeing Mark and me to-morrow, will you? Are you afraid to stay alone? I'll sit on the steps all night if you say the word."

"No, no, run along. Father has vented his rage upon you, and I shall not have any more trouble. God bless and keep you, darling. Run along!"

"And you're not angry with me now, Waity? You still love me? And you'll forgive Mark and come to stay with us soon, soon, soon?"

"We'll see, dear, when all this unhappy business is settled, and you are safe and happy in your own home. I shall have much to tell you when we meet to-morrow."

XXIX. WAITSTILL SPEAKS HER MIND

Patty had the most ardent love for her elder sister, and something that resembled reverence for her unselfishness, her loyalty, and her strength of character; but if the truth were told she had no great opinion of Waitstill's ability to feel righteous wrath, nor of her power to avenge herself in the face of rank injustice. It was the conviction of her own superior finesse and audacity that had sustained patty all through her late escapade. She felt herself a lucky girl, indeed, to achieve liberty and happiness for herself, but doubly lucky if she had chanced to open a way of escape for her more docile and dutiful sister.

She would have been a trifle astonished had she surmised the existence of certain mysterious waves that had been sweeping along the coasts of Waitstill's mind that afternoon, breaking down all sorts of defences and carrying her will along with them by sheer force: but it is a truism that two human beings can live beside each other for half a century and yet continue strangers.

Patty's elopement with the youth of her choice, taking into account all its attendant risks, was Indeed an exhibition of courage and initiative not common to girls of seventeen; but Waitstill was meditating a mutiny more daring yet—a mutiny, too, involving a course of conduct most unusual in maidens of puritan descent.

She walked back into the kitchen to find her father sitting placidly in the rocking-chair by the window. He had lighted his corn-cob pipe, in which he always smoked a mixture of dried sweet-fern as being cheaper than tobacco, and his face wore something resembling a smile—a foxy smile—as he watched his youngest-born ploughing down the hill through the deep snow, while the more obedient Waitstill moved about the room, setting supper on the table.

Conversation was not the Deacon's forte, but it seemed proper for some one to break the ice that seemed suddenly to be very thick in the immediate vicinity.

"That little Jill-go-over-the-ground will give the neighbors a pleasant evenin' tellin' 'em 'bout me," he chuckled. "Aunt Abby Cole will run the streets o' the three villages by sun-up to-morrer; but nobody pays any 'tention to a woman whose tongue is hung in the middle and wags at both ends. I wa'n't intending to use the whip on your sister, Waitstill," continued the Deacon, with a crafty look at his silent daughter, "though a trouncin' would 'a' done her a sight o' good; but I was only tryin' to frighten her a little mite an' pay her up for bringin' disgrace on us the way she's done, makin' us the talk o' the town. Well, she's gone, an' good riddance to bad rubbish, say I! One less mouth to feed, an' one less body to clothe. You'll miss her jest at first, on account o' there bein' no other women-folks on the hill, but 't won't last long. I'll have Bill Morrill do some o' your outside chores, so 't you can take on your sister's work, if she ever done any."

This was a most astoundingly generous proposition on the Deacon's part, and to tell the truth he did not himself fully understand his mental processes when he made it; but it seemed to be drawn from him by a kind of instinct that he was not standing well in his elder daughter's books. Though the two girls had never made any demonstration of their affection in his presence, he had a fair idea of their mutual dependence upon each other. Not that he placed the slightest value on Waitstill's opinion of him, or cared in the smallest degree what she, or any one else in the universe, thought of his conduct; but she certainly did appear to advantage when contrasted with the pert little hussy who had just left the premises. Also, Waitstill loomed large in his household comforts and economies, having a clear head, a sure hand, and being one of the steady-going, reliable sort that can be counted on in emergencies, not, like Patty, going off at half-cock at the smallest provocation. Yes, Waitstill, as a product of his masterly training for the last seven years, had settled down, not without some trouble and friction, into a tolerably dependable pack-horse, and he intended in the future to use some care in making permanent so valuable an aid and ally. She did not pursue nor attract the opposite sex, as his younger daughter apparently did; so by continuing his policy of keeping all young men rigidly at a distance he could count confidently on having', Waitstill serve his purposes for the next fifteen or twenty years, or as long as he, himself, should continue to ornament and enrich the earth. He would go to Saco the very next day, and cut Patty out of his will, arranging his property so that Waitstill should be the chief legatee as long as she continued to live obediently under his roof. He intended to make the last point clear if he had to consult every lawyer in York County; for he wouldn't take risks on any woman alive.

If he must leave his money anywhere—and it was with a bitter pang that he faced the inexorable conviction that he could neither live forever, nor take his savings with him to the realms of bliss prepared for members of the Orthodox Church in good and regular standing—if he must leave his money behind him, he would dig a hole in the ground and bury it, rather than let it go to any one who had angered him in his lifetime.

These were the thoughts that caused him to relax his iron grip and smile as he sat by the window, smoking his corn-cob pipe and taking one of his very rare periods of rest.

Presently he glanced at the clock. "It's only quarter-past four," he said. "I thought 't was later, but the snow makes it so light you can't jedge the time. The moon fulls to-night, don't it? Yes; come to think of it, I know it does. Ain't you settin' out supper a little mite early, Waitstill?" This was a longer and more amiable speech than he had made in years, but Waitstill never glanced at him as she said: "It is a little early, but I want to get it ready before I leave."

"Be you goin' out? Mind, I won't have you follerin' Patience round; you'll only upset what I've done, an' anyhow I want you to keep away from the neighbors for a few days, till all this blows over."

He spoke firmly, though for him mildly, for he still had the uneasy feeling that he stood on the brink of a volcano; and, as a matter of fact, he tumbled into it the very next moment.

The meagre supper was spread; a plate of cold; soda biscuits, a dried-apple pie, and the usual brown teapot were in evidence; and as her father ceased speaking Waitstill opened the door of the brick oven where the bean-pot reposed, set a chair by the table, and turning, took up her coat (her mother's old riding-cloak, it was), and calmly put it on, reaching then for her hood and her squirrel tippet.

"You are goin' out, then, spite o' what I said?" the Deacon inquired sternly.

"Did you really think, father, that I would sleep under your roof after you had turned my sister out into the snow to lodge with whoever might take her in—my seventeen year-old-sister that your wife left to my care; my little sister, the very light of my life?"

Waitstill's voice trembled a trifle, but other-wise she was quite calm and free from heroics of any sort.

The Deacon looked up in surprise. "I guess you're kind o' hystericky," he said. "Set down—set down an' talk things over. I ain't got nothin' ag'in' you, an' I mean to treat you right. Set down!"

The old man was decidedly nervous, and intended to keep his temper until there was a safer chance to let it fly.

Waitstill sat down. "There's nothing to talk over," she said. "I have done all that I promised my stepmother the night she died, and now I am going. If there's a duty owed between daughter and father, it ought to work both ways. I consider that I have done my share, and now I intend to seek happiness for myself. I have never had any, and I am starving for it."

"An' you'd leave me to git on the best I can, after what I've done for you?" burst out the Deacon, still trying to hold down his growing passion.

"You gave me my life, and I'm thankful to you for that, but you've given me little since, father."

"Hain't I fed an' clothed you?"

"No more than I have fed and clothed you. You've provided the raw food, and I've cooked and served it. You've bought and I have made shirts and overalls and coats for you, and knitted your socks and comforters and mittens. Not only have I toiled and saved and scrimped away my girlhood as you bade me, but I've earned for you. Who made the butter, and took care of the hens, and dried the apples, and 'drew in' the rugs? Who raised and ground the peppers for sale, and tended the geese that you might sell the feathers? No, father, I don't consider that I'm in your debt!"

XXX. A CLASH OF WILLS

DEACON FOXWELL BAXTER was completely non-plussed for the first time in his life. He had never allowed "argyfyin'" in his household, and there had never been a clash of wills before this when he had not come off swiftly and brutally triumphant. This situation was complicated by the fact that he did not dare to apply the brakes as usual, since there were more issues involved than ever before. He felt too stunned to deal properly with this daughter, having emptied all the vials of his wrath upon the other one, and being, in consequence, somewhat enfeebled. It was always easy enough to cope with Patty, for her impertinence evoked such rage that the argument took care of itself; but this grave young woman was a different matter. There she sat composedly on the edge of her wooden chair, her head lifted high, her color coming and going, her eyes shining steadily, like fixed stars; there she sat, calmly announcing her intention of leaving her father to shift for himself; yet the skies seemed to have no thought of falling! He felt that he must make another effort to assert his authority.

"Now, you take off your coat," he said, the pipe in his hand trembling as he stirred nervously in his chair. "You take your coat right off an' set down to the supper-table, same as usual, do you hear? Eat your victuals an' then go to your bed an' git over this crazy fit that Patience has started workin' in you. No more nonsense, now; do as I tell you!"

"I have made up my mind, father, and it's no use arguing. All who try to live with you fail, sooner or later. You have had four children, father. One boy ran away; the other did not mind being drowned, I fear, since life was so hard at home. You have just turned the third child out for a sin of deceit and disobedience she would never have committed—for her nature is as clear as crystal—if you had ever loved her or considered her happiness. So I have done with you, unless in your old age God should bring you to such a pass that no one else will come to your assistance; then I'd see somehow that you were cared for and nursed and made comfortable. You are not an old man; you are strong and healthy, and you have plenty of money to get a good house-keeper. I should decide differently, perhaps, if all this were not true."

"You lie! I haven't got plenty of money!" And the Deacon struck the table a sudden blow that made the china in the cupboard rattle. "You've no notion what this house costs me, an' the feed for the stock, an' you two girls, an' labor at the store, an' the hay-field, an' the taxes an' insurance! I've slaved from sunrise to sunset but I ain't hardly been able to lay up a cent. I s'pose the neighbors have been fillin' you full o' tales about my mis'able little savin's an' makin' 'em into a fortune. Well, you won't git any of 'em, I promise you that!"

"You have plenty laid away; everybody knows, so what's the use of denying it? Anyway, I don't want a penny of your money, father, so good-bye. There's enough cooked to keep you for a couple of days"; and Waitstill rose from her chair and drew on her mittens.

Father and daughter confronted each other, the secret fury of the man met by the steady determination of the girl. The Deacon was baffled, almost awed, by Waitstill's quiet self-control; but at the very moment that he was half-uncomprehendingly glaring at her, it dawned upon him that he was beaten, and that she was mistress of the situation.

Where would she go? What were her plans?—for definite plans she had, or she could not meet his eye with so resolute a gaze. If she did leave him, how could he contrive to get her back again, and so escape the scorn of the village, the averted look, the lessened trade?

"Where are you goin' now?" he asked, and though he tried his best he could not for the life of him keep back one final taunt. "I s'pose, like your sister, you've got a man in your eye?" He chose this, to him, impossible suggestion as being the most insulting one that he could invent at the moment.

"I have," replied Waitstill, "a man in my eye and in my heart. We should have been husband and wife before this had we not been kept apart by obstacles too stubborn for us to overcome. My way has chanced to open first, though it was none of my contriving."

Had the roof fallen in upon him, the Deacon could not have been more dumbfounded. His tongue literally clove to the roof of his mouth; his face fell, and his mean, piercing eyes blinked under his shaggy brows as if seeking light.

Waitstill stirred the fire, closed the brick oven and put the teapot on the back of the stove, hung up the long-handled dipper on its accustomed nail over the sink, and went to the door.

Her father collected his scattered wits and pulled himself to his feet by the arms of the high-backed rocker. "You shan't step outside this 306 room till you tell me where you're goin'," he said when he found his voice.

"I have no wish to keep it secret: I am going to see if Mrs. Mason will keep me to-night. To-morrow I shall walk down river and get work at the mills, but on my way I shall stop at the Boyntons' to tell Ivory I am ready to marry him as soon as he's ready to take me."

This was enough to stir the blood of the Deacon into one last fury.

"I might have guessed it if I hadn't been blind as a bat an' deaf as an adder!" And he gave the table another ringing blow before he leaned on it to gather strength. "Of course, it would be one o' that crazy Boynton crew you'd take up with," he roared. "Nothin' would suit either o' you girls but choosin' the biggest enemies I've got in the whole village!"

"You've never taken pains to make anything but enemies, so what could we do?"

"You might as well go to live on the poor-farm! Aaron Boynton was a disrep'table hound; Lois Boynton is as crazy as a loon; the boy is a nobody's child, an' Ivory's no better than a common pauper."

"Ivory's a brave, strong, honorable man, and a scholar, too. I can work for him and help him earn and save, as I have you."

"How long's this been goin' on?" The Deacon was choking, but he meant to get to the bottom of things while he had the chance.

"It has not gone on at all. He has never said a word to me, and I have always obeyed your will in these matters; but you can't hide love, any more than you can hide hate. I know Ivory loves me, so I'm going to tell him that my duty is done here and I am ready to help him."

"Goin' to throw yourself at his head, be you?" sneered the Deacon. "By the Lord, I don' know where you two girls got these loose ways o' think-in' an' acting mebbe he won't take you, an' then where'll you be? You won't git under my roof again when you've once left it, you can make up your mind to that!"

"If you have any doubts about Ivory's being willing to take me, you'd better drive along behind me and listen while I ask him."

Waitstill's tone had an exultant thrill of certainty in it. She threw up her head, glorying in what she was about to do. If she laid aside her usual reserve and voiced her thoughts openly, it was not in the hope of convincing her father, but for the bliss of putting them into words and intoxicating herself by the sound of them.

"Come after me if you will, father, and watch the welcome I shall get. Oh! I have no fear of being turned out by Ivory Boynton. I can hardly wait to give him the joy I shall be bringing! It 's selfish to rob him of the chance to speak first, but I'll do it!" And before Deacon Baxter could cross the room, Waitstill was out of the kitchen door into the shed, and flying down Town-House Hill like an arrow shot free from the bow.

The Deacon followed close behind, hardly knowing why, but he was no match for the girl, and at last he stood helpless on the steps of the shed, shaking his fist and hurling terrible words after her, words that it was fortunate for her peace of mind she could not hear.

"A curse upon you both!" he cried savagely. "Not satisfied with disobeyin' an' defyin' me, you've put me to shame, an' now you'll be settin' the neighbors ag'in' me an' ruinin' my trade. If you was freezin' in the snow I wouldn't heave a blanket to you! If you was starvin' I wouldn't fling either of you a crust! Never shall you darken my doors again, an' never shall you git a penny o' my money, not if I have to throw it into the river to spite you!"

Here his breath failed, and he stumbled out into the barn whimpering between his broken sentences like a whipped child.

"Here I am with nobody to milk, nor feed the hens; nobody to churn tomorrow, nor do the chores; a poor, mis'able creeter, deserted by my children, with nobody to do a hand's turn 'thout bein' paid for every step they take! I'll give 'em what they deserve; I don' know what, but I'll be even with 'em yet." And the Deacon set his Baxter jaw in a way that meant his determination to stop at nothing.

XXXI. SENTRY DUTY

IVORY BOYNTON drove home from the woods that same afternoon by way of the bridge, in order to buy some provisions at the brick store. When he was still a long distance from the bars that divided the lane from the highroad, he espied a dark-clad little speck he knew to be Rodman leaning over the fence, waiting and longing as usual for his home-coming, and his heart warmed at the thought of the boyish welcome that never failed.

The sleigh slipped quickly over the hard-packed, shining road, and the bells rang merrily in the clear, cold air, giving out a joyous sound that had no echo in Ivory's breast that day. He had just had a vision of happiness through another man's eyes. Was he always to stand outside the banqueting-table, he wondered, and see others feasting while he hungered.

Now the little speck bounded from the fence, flew down the road to meet the sleigh, and jumped in by the driver's side.

"I knew you'd come to-night," Rodman cried eagerly. "I told Aunt Boynton you'd come."

"How is she, well as common?"

"No, not a bit well since yesterday morning, but Mrs. Mason says it's nothing worse than a cold. Mrs. Mason has just gone home, and we've had a grand house-cleaning to-day. She's washed and ironed and baked, and we've put Aunt Boynton in clean sheets and pillow-cases, and her room's nice and warm, and I carried the cat in and put it on her bed to keep her company while I came to watch for you. Aunt Boynton let Mrs. Mason braid her hair, and seemed to like her brushing it. It's been dreadful lonesome, and oh! I am glad you came back, Ivory. Did you find any more spruce gum where you went this time?"

"Pounds and pounds, Rod; enough to bring me in nearly a hundred dollars. I chanced on the greatest place I've found yet. I followed the wake of an old whirlwind that had left long furrows in the forest,—I've told you how the thing works,—and I tracked its course by the gum that had formed wherever the trees were wounded. It's hard, lonely work, Rod, but it pays well."

"If I could have been there, maybe we could have got more. I'm good at shinning up trees."

"Yes, sometime we'll go gum-picking together. We'll climb the trees like a couple of cats, and take our knives and serape off the precious lumps that are worth so much money to the druggists. You've let down the bars, I see."

"'Cause I knew you'd come to-night," said Rodman. "I felt it in my bones. We're going to have a splendid supper."

"Are we? That's good news." Ivory tried to make his tone bright and interested, though his heart was like a lump of lead in his breast. "It's the least I can do for the poor little chap," he thought, "when he stays as caretaker in this lonely spot.—I wonder if I hadn't better drive into the barn, Rod, and leave the harness on Nick till I go in and see mother? Guess I will."

"She's hot, Aunt Boynton is, hot and restless, but Mrs. Mason thinks that's all."

Ivory found his mother feverish, and her eyes were unnaturally bright; but she was clear in her mind and cheerful, too, sitting up in bed to breathe the better, while the Maltese cat snuggled under her arm and purred peacefully.

"The cat is Rod's idea," she said smilingly but in a very weak voice. "He is a great nurse I should never have thought of the cat myself but she gives me more comfort than all the medicine."

Ivory and Rodman drew up to the supper table, already set in the kitchen, but before Ivory took his seat he softly closed the door that led into the living-room. They ate their beans and brown bread and the mince pie that had been the "splendid" feature of the meal, as reported by the boy; and when they had finished, and Rodman was clearing the table, Ivory walked to the window, lighting his pipe the while, and stood soberly looking out on the snowy landscape. One could scarcely tell it was twilight, with such sweeps of whiteness to catch every gleam of the dying day.

"Drop work a minute and come here, Rod," he said at length. "Can you keep a secret?"

"'Course I can! I'm chock full of 'em now, and nobody could dig one of 'em out o' me with a pickaxe!"

"Oh, well! If you're full you naturally couldn't hold another!"

"I could try to squeeze it in, if it's a nice one," coaxed the boy.

"I don't know whether you'll think it's a nice one, Rod, for it breaks up one of your plans. I'm not sure myself how nice it is, but it's a very big, unexpected, startling one. What do you think? Your favorite Patty has gone and got married."

"Patty! Married!" cried Rod, then hastily putting his hand over his mouth to hush his too-loud speaking.

"Yes, she and Mark Wilson ran away last Monday, drove over to Allentown, New Hampshire, and were married without telling a soul. Deacon Baxter discovered everything this afternoon, like the old fox that he is, and turned Patty out of the house."

"Mean old skinflint!" exclaimed Rod excitedly, all the incipient manhood rising in his ten-year-old breast. "Is she gone to live with the Wilsons?"

"The Wilsons don't know yet that Mark is married to her, but I met him driving like Jehu, just after I had left Patty, and told him everything that had happened, and did my best to cool him down and keep him from murdering his new father-in-law by showing him it would serve no real purpose now."

"Did he look married, and all different?" asked Rod curiously.

"Yes, he did, and more like a man than ever he looked before in his life. We talked everything over together, and he went home at once to break the news to his family, without even going to take a peep at Patty. I couldn't bear to have them meet till he had something cheerful to say to the poor little soul. When I met her by Uncle Bart's shop, she was trudging along in the snow like a draggled butterfly, and crying like a baby."

Sympathetic tears dimmed Rodman's eyes. "I can't bear to see girls cry, Ivory. I just can't bear it, especially Patty."

"Neither can I, Rod. I came pretty near wiping her eyes, but pulled up, remembering she wasn't a child but a married lady. Well, now we come to the point."

"Isn't Patty's being married the point?"

"No, only part of it. Patty's being sent away from home leaves Waitstill alone with the Deacon, do you see? And if Patty is your favorite, Waitstill is mine—I might as well own up to that."

"She's mine, too," cried Rod. "They're both my favorites, but I always thought Patty was the suitablest for me to marry if she'd wait for me. Waitstill is too grand for a boy!"

"She's too grand for anybody, Rod. There isn't a man alive that's worthy to strap on her skates."

"Well, she's too grand for anybody except—" and here Rod's shy, wistful voice trailed off into discreet silence.

"Now I had some talk with Patty, and she thinks Waitstill will have no trouble with her father just at present. She says he lavished so much rage upon her that there'll be none left for anybody else for a day or two. And, moreover, that he will never dare to go too far with Waitstill, because she's so useful to him. I'm not afraid of his beating or injuring her so long as he keeps his sober senses, if he's ever rightly had any; but I don't like to think of his upbraiding her and breaking her heart with his cruel talk just after she's lost the sister that's been her only companion." And Ivory's hand trembled as he filled his pipe. He had no confidant but this quaint, tender-hearted, old-fashioned little lad, to whom he had grown to speak his mind as if he were a man of his own age; and Rod, in the same way, had gradually learned to understand and sympathize.

"It's dreadful lonesome on Town-House Hill," said the boy in a hushed tone.

"Dreadful lonesome," echoed Ivory with a sigh; "and I don't dare leave mother until her fever dies down a bit and she sleeps. Now do you remember the night that she was taken ill, and we shared the watch?"

Rodman held his breath. "Do you mean you're going to let me help just as if I was big?" he asked, speaking through a great lump in his throat.

"There are only two of us, Rod. You're rather young for this piece of work, but you're trusty—you're trusty!"

"Am I to keep watch on the Deacon?"

"That's it, and this is my plan: Nick will have had his feed; you're to drive to the bridge when it gets a little darker and hitch in Uncle Bart's horse-shed, covering Nick well. You're to go into the brick store, and while you're getting some groceries wrapped up, listen to anything the men say, to see if they know what's happened. When you've hung about as long as you dare, leave your bundle and say you'll call in again for it. Then see if Baxter's store is open. I don't believe it will be, and if it isn't, look for a light in his kitchen window, and prowl about till you know that Waitstill and the Deacon have gone up to their bedrooms. Then go to Uncle Bart's and find out if Patty is there."

Rod's eyes grew bigger and bigger: "Shall I talk to her?" he asked; "and what'll I say?"

"No, just ask if she's there. If she's gone, Mark has made it right with his family and taken her home. If she hasn't, why, God knows how that matter will be straightened out. Anyhow, she has a husband now, and he seems to value her; and Waitstill is alone on the top of that wind-swept hill!"

"I'll go. I'll remember everything," cried Rodman, in the seventh heaven of delight at the responsibilities Ivory was heaping upon him.

"Don't stay beyond eight o'clock; but come back and tell me everything you've learned. Then, if mother grows no worse, I'll walk back to Uncle Bart's shop and spend the night there, just—just to be near, that's all."

"You couldn't hear Waitstill, even if she called," Rod said.

"Couldn't I? A man's ears are very sharp under certain circumstances. I believe if Waitstill needed help I could hear her—breathe! Besides, I shall be up and down the hill till I know all's well; and at sunrise I'll go up and hide behind some of Baxter's buildings till I see him get his breakfast and go to the store. Now wash your dishes"; and Ivory caught up his cap from a hook behind the door.

"Are you going to the barn?" asked Rodman.

"No, only down to the gate for a minute. Mark said that if he had a good chance he'd send a boy with a note, and get him to put it under the stone gate-post. It's too soon to expect it, perhaps, but I can't seem to keep still."

Rodman tied a gingham apron round his waist, carried the tea-kettle to the sink, and poured the dishpan full of boiling water; then dipped the cups and plates in and out, wiped them and replaced them on the table' gave the bean-platter a special polish, and set the half mince pie and the butter-dish in the cellar-way.

"A boy has to do most everything in this family!" He sighed to himself. "I don't mind washing dishes, except the nasty frying-pan and the sticky bean-pot; but what I'm going to do to-night is different." Here he glowed and tingled with anticipation. "I know what they call it in the story-books—it's sentry duty; and that's braver work for a boy than dish-washing!"

Which, however, depends a good deal upon circumstances, and somewhat on the point of view.

XXXII. THE HOUSE OF AARON

A FEELING that the day was to bring great things had dawned upon Waitstill when she woke that morning, and now it was coming true.

Climbing Saco Hill was like climbing the hill of her dreams; life and love beckoned to her across the snowy slopes.

At rest about Patty's future, though troubled as to her sorry plight at the moment, she was conscious chiefly of her new-born freedom. She revelled in the keen air that tingled against her cheek, and drew in fresh hope with every breath. As she trod the shining pathway she was full of expectancy, her eyes dancing, her heart as buoyant as her step. Not a vestige of confusion or uncertainty vexed her mind. She knew Ivory for her true mate, and if the way to him took her through dark places it was lighted by a steadfast beacon of love.

At the top of the hill she turned the corner breathlessly, and faced the length of road that led to the Boynton farm. Mrs. Mason's house was beyond, and oh, how she hoped that Ivory would be at home, and that she need not wait another day to tell him all, and claim the gift she knew was hers before she asked it. She might not have the same exaltation tomorrow, for now there were no levels in her heart and soul. She had a sense of mounting from height to height and lighting fires on every peak of her being. She took no heed of the road she was travelling; she was conscious only of a wonderful inward glow.

The house was now in sight, and a tall figure was issuing from the side door, putting on a fur cap as it came out on the steps and down the lane. Ivory was at home, then, and, best of all, he was unconsciously coming to meet her—although their hearts had been coming to meet each other, she thought, ever since they first began to beat.

As she neared the bars she called Ivory's name. His hands were in the pockets of his great-coat, and his eyes were fixed on the ground. Sombre he was, distinctly sombre, in mien and gait; could she make him smile and flush and glow, as she was smiling and flushing and glowing? As he heard her voice he raised his head quickly and uncomprehendingly.

"Don't come any nearer," she said, "until I have told you something!" His mind had been so full of her that the sight of her in the flesh, standing twenty feet away, bewildered him.

She took a few steps nearer the gate, near enough now for him to see her rosy face framed in a blue hood, and to catch the brightness of her eyes under their lovely lashes. Ordinarily they were cool and limpid and grave, Waitstill's eyes; now a sunbeam danced in each of them. And her lips, almost always tightly closed, as if she were holding back her natural speech,—her lips were red and parted, and the soul of her, free at last, shone through her face, making it luminous with a new beauty.

"I have left home for good and all," she said. "I'll tell you more of this later on, but I have left my father's house with nothing to my name but the clothes I stand in. I am going to look for work in the mills to-morrow, but I stopped here to say that I'm ready to marry you whenever you want me—if you do want me."

Ivory was bewildered, indeed, but not so much so that he failed to apprehend, and instantly, too, the real significance of this speech.

He took a couple of long strides, and before Waitstill had any idea of his intentions he vaulted over the bars and gathered her in his arms.

"Never shall you go to the mills, never shall you leave my sight for a single hour again, my one-woman-in-all-the-world! Come to me, to be loved and treasured all your life long! I've worshipped you ever since I was a boy; I've kept my heart swept and garnished for you and no other, hoping I might win you at last."

How glorious to hear all this delicious poetry of love, and to feel Ivory's arms about her, making the dream seem surer!

"Oh, how like you to shorten the time of my waiting!" he went on, his words fairly chasing one another in their eagerness to be spoken. "How like you to count on me, to guess my hunger for your love, to realize the chains that held me back, and break them yourself with your own dear, womanly hands! How like you, oh, wonderful Waitstill!"

Ivory went on murmuring phrases that had been lying in his heart unsaid for years, scarcely conscious of what he was saying, realizing only that the miracle of miracles had happened.

Waitstill, for her part, was almost dumb with joy to be lying so close to his heart that she could hear it beating; to feel the passionate tenderness of his embrace and his kiss falling upon her hair.

"I did not know a girl could be so happy!" she whispered. "I've dreamed of it, but it was nothing like this. I am all a-tremble with it."

Ivory held her off at arm's length for a moment, reluctantly, grudgingly. "You took me fairly off my feet, dearest," he said, "and forgot everything but the one supreme fact you were telling me. Had I been on guard I should have told you that I am no worthy husband for you, Waitstill. I haven't enough to offer such a girl as you."

"You're too late, Ivory! You showed me your heart first, and now you are searching your mind for bugbears to frighten me."

"I am a poor man."

"No girl could be poorer than I am."

"After what you've endured, you ought to have rest and comfort."

"I shall have both—in you!" This with eyes, all wet, lifted to Ivory's.

"My mother is a great burden—a very dear and precious, but a grievous one."

"She needs a daughter. It is in such things that I shall be your helpmate."

"Will not the boy trouble you and add to your cares?"

"Rod? I love him; he shall be my little brother."

"What if my father were not really dead?—I think of this sometimes in the night!—What if he should wander back, broken in spirit, feeble in body, empty in purse?"

"I do not come to you free of burdens. If my father is deserted by all, I must see that he is made comfortable. He never treated me like a daughter, but I acknowledge his claim."

"Mine is such a gloomy house!"

"Will it be gloomy when I am in it?" and Waitstill, usually so grave, laughed at last like a care-free child.

Ivory felt himself hidden in the beautiful shelter of the girl's love. It was dark now, or as dark as the night ever is that has moonlight and snow. He took Waitstill in his arms again reverently, and laid his cheek against her hair. "I worship God as well as I know how," he whispered; "worship him as the maker of this big heaven and earth that surrounds us. But I worship you as the maker of my little heaven and earth, and my heart is saying its prayers to you at this very moment!"

"Hush, my dear! hush! and don't value me too much, or I shall lose my head—I that have never known a sweet word in all my life save those that my sister has given me.—I must tell you all about Patty now."

"I happen to know more than you, dear. I met her at the bridge when I was coming home from the woods, and I saw her safely to Uncle Bart's door.—I don't know why we speak of it as Uncle Bart's when it is really Aunt

Abby's!—I next met Mark, who had fairly flown from Bridgton on the wings of love, arriving hours ahead of time. I managed to keep him from avenging the insults heaped upon his bride, and he has driven to the Mills to confide in his father and mother. By this time Patty is probably the centre of the family group, charming them all as is her custom."

"Oh, I am so glad Mark is at home! Now I can be at rest about Patty. And I must not linger another moment, for I am going to ask Mrs. Mason to keep me overnight," cried Waitstill, bethinking herself suddenly of time and place.

"I will take you there myself and explain everything. And the moment I've lighted a fire in Mrs. Mason's best bedroom and settled you there, what do you think I am going to do? I shall drive to the town clerk's house, and if he is in bed, rout him out and have the notice of our intended marriage posted in a public place according to law. Perhaps I shall save a day out of the fourteen I've got to wait for my wife. 'Mills,' indeed! I wonder at you, Waitstill! As if Mrs. Mason's house was not far enough away, without your speaking of 'mills.'"

"I only suggested mills in case you did not want to marry me," said Waitstill.

"Walk up to the door with me," begged Ivory.

"The horse is all harnessed, and Rod will slip him into the sleigh in a jiffy."

"Oh, Ivory! do you realize what this means?"—and Waitstill clung to his arm as they went up the lane together—"that whatever sorrow, whatever hardship comes to us, neither of us will ever have to bear it alone again?"

"I believe I do realize it as few men could, for never in my five-and-twenty years have I had a human creature to whom I could pour myself out, in whom I could really confide, with whom I could take counsel. You can guess what it will be to have a comprehending woman at my side. Shall we tell my mother? Do say 'yes'; I believe she will understand.—Rod, Rod! come and see who's stepping in the door this very minute!"

Rodman was up in his bedroom, attiring himself elaborately for sentry duty. His delight at seeing Waitstill was perhaps slightly tempered by the thought that flashed at once through his mind,—that if she was safe, he would not be required to stand guard in the snow for hours as he had hoped. But this grief passed when he fully realized what Waitstill's presence at the farm at this unaccustomed hour really meant. After he had been told, he hung about her like the child that he was,—though he had a bit of the hero in him, at bottom, too,—embracing her waist fondly, and bristling with wondering questions.

"Is she really going to stay with us for always, Ivory?" he asked.

"Every day and all the days; every night and all the nights. 'Praise God from whom all blessings flow!'" said Ivory, taking off his fur cap and opening the door of the living-room. "But we've got to wait for her a whole fortnight, Rod. Isn't that a ridiculous snail of a law?"

"Patty didn't wait a fortnight."

"Patty never waited for anything," Ivory responded with a smile; "but she had a good reason, and, alas! we haven't, or they'll say that we haven't. And I am very grateful to the same dear little Patty, for when she got herself a husband she found me a wife!"

Rodman did not wholly understand this, but felt that there were many mysteries attending the love affairs of grown-up people that were too complicated for him to grasp; and it did not seem to be just the right moment for questions.

Waitstill and Ivory went into Mrs. Boynton's room quietly, hand in hand, and when she saw Waitstill she raised herself from her pillow and held out her arms with a soft cry of delight.

"I haven't had you for so long, so long!" she said, touching the girl's cheek with her frail hand.

"You are going to have me every day now, dear," whispered Waitstill, with a sob in her voice; for she saw a change in the face, a new transparency, a still more ethereal look than had been there before.

"Every day?" she repeated, longingly. Waitstill took off her hood, and knelt on the floor beside the bed, hiding her face in the counterpane to conceal the tears.

"She is coming to live with us, dear.—Come in, Rod, and hear me tell her.—Waitstill is coming to live with us: isn't that a beautiful thing to happen to this dreary house?" asked Ivory, bending to take his mother's hand.

"Don't you remember what you thought the first time I ever came here, mother?" and Waitstill lifted her head, and looked at Mrs. Boynton with swimming eyes and lips that trembled. "Ivory is making it all come true, and I shall be your daughter!"

Mrs. Boynton sank farther back into her pillows, and closing her eyes, gave a long sigh of infinite content. Her voice was so faint that they had to stoop to catch the words, and Ivory, feeling the strange benediction that seemed to be passing from his mother's spirit to theirs, took Rod's hand and knelt beside Waitstill.

The verse of a favorite psalm was running through Lois Boynton's mind, and in a moment the words came clearly, as she opened her eyes, lifted her hands, and touched the bowed heads. "Let the house of Aaron now say that his mercy endureth forever!" she said, slowly and reverently; and Ivory, with all his heart, responded, "Amen!"

XXXIII. AARON'S ROD

"IVORY! IVORY!"

Ivory stirred in a sleep that had been troubled by too great happiness. To travel a dreary path alone, a path leading seemingly nowhere, and then suddenly to have a companion by one's side, the very sight of whom enchanted the eye, the very touch of whom delighted the senses—what joy unspeakable! Who could sleep soundly when wakefulness brought a train of such blissful thoughts?

"Ivory! Ivory!"

He was fully awake now, for he knew his mother's voice. In all the years, ever thoughtful of his comfort and of the constant strain upon his strength, Lois had never wakened her son at night.

"Coming, mother, coming!" he said, when he realized she was calling him; and hastily drawing on some clothing, for the night was bitterly cold, he came out of his room and saw his mother standing at the foot of the stairway, with a lighted candle in her hand.

"Can you come down, Ivory? It is a strange hour to call you but I have something to tell you; something I have been piecing together for weeks; something I have just clearly remembered."

"If it's something that won't keep till morning, mother, you creep back into bed and we'll hear it comfortably," he said, coming downstairs and leading her to her room. "I'll smooth the covers, so; beat up the pillows,—there, and throw another log on the sitting-room fire. Now, what's the matter? Couldn't you sleep?"

"All summer long I have been trying to remember something; something untrue that you have been believing, some falsehood for which I was responsible. I have pursued and pursued it, but it has always escaped me. Once it was clear as daylight, for Rodman read me from the Bible a plain answer to all the questions that tortured me."

"That must have been the night that she fainted," thought Ivory.

"When I awoke next morning from my long sleep, the old puzzle had come back, a thousand times worse than before, for then I knew that I had held the clue in my own hand and had lost it. Now, praise God! I know the truth, and you, the only one to whom I can tell it, are close at hand."

Ivory looked at his mother and saw that the veil that had separated them mentally seemed to five vanished in the night that had passed. Often and often it had blown away, as it were, for the fraction of a moment and then blown back again. Now her eyes met his with an altogether new clearness that startled him, while her health came with ease and she seemed stronger than for many days.

"You remember the winter I was here at the farm alone, when you were at the Academy?"

"Yes; it was then that I came home and found you so terribly ill. Do you think we need go back to that old time now, mother dear?"

"Yes, I must, I must! One morning I received a strange letter, bearing no signature, in which the writer said that if I wished to see my husband I had only to go to a certain address in Brentville, New Hampshire. The letter went on to say that Mr. Aaron Boynton was ill and longed for nothing so much as to speak with me; but there were reasons why he did not wish to return to Edgewood,—would I come to him without delay."

Ivory now sat straight in his chair and listened keenly, feeling that this was to be no vague, uncertain, and misleading memory, but something true and tangible.

"The letter excited me greatly after your father's long absence and silence. I knew it could mean nothing but sorrow, but although I was half ill at the time, my plain duty was to go, so I thought, and go without making any explanation in the village."

All this was new to Ivory and he hung upon his mother's words, dreading yet hoping for the light that they might shed upon the past.

"I arrived at Brentville quite exhausted with the journey and weighed down by anxiety and dread. I found the house mentioned in the letter at seven o'clock in the evening, and knocked at the door. A common, hard-featured woman answered the knock and, seeming to expect me, ushered me in. I do not remember the room; I remember only a child leaning patiently against the window-sill looking out into the dark, and that the place was bare and cheerless.

"I came to call upon Mr. Aaron Boynton,' I said, with my heart sinking lower and lower as I spoke. The woman opened a door into the next room and when I walked in, instead of seeing your father, I confronted a haggard, death-stricken young woman sitting up in bed, her great eyes bright with pain, her lips as white as her hollow cheeks, and her long, black hair streaming over the pillow. The very sight of her struck a knell to the little hope I had of soothing your father's sick bed and forgiving him if he had done me any wrong.

"'Well, you came, as I thought you would,' said the girl, looking me over from head to foot in a way that somehow made me burn with shame. 'Now sit down in that chair and hear what I've got to say while I've got the strength to say it. I haven't the time nor the desire to put a gloss on it. Aaron Boynton isn't here, as you plainly see, but that's not my fault, for he belongs here as much as anywhere, though he wouldn't have much interest in a dying woman. If you have suffered on account of him, so have I and you haven't had this pain boring into you and eating your life away for months, as I have.'

"I pitied her, she seemed so distraught, but I was in terror of her all the same, and urged her to tell her story calmly and I would do my best to hear it in the same way.

"'Calm,' she exclaimed, 'with this agony tearing me to pieces! Well, to make beginning and end in one, Aaron Boynton was my husband for three years.'

"I caught hold of the chair to keep myself from falling and cried: 'I do not believe it!' 'Believe it or not, she answered scornfully, 'it makes no difference to me, but I can give you twenty proofs in as many seconds. We met at a Cochrane meeting and he chose me from all the others as his true wife. For two years we travelled together, but long before they came to an end there was no happiness for either of us. He had a conscience—not much of a one, but just enough to keep him miserable. At last I felt he was not believing the doctrines he preached and I caught him trying to get news of you and your boy, just because you were out of reach, and neglecting my boy and me, who had given up everything to wander with him and live on whatever the brethren and sisters chose to give us.'

"'So there was a child, a boy,' I gasped. 'Did—did he live?' 'He's in the next room,' she answered, 'and it's him I brought you here for. Aaron Boynton has served us both the same. He left you for me and me for Heaven knows who. If I could live I wouldn't ask any favors, of you least of all, but I haven't a penny in the world, though I shan't need one very long. My friend that's nursing me hasn't a roof to her head and she wouldn't share it with the boy if she had—she's a bigoted Orthodox.'

"'But what do you expect me to do?' I asked angrily, for she was stabbing me with every word.

"'The boy is your husband's child and he always represented you as a saint upon earth. I expect you to take him home and provide for him. He doesn't mean very much to me—just enough so that I don't relish his going to the poorhouse, that's all.'

"'He'll go to something very like that if he comes to mine,' I said.

"'Don't worry me with talk, for I can't stand it,' she wailed, clutching at her nightgown and flinging back her hair. 'Either you take the child or I send somebody to Edgewood with him, somebody to tell the whole story. Some of the Cochranites can support him if you won't; or, at the worst, Aaron Boynton's town can take care of his son. The doctor has given me two days to live. If it's a minute longer I've warned him and I warn you, that I'll end it myself; and if you don't take the boy I'll do the same for him. He's a good sight better off dead than knocking about the world alone; he's innocent and there's no sense in his being punished for the sins of other folks.'"

"I see it all! Why did I never think of it before; my poor, poor Rod!" said Ivory, clenching his hands and burying his head in them.

"Don't grieve, Ivory; it has all turned out so much better than we could have hoped; just listen to the end. She was frightful to hear and to look at, the girl was, though all the time I could feel that she must have had a gipsy beauty and vigor that answered to something in your father.

"'Go along out now,' she cried suddenly. 'I can't stand anybody near. The doctor never gives me half enough medicine and for the hour before he comes I fairly die for lack of it—though little he cares! Go upstairs and have your sleep and to-morrow you can make up your mind.'

"'You don't leave me much freedom to do that,' I tried to answer; but she interrupted me, rocking her body to and fro. 'Neither of us will ever see Aaron Boynton again; you no more than I. He's in the West, and a man with two families and no means of providing for them doesn't come back where he's known.—Come and take her away, Eliza! Take her away, quick!' she called.

"I stumbled out of the room and the woman waved me upstairs. 'You mustn't mind Hetty,' she apologized; 'she never had a good disposition at the best, but she's frantic with the pain now, and good reason, too. It's about over and I'll be thankful when it is. You'd better swallow the shame and take the child; I can't and won't have him and it'll be easy enough for you to say he belongs to some of your own folks.'

"By this time I was mentally bewildered. When the iron first entered my soul, when I first heard the truth about your father, at that moment my mind gave way—I know it now."

"Poor, poor mother! My poor, gentle little mother!" murmured Ivory brokenly, as he asked her hand.

"Don't cry, my son; it is all past; the sorrow and the bitterness and the struggle. I will just finish the story and then we'll close the book forever.

The woman gave me some bread and tea, and I flung myself on the bed without undressing. I don't know how long afterward it was, but the door opened and a little boy stole in; a sad, strange, dark-eyed little boy who said: 'Can I sleep up here? Mother's screaming and I'm afraid.' He climbed to the couch. I covered him with a blanket, and I soon heard his deep breathing. But later in the night, when I must have fallen asleep myself, I suddenly awoke and felt him lying beside me. He had dragged the blanket along and crept up on the bed to get close to my side for the warmth I could give, or the comfort of my nearness. The touch of him almost broke my heart; I could not push the little creature away when he was lying there so near and warm and confiding—he, all unconscious of the agony his mere existence was to me. I must have slept again and when the day broke I was alone. I thought the presence of the child in the night was a dream and I could not remember where I was, nor why I was there."

"Mother, dear mother, don't tell me any more to-night. I fear for your strength," urged Ivory, his eyes full of tears at the remembrance of her sufferings.

"There is only a little more and the weight will be off my heart and on yours, my poor son. Would that I need not tell you! The house was still and I thought at first that no one was awake, but when I opened the sitting-room door the child ran towards me and took my hand as the woman came in from the sick-room. 'Go into the kitchen, Rodman,' she said, 'and lace up your boots; you're going right out with this lady. Hetty died in the night,' she continued impassively. 'The doctor was here about ten o'clock and I've never seen her so bad. He gave her a big dose of sleeping powder and put another in the table drawer for me to mix for her towards morning. She was helpless to move, we thought, but all the same she must have got out of bed when my back was turned and taken the powder dry on her tongue, for it was gone when I looked for it. It didn't hasten things much and I don't blame her. If ever there was a wild, reckless creature it was Hetty Rodman, but I, who am just the opposite, would have done the same if I'd been her.'

"She hurriedly gave me a cup of coffee, and, putting a coat and a cap on the boy, literally pushed me out of the house. 'I've got to report things to the doctor,' she said, 'and you're better out of the way. Go down that side street to the station and mind you say the boy belonged to your sister who died and left him to you. You're a Cochranite, ain't you? So was Hetty, and they're all sisters, so you'll be telling no lies. Good-bye, Rodman, be a good boy and don't be any trouble to the lady.'

"How I found the station I do not know, nor how I made the journey, nor where I took the stage-coach. The snow began to fall and by noon there was a drifting storm. I could not remember where I was going, nor who the boy was, for just as the snow was whirling outside, so it was whirling in my brain."

"Mother, I can hardly bear to hear any more; it is too terrible!" cried Ivory, rising from his chair and pacing the floor.

"I can recall nothing of any account till I awoke in my own bed weeks afterwards. The strange little boy was there, but Mrs. Day and Dr. Perry told me what I must have told them—that he was the child of my dead sister. Those were the last words uttered by the woman in Brentville; I carried them straight through my illness and brought them out on the other side more firmly intrenched than ever."

"If only the truth had come back to you sooner!" sighed Ivory, coming back to her bedside. "I could have helped you to bear it all these years. Sorrow is so much lighter when you can share it with some one else. And the girl who died was called Hetty Rodman, then, and she simply gave the child her last name?"

"Yes, poor suffering creature. I feel no anger against her now; it has burned itself all away. Nor do I feel any bitterness against your father. I forgot all this miserable story for so long, loving and watching for him all the time, that it is as if it did not belong to my own life, but had to do with some unhappy stranger. Can you forgive, too, Ivory?"

"I can try," he answered. "God knows I ought to be able to if you can!"

"And will it turn you away from Rod?"

"No, it draws me nearer to him than ever. He shall never know the truth— why should he? Just as he crept close to you that night, all unconscious of the reason you had for shrinking from him, so he has crept close to me in these years of trial, when your mind has been wandering."

"Life is so strange. To think that this child, of all others, should have been a comfort to you. The Lord's hand is in it!" whispered Mrs. Boynton feebly.

"His boyish belief in me, his companionship, have kept the breath of hope alive in me—that's all I can say."

"The Bible story is happening over again in our lives, then. Don't you remember that Aaron's rod budded and blossomed and bore fruit, and that the miracle kept the rebels from murmuring?"

"This rebel never will murmur again, mother," and Ivory rose to leave the room. "Now that you have shed your burden you will grow stronger and life will be all joy, for Waitstill will come to us soon and we can shake off these miseries and be a happy family once more."

"It is she who has helped me most to find the thread; pouring sympathy and strength into me, nursing me, loving me, because she loved my wonderful son. Oh! how blest among women I am to have lived long enough to see you happy!"

And as Ivory kissed his mother and blew out the candle, she whispered to herself: "Even so, Lord Jesus, come quickly!"

XXXIV. THE DEACON'S WATERLOO

MRS. MASON'S welcome to Waitstill was unexpectedly hearty—much heartier than it would have been Six months before, when she regarded Mrs. Boynton as little less than a harmless lunatic, of no use as a neighbor; and when she knew nothing more of Ivory than she could gather by his occasional drive or walk past her door with a civil greeting. Rodman had been until lately the only member of the family for whom she had a friendly feeling; but all that had changed in the last few weeks, when she had been allowed to take a hand in the Boyntons' affairs. As to this newest development in the life of their household, she had once been young herself, and the veriest block of stone would have become human when the two lovers drove up to the door and told their exciting story.

Ivory made himself quickly at home, and helped the old lady to get a room ready for Waitstill before he drove back for a look at his mother and then on to carry out his impetuous and romantic scheme of routing out the town clerk and announcing his intended marriage. 345

Waitstill slept like the shepherd boy in "The Pilgrim's Progress," with the "herb called Heart's Ease" in her bosom. She opened her eyes next morning from the depths of Mrs. Mason's best feather bed, and looked wonderingly about the room, with all its unaccustomed surroundings. She heard the rattle of fire-irons and the flatter of dishes below; the first time in all her woman's life that preparations for breakfast had ever greeted her ears when she had not been an active participator in them.

She lay quite still for a quarter of an hour, tired in body and mind, but incredibly happy in spirit, marvelling at the changes wrought in her during the day preceding, the most eventful one in her history. Only yesterday her love had been a bud, so closely folded that she scarcely recognized its beauty or color or fragrance; only yesterday, and now she held in her hand a perfect flower. When and how had it grown, and by what magic process?

The image of Ivory had been all through the night in the foreground of her dreams and in her moments of wakefulness, both made blissful by the heaven of anticipation that dawned upon her. Was ever man so wise, so tender and gentle, so strong, so comprehending? What mattered the absence of worldly goods, the presence of care and anxiety, when n woman had a steady hand to hold, a steadfast heart to trust, a man who would love her and stand by her, whate'er befell?

Then the face of Ivory's mother would swim into the mental picture; the pale face, as white as the pillow it lay upon; the face with its aureole of ashen hair, and the wistful blue eyes that begged of God and her children some peace before they closed on life.

The vision of her sister was a joyful one, and her heart was at peace about her, the plucky little princess who had blazed the way out of the ogre's castle.

She saw Patty clearly as a future fine lady, in velvets and satins and furs, bewitching every-body by her gay spirits, her piquant vivacity, and the loving heart that lay underneath all the nonsense and gave it warmth and color.

The remembrance of her father alone on the hilltop did indeed trouble Waitstill. Self-reproach, in the true sense of the word, she did not, could not, feel. Never since the day she was born had she been fathered, and daughterly love was absent; but she suffered when she thought of the fierce, self-willed old man, cutting himself off from all possible friendships, while his vigor was being sapped daily and hourly by his terrible greed of money.

True housewife that Waitstill was, her mind reverted to every separate crock and canister in her cupboards, every article of her baking or cooking that reposed on the swing-sheh in the cellar, thinking how long her father could be comfortable without her ministrations, and so, how long he would delay before engaging the u inevitable housekeeper. She revolved the number of possible persons to whom the position would be offered, and wished that Mrs. Mason, who so needed help, might be the chosen one: but the fact of her having been friendly to the Boyntons would strike her at once from the list.

When she was thankfully eating her breakfast with Mrs. Mason a little later, and waiting for Ivory to call for them both and take them to the Boynton farm, she little knew what was going on at her old home in these very hours, when to tell the truth she would have liked to slip in, had it been possible, wash the morning dishes, skim the cream, do the week's churning, make her father's bed, and slip out again into the dear shelter of love that awaited her.

The Deacon had passed a good part of the night in scheming and contriving, and when he drank his self-made cup of muddy coffee at seven o'clock next morning he had formed several plans that were to be immediately frustrated, had he known it, by the exasperating and suspicious nature of the ladies involved in them.

At eight he had left the house, started Bill Morrill at the store, and was on the road in search of vengeance and a housekeeper. Old Mrs. Atkins of Deerwander sniffed at the wages offered. Miss Peters, of Union Falls, an aged spinster with weak lungs, had the impertinence to tell him that she feared she couldn't stand the cold in his house; she had heard he was very particular about the amount of wood that was burned. A four-mile drive brought him to the village poetically named the Brick Kiln, where he offered to Mrs. Peter Upham an advance of twenty-five cents a week over and above the salary with which he had sought to tempt Mrs. Atkins. Far from being impressed, Mrs. Uphill, being of a high temper and candid turn of mind, told him she'd prefer to starve at home. There was not another free woman within eight miles, and the Deacon was chafing under t e mortification of being continually obliged to state the reason for his needing a housekeeper. The only hope, it seemed, lay in going to Saco and hiring a stranger, a plan not at all to his liking, as it was sure to involve him in extra expense.

Muttering threats against the universe in general, he drove home by way of Milliken's Mills, thinking of the unfed hens, the unmilked cow, the unwashed dishes, the unchurned cream and above all of his unchastened daughters; his rage increasing with every step until it was nearly at the white heat of the night before.

A long stretch of hill brought the tired old mare to a slow walk, and enabled the Deacon to see the Widow Tillman clipping the geraniums that stood in tin cans on the shelf of her kitchen window.

Now, Foxwell Baxter had never been a village Lothario at any age, nor frequented the society of such. Of late years, indeed, he had frequented no society of any kind, so that he had missed, for instance, Abel Day's description of the Widow Tillman as a "reg'lar syreen," though he vaguely remembered that some of the Baptist sisters had questioned the authenticity of her conversion by their young and attractive minister. She made a pleasant picture at the window; she was a free woman (a little too free, the neighbors would have said; but the Deacon didn't know that); she was a comparative newcomer to the village, and her mind had not been poisoned with feminine gossip—in a word, she was a distinctly hopeful subject, and, acting on a blind and sudden impulse, he turned into the yard, 'dung the reins over the mare's neck, and knocked at the back door.

"Her character 's no worse than mine by now if Aunt Abby Cole's on the road," he thought grimly, "an' if the Wilsons see my sleigh inside of widder's fence, so much the better; it'll give 'em a jog.—Good morning Mis' Tillman," he said to the smiling lady. "I'll come to the p'int at once. My youngest daughter has married Mark Wilson against my will, an' gone away from town, an' the older one's chosen a husband still less to my likin'. Do you want to come and housekeep for me?"

"I surmised something was going on," re-turned Mrs. Tillman. "I saw Patty and Mark drive away early this morning, with Mr. and Mrs. Wilson wrapping the girl up and putting a hot soapstone in the sleigh, and consid'able kissing and hugging thrown in."

This knowledge added fuel to the flame that was burning fiercely in the Deacon's breast. "Well, how about the housekeeping he asked, trying not to show his eagerness, and not recognizing himself at all in the enterprise in which he found himself indulging.

"I 'm very comfortable here," the lady responded artfully, "and I don't know 's I care to make any change, thank you. I didn't like the village much at first, after living in larger places, but now I'm acquainted, it kind of gains on me."

Her reply was carefully framed, for her mind worked with great rapidity, and she was mistress of the situation almost as soon as she saw the Deacon alighting from his sleigh. He was not the sort of man to be a casual caller, and his manner bespoke an urgent errand. She had a pension of six dollars a month, but over and above that sum her living was precarious. She made coats, and she had never known want, for she was a master hand at dealing with the opposite sex. Deacon Baxter, according to common report, had ten or fifteen thousand dollars stowed away in the banks, so the situation would be as simple as possible under ordinary circumstances; it was as easy to turn out one man's pockets as all-other's when he was a normal human being; but Deacon Baxter was a different proposition.

"I wonder how long he's likely to live," she thought, glancing at him covertly, out of the tail of her eye. "His evil temper must have driven more than one nail in his coffin. I wonder, if I refuse to housekeep, whether I 'll get—a better offer. I wonder if I could manage him if I got him! I'd rather like to sit in the Baxter pew at the Orthodox meeting-house after the way some of the Baptist sisters have snubbed me since I come here."

Not a vestige of these incendiary thoughts showed in her comely countenance, and her soul might have been as white as the high-bibbed apron that covered it, to judge by her genial smile.

"I'd make the wages fair," urged the Deacon, looking round the clean kitchen, with the break-fast-table sitting near the sunny window and the odor of corned beef and cabbage issuing temptingly from a boiling pot on the fire. "I hope she ain't a great meat-eater," he thought, "but it's too soon to cross that bridge yet a while."

"I've no doubt of it," said the widow, wondering if her voice rang true; "but I've got a pension, and why should I leave this cosy little home? Would I better myself any, that's the question? I'm kind of lonesome here, that's the only reason I'd consider a move."

"No need o' bein' lonesome down to the Falls," said the Deacon. "And I'm in an' out all day, between the barn an' the store."

This, indeed, was not a pleasant prospect, but Jane Tillman had faced worse ones in her time.

"I'm no hand at any work outside the house," she observed, as if reflecting. "I can truthfully say I'm a good cook, and have a great faculty for making a little go a long ways." (She considered this a master-stroke, and in fact it was; for the Deacon's mouth absolutely watered at this apparently unconscious comprehension of his disposition.) "But I'm no hand at any chores in the barn or shed," she continued. "My first husband would never allow me to do that kind of work."

"Perhaps I could git a boy to help out; I've been kind o' thinkin' o' that lately. What wages would you expect if I paid a boy for the rough work?" asked the Deacon tremulously. "Well, to tell the truth, I don't quite fancy the idea of taking wages. Judge Dickinson wants me to go to Alfred and housekeep for him, and I'd named twelve dollars a month. It's good pay, and I haven't said 'No'; but my rent is small here, I'm my own mistress, and I don't feel like giving up my privileges."

"Twelve dollars a month!" He had never thought of approaching that sum; and he saw the heap of unwashed dishes growing day by day, and the cream souring on the milk-pans. Suddenly an idea sprang full-born into the Deacon's mind (Jed Morrill's "Old Driver" must have been close at hand!). Would Jane Tillman marry him? No woman in the three villages would be more obnoxious to his daughters; that in itself was a distinct gain. She was a fine, robust figure of a woman in her early forties, and he thought, after all, that the hollow-chested, spindle-shanked kind were more ex-pensive to feed, on the whole, than their better-padded sisters. He had never had any difficulty in managing wives, and thought himself quite equal to one more bout, even at sixty-five, though he had just the faintest suspicion that the high color on Mrs. Tillman's prominent cheek-bones, the vigor shown in the coarse black hair and handsome eyebrows, might make this task a little more difficult than his previous ones. But this fear vanished almost as quickly as it appeared, for he kept saying to himself: "A judge of the County Court wants her at twelve dollars a month; hadn't I better bid high an' git settled?

"If you'd like to have a home o' your own 'thout payin' rent, you've only got to say the word an' I'll make you Mis' Baxter," said the Deacon. "There'll be nobody to interfere with you, an' a handsome legacy if I die first; for none o' my few savin's is goin' to my daughters, I can promise you that!"

The Deacon threw out this tempting bait advisedly, for at this moment he would have poured his hoard into the lap of any woman who would help him to avenge his fancied wrongs.

This was information, indeed! The "few savings" alluded to amounted to some thousands, Jane Tillman knew. Had she not better burn her ships behind her, take the risks, and have faith in her own powers? She was getting along in ears, and her charms of person were lessening with every day that passed over her head. If the Deacon's queer ways grew too queer, she thought an appeal to the doctor and the minister might provide a way of escape and a neat little income to boot; so, on the whole, the marriage, though much against her natural inclinations, seemed to be providentially arranged.

The interview that succeeded, had it been reported verbatim, deserved to be recorded in local history. Deacon Baxter had met in Jane Tillman a foeman more than worthy of his steel. She was just as crafty as he, and in generalship as much superior to him as Napoleon Bonaparte to Cephas Cole. Her knowledge of and her experiences with men, all very humble, it is true, but decidedly varied, enabled her to play on every weakness of this particular one she had in hand, and at the same time skilfully to avoided alarming him.

Heretofore, the women with whom the Deacon had come in contact had timidly steered away from the rocks and reefs in his nature, and had been too ignorant or too proud to look among them for certain softer places that were likely to be there—since man is man, after all, even when he is made on a very small pattern.

If Jane Tillman became Mrs. Baxter, she intended to get the whip hand and keep it; but nothing was further from her intention than to make the Deacon miserable if she could help it. That was not her disposition; and so, when the deluded man left her house, he had made more concessions in a single hour than in all the former years of his life.

His future spouse was to write out a little paper for his signature; just a friendly little paper to be kept quite private and confidential between themselves, stating that she was to do no work outside of the house; that her pension was to be her own; that she was to have five dollars in cash on the first of every month in lieu of wages; and that in ease of his death occurring first she was to have a third of his estate, and the whole of it if at the time of his decease he was still pleased with his bargain. The only points in this contract that the Deacon really understood were that he was paying only five dollars a month for a housekeeper to whom a judge had offered twelve; that, as he had expected to pay at least eight, he could get a boy for the remaining three, and so be none the worse in pocket; also, that if he could keep his daughters from getting his money, he didn't care a hang who had it, as he hated the whole human race with entire impartiality. If Jane Tillman didn't behave herself, he had pleasing visions of converting most of his fortune into cash and having it dropped off the bridge some dark night, when the doctor had given him up and proved to his satisfaction that death would occur in the near future.

All this being harmoniously settled, the Deacon drove away, and caused the announcement of his immediate marriage to be posted directly below that of Waitstill and Ivory Boynton.

"Might as well have all the fat in the fire to once," he chuckled. "There won't be any house-work done in this part of the county for a week to come. If we should have more snow, nobody'll have to do any shovellin', for the women-folks'll keep all the paths in the village trod down from door to door, travellin' round with the news."

A "spite match," the community in general called the Deacon's marriage; and many a man, and many a woman, too, regarding the amazing publishing notice in the frame up at the meeting-house, felt that in Jane Tillman Deacon Baxter had met his Waterloo.

"She's plenty good enough for him," said Aunt Abby Cole, "though I know that's a terrible poor compliment. If she thinks she'll ever break into s'ciety here at the Falls, she'll find herself mistaken! It's a mystery to me why the poor deluded man ever done it; but ain't it wonderful the ingenuity the Lord shows in punishin' sinners? I couldn't 'a' thought out such a good comeuppance myself for Deacon Baxter, as marryin' Jane Tillman! The thing that troubles me most, is thinkin' how tickled the Baptists'll be to git her out o' their meetin' an' into ourn!"

XXXV. TWO HEAVENS

AT the very moment that Deacon Baxter was I starting out on his quest for a housekeeper, Patty and Mark drove into the Mason dooryard and the sisters flew into each other's arms. The dress that Mark had bought for Patty was the usual charting and unsuitable offering of a man's spontaneous affection, being of dark violet cloth with a wadded cape lined with satin. A little brimmed hat of violet velvet tied under her chin with silk ribbons completed the costume, and before the youthful bride and groom had left the ancestral door Mrs. Wilson had hung her own ermine victorine (the envy of all Edgewood) around Patty's neck and put her ermine willow muff into her new daughter's hands; thus she was as dazzling a personage, and as improperly dressed for the journey, as she could well be.

Waitstill, in her plain linsey-woolsey, was entranced with Patty's beauty and elegance, and the two girls had a few minutes of sisterly talk, of interchange of radiant hopes and confidences before Mark tore them apart, their cheeks wet with happy tears.

As the Mason house faded from view, Patty having waved her muff until the last moment, turned in her seat and said:—

"Mark, dear, do you think your father would care if I spent the twenty-dollar gold-piece he gave me, for Waitstill? She will be married in a fortnight, and if my father does not give her the few things she owns she will go to her husband more ill-provided even than I was. I have so much, dear Mark, and she so little."

"It's your own wedding-present to use as you wish," Mark answered, "and it's exactly like you to give it away. Go ahead and spend it if you want to; I can always earn enough to keep you, without anybody's help!" and Mark, after cracking the whip vaingloriously, kissed his wife just over the violet ribbons, and with sleigh-bells jingling they sped over the snow towards what seemed Paradise to them, the New Hampshire village where they had been married and where—

So a few days later, Waitstill received a great parcel which relieved her of many feminine anxieties and she began to shape and cut and stitch during all the hours she had to herself. They were not many, for every day she trudged to the Boynton farm and began with youthful enthusiasm the household tasks that were so soon to be hers by right.

"Don't waste too much time and strength here, my dearest," said Ivory. "Do you suppose for a moment I shall keep you long on this lonely farm? I am ready for admission to the Bar or I am fitted to teach in the best school in New England. Nothing has held me here but my mother, and in her present condition of mind we can safely take her anywhere. We will never live where there are so many memories and associations to sadden and hamper us, but go where the best opportunity offers, and as soon as may be. My wife will be a pearl of great price," he added fondly, "and I intend to provide a right setting for her!"

This was all said in a glow of love and joy, pride and ambition, as Ivory paced up and down before the living-room fireplace while Waitstill was hanging the freshly laundered curtains.

Ivory was right; Waitstill Baxter was, indeed, a jewel of a woman. She had little knowledge, but much wisdom, and after all, knowledge stands for the leaves on a tree and wisdom for the fruit. There was infinite richness in the girl, a richness that had been growing and ripening through the years that she thought so gray and wasted. The few books she owned and loved had generally lain unopened, it is true, upon her bedroom table, and she held herself as having far too little learning to be a worthy companion for Ivory Boynton; but all the beauty and cheer a comfort that could ever be pressed into the arid life of the Baxter household had come from Waitstill's heart, and that heart had grown in warmth and plenty year by year.

Those lonely tasks, too hard for a girl's hands, those unrewarded drudgeries, those days of faithful labor in and out of doors, those evenings of self-sacrifice over the mending-basket; the quiet avoidance of all that might vex her father's crusty temper, her patience with his miserly exactions; the hourly holding back of the hasty word,—all these had played their part; all these had been somehow welded into a strong, sunny, steady, life-wisdom, there is no better name for it; and so she had unconsciously the best of all harvests to bring as dower to a husband who was worthy of her. Ivory's strength called to hers and answered it, just as his great need awoke such a power of helpfulness in her as she did not know she possessed. She loved the man, but she loved the task that beckoned her, too. The vision of it was like the breath of wind from a hill-top, putting salt and savor into the new life that opened before her.

These were quietly happy days at the farm, for Mrs. Boynton took a new, if transient, hold upon life that deceived even the doctor. Rodman was nearly as ardent a lover as Ivory, hovering about Waitstill and exclaiming, "You never stay to supper and it's so lonesome evenings without you! Will it never be time for you to come and live with us, Waity dear? The days crawl so slowly!" At which Ivory would laugh, push him away and draw Waitstill nearer to his own side, saying: "If you are in a hurry, you young cormorant, what do you think of me?" And Waitstill would look from one to the other and blush at the heaven of love that surrounded her on every side.

"I believe you are longing to begin on my cooking, you two big greedy boys!" she said teasingly. "What shall we have for New Year's dinner, Rod? Do you like a turkey, roasted brown and crispy, with giblet gravy and cranberry jelly? Do you fancy an apple dumpling afterwards,—an apple dumpling with potato crust,—or will you have a suet pudding with foamy sauce?"

"Stop, Waitstill!" cried Ivory. "Don't put hope into us until you are ready to satisfy it; we can't bear it!"

"And I have a box of goodies from my own garden safely stowed away in Uncle Bart's shop," Waitstill went on mischievously. "They were to be sold in Portland, but I think they'll have to be my wedding-present to my husband, though a very strange one, indeed! There are peaches floating in sweet syrup; there are tumblers of quince jelly; there are jars of tomato and citron preserves, and for supper you shall eat them with biscuits as light as feathers and white as snowdrifts."

"We can never wait two more days, Rod; let us kidnap her! Let us take the old bob-sled and run over to New Hampshire where one can be married the minute one feels like it. We could do it between sunrise and moonrise and be at home for a late supper. Would she be too tired to bake the biscuits for us, do you think? What do you say, Rod, will you be best man?" And there would be youthful, unaccustomed laughter floating out from the kitchen or living-room, bringing a smile of content to Lois Boynton's face as she lay propped up in bed with her open Bible beside her. "He binds up the broken-hearted," she whispered to herself. "He gives unto them a garland for ashes; the oil of joy for mourning; the garment of praise for the spirit of heaviness."

The quiet wedding was over. There had been neither feasting, nor finery, nor presents, nor bridal journey; only a home-coming that meant deep and sacred a joy, as fervent gratitude as any four hearts ever contained in all the world. But the laughter ceased, though the happiness flowed silently underneath, almost forgotten in the sudden sorrow that overcame them, for it fell out that Lois Boynton had only waited, as it were, for the marriage, and could stay no longer.

"... There are two heavens...

Both made of love,—one, inconceivable

Ev'n by the other, so divine it is;

The other, far on this side of the stars,

By men called home."

And these two heavens met, over at Boyntons', during these cold, white, glistening December days.

Lois Boynton found hers first. After a windy moonlit night a morning dawned in which a hush seemed to be on the earth. The cattle huddled together in the farmyards and the fowls shrank into their feathers. The sky was gray, and suddenly the first white heralds came floating down like scouts seeking for paths and camping-places.

Waitstill turned Mrs. Boynton's bed so that she could look out of the window. Slope after slope, dazzling in white crust, rose one upon another and vanished as they slipped away into the dark green of the pine forests. Then,

"... there fell from out the skies

A feathery whiteness over all the land;

A strange, soft, spotless something, pure as light."

It could not be called a storm, for there had been no wind since sunrise, no whirling fury, no drifting; only a still, steady, solemn fall of crystal flakes, hour after hour, hour after hour.

Mrs. Boynton's Book of books was open on the bed and her finger marked a passage in her favorite Bible-poet.

"Here it is, daughter," she whispered. "I have found it, in the same chapter where the morning stars sing together and the sons of God shout for joy. The Lord speaks to Job out of the whirlwind and says: 'HAST THOU ENTERED INTO THE TREASURES OF THE SNOW? OR HAST THOU SEEN THE TREASURES OF THE HAIL?' Sit near me, Waitstill, and look out on the hills. 'HAST THOU ENTERED INTO THE TREASURES OF THE SNOW?' No, not yet, but please God, I shall, and into many other treasures, soon"; and she closed her eyes.

All day long the air-ways were filled with the glittering army of the snowflakes; all day long the snow grew deeper and deeper on the ground; and on the breath of some white-winged wonder that passed Lois Boynton's window her white soul forsook its "earth-lot" and took flight at last.

They watched beside her, but never knew the moment of her going; it was just a silent flitting, a ceasing to be, without a tremor, or a flutter that could be seen by mortal eye. Her face was so like an angel's in its shining serenity that the few who loved her best could not look upon her with anything but reverent joy. On earth she had known nothing but the "broken arcs," but in heaven she would find the "perfect round"; there at last, on the other side of the stars, she could remember right, poor Lois Boynton!

For weeks afterwards the village was shrouded in snow as it had never been before within memory, but in every happy household the home-life deepened day by day. The books came out in the long evenings; the grandsires told old tales under the inspiration of the hearth-fire: the children gathered on their wooden stools to roast apples and pop corn; and hearts came closer together than when summer called the housemates to wander here and there in fields and woods and beside the river.

Over at Boyntons', when the snow was whirling and the wind howling round the chimneys of the high-gabled old farmhouse; when every window had its frame of ermine and fringe of icicles, and the sleet rattled furiously against the glass, then Ivory would throw a great back log on the bank of coals between the fire-dogs, the kettle would begin to sing, and the eat come from some snug corner to curl and purr on the braided hearth-rug.

School was in session, and Ivory and Rod had their textbooks of an evening, but oh! what a new and strange joy to study when there was a sweet woman sitting near with her workbasket; a woman wearing a shining braid of hair as if it were a coronet; a woman of clear eyes and tender lips, one who could feel as well as think, one who could be a man's comrade as well as his dear love.

Truly the second heaven, the one on "this side of the stars, by men called home," was very present over at Boyntons'.

Sometimes the broad-seated old haircloth sofa would be drawn in front of the fire, and Ivory, laying his pipe and his Greek grammar on the table, would take some lighter book and open it on his knee. Waitstill would lift her eyes from her sewing to meet her husband's glance that spoke longing for her closer companionship, and gladly leaving her work, and slipping into the place by his side, she would put her elbow on his shoulder and read with him.

Once, Rod, from his place at a table on the other side of the room, looked and looked at them with a kind of instinct beyond his years, and finally crept up to Waitstill, and putting an arm through hers, nestled his curly head on her shoulder with the quaint charm and grace that belonged to him.

It was a young and beautiful shoulder, Waitstill's, and there had always been, and would always be, a gracious curve in it where a child's head might lie in comfort. Presently with a shy pressure, Rod whispered: "Shall I sit in the other room, Waitstill and Ivory?—Am I in the way?"

Ivory looked up from his book quietly shaking his head, while Waitstill put her arm around the boy and drew him closer.

"Our little brother is never in the way," she said, as she bent and kissed him.

Men may come and men may go; Saco Water still tumbles tumultuously over the dam and rushes under the Edgewood bridge on its way to the sea; and still it listens to the story of to-day that will sometime be the history of yesterday.

On midsummer evenings the windows of the old farmhouse over at Boyntons' gleam with unaccustomed lights and voices break the stillness, lessening the gloom of the long grass-grown lane of Lois Boynton's watching in days gone by. On sunny mornings there is a merry babel of children's chatter, mingled with gentle maternal warnings, for this is a new brood of young things and the river is calling them as it has called all the others who ever came within the circle of its magic. The fragile harebells hanging their blue heads from the crevices of the rocks; the brilliant columbines swaying to and fro on their tall stalks; the patches of gleaming sand in shallow places beckoning little bare feet to come and tread them; the glint of silver minnows darting hither and thither in some still pool; the tempestuous journey of some weather-beaten log, fighting its way downstream;—here is life in abundance, luring the child to share its risks and its joys.

When Waitstill's boys and Patty's girls come back to the farm, they play by Saco Water as their mothers and their fathers did before them. The paths through the pine woods along the river's brink are trodden smooth by their restless, wandering feet; their eager, curious eyes search the waysides for adventure, but their babble and laughter are oftenest heard from the ruins of an old house hidden by great trees. The stones of the cellar, all overgrown with blackberry vines, are still there; and a fragment of the brick chimney, where swallows build their nests from year to year. A wilderness of weeds, tall and luxuriant, springs up to hide the stone over which Jacob Cochrane stepped daily when he issued from his door; and the polished stick with which three-year-old Patty beats a tattoo may be a round from the very chair in which he sat, expounding the Bible according to his own vision. The thickets of sweet clover and red-tipped grasses, of waving ferns and young alder bushes hide all of ugliness that belongs to the deserted spot and serve as a miniature forest in whose shade the younglings foreshadow the future at their play of home-building and housekeeping. In a far corner, altogether concealed from the passer-by, there is a secret treasure, a wonderful rosebush, its green leaves shining with health and vigor. When the July sun is turning the hay-fields yellow, the children part the bushes in the leafy corner and little Waitstill Boynton steps cautiously in, to gather one splendid rose, "for father and mother."

Jacob Cochrane's heart, with all its faults and frailties has long been at peace. On a chill, dreary night in November, all that was mortal of him was raised from its unhonored resting-place not far from the ruins of his old abode, and borne by three of his disciples far away to another state. The gravestones were replaced, face downward, deep, deep in the earth, and the sod laid back upon them, so that no man thence forward could mark the place of the prophet's transient burial amid the scenes of his first and only triumphant ministry.

"It is a sad story, Jacob Cochrane's," Waitstill said to her husband when she first discovered that her children had chosen the deserted spot for their play; "and yet, Ivory, the red rose blooms and blooms in the ruins of the man's house, and perhaps, somewhere in the world, he has left a message that matches the rose."